"YOU ARE A CLOSET ROMANTIC,"

Donis said as he sat beside Karen on the grass. "Has anyone ever told you?"

"Not that I recall. But what makes you think so?"

"I saw that look on your face, faraway, dreamy."

"There is a sentimental streak in me somewhere, I suppose," Karen replied a little self-consciously.

Donis stretched out beside her. "What does a fair-haired, green-eyed Canadian woman see when she gazes so far away?"

Karen's mind seemed to go blank with Donis so near. "I don't know. I don't form a definite image or anything. It's more like . . . a feeling. I feel as though I'm thousands of miles away, doing something wonderful, something adventurous . . ."

"You are."

Karen laughed. "Working for the federal government?"

"But look at the people you meet, the stories you've heard—not bad for a girl who was born and raised in rural Ontario."

"Funny, I've never looked at it that way before. . . ." But suddenly Karen was aware that Donis was right. Since he'd come into her life, that something wonderful and adventurous really wasn't thousands of miles away. It was here and now. . . .

ABOUT THE AUTHOR

Award-winning author Elaine K. Stirling is always
on the move! Just recently she and her two boys,
Nicholas and Benjamin, pulled up their Toronto
roots and settled anew in beautiful British
Columbia. Elaine's had several different careers,
too—one of which was as an immigration
counselor in the small Canadian cities of London
and Windsor. And while Elaine found her work
with Immigration rewarding, she is the first to
admit that becoming an author was the perfect
career choice for a woman with more than a touch
of Gypsy in her blood. "After all," says Elaine,
"a writer can write anywhere!"

Books by Elaine K. Stirling

HARLEQUIN SUPERROMANCE
261–THIS TIME FOR US

HARLEQUIN INTRIGUE
28–UNSUSPECTED CONDUCT
35–MIDNIGHT OBSESSION
53–FOUL PLAY
85–CHAIN LETTER

HARLEQUIN TEMPTATION
139–ALMOST HEAVEN

Don't miss any of our special offers. Write to us at the
following address for information on our newest releases.

Harlequin Reader Service
901 Fuhrmann Blvd., P.O. Box 1397, Buffalo, NY 14240
Canadian address: P.O. Box 603,
Fort Erie, Ont. L2A 5X3

Elaine K. Stirling

MORE THAN A FEELING

Harlequin Books

TORONTO • NEW YORK • LONDON
AMSTERDAM • PARIS • SYDNEY • HAMBURG
STOCKHOLM • ATHENS • TOKYO • MILAN

Published February 1989

First printing December 1988

ISBN 0-373-70345-7

To Marsha,
who makes wishes come true

PROLOGUE

THE PEOPLE OF SANVITO hold their legends dear. They claim that their island is a slumbering giant; the sea, a temptress who longs to rouse them. Her sighs are the winds on the limestone cliffs; the billowing surf is her gown.

So fervent is her love for the giant, the sea cannot be appeased by other men. They say that when a man falls from the cliffs of Sanvito, the temptress turns away, yanking her skirt so that he lands on bare rock and dies. But if a woman falls, the sea, à kindred spirit, takes pity. She throws out her aqueous robe, catches the woman and spirits her to safety.

Legends, however, held little interest for the two men walking the cliff's pathways that morning. Caught up in the heat of debate, each was aware only of his own unshakable rightness.

They had no fear of eavesdroppers. People seldom came to this part of the island, especially not at dawn when the Mediterranean mist was heavy and the rocky pathways slick.

"You are not yet twenty years old, Salvo," the taller one said. "How can you presume to know what is right for our people?"

"You're the same age. How can you presume that I don't?"

"All I am saying is that Sanvitans are comfortable with things as they are. First, you must convince them there is need for improvement, and that is no easy task."

Salvo's heavy jaw thrust out when he laughed. "On that, at least, we agree. Given the choice, Sanvitans would quite happily wallow in their superstition for another two thousand years." He kicked loose a stone and watched it career over the cliff's edge. "Mark my words, Donis. One day... one day the people of Sanvito will revere the name of Salvo Gibrian. They will fall to their knees, grateful for the prosperity I have brought them."

Andonis had been audience to his cousin's fantasies since childhood. They no longer shocked him, these notions, but neither did they amuse. More than anything, Andonis pitied his cousin. Such idealism could only bring about despair.

They continued to walk in silence, while Andonis scanned the island's southern horizon. From this bleak vantage, there was little evidence of civilization. Only the cathedral could be seen, fog muting its gilt dome and softening the edges of the stonework. The structure was squat and archaic, but it was impressive nonetheless. To Andonis, the cathedral embodied the Sanvitan people themselves: pious, proud, resilient.

Salvo, frowning, followed the direction of his friend's gaze. "That decrepit old eyesore. Little wonder we're still in the Middle Ages with such relics around."

Andonis looked at Salvo and said nothing. It would be difficult to find two family members as dissimilar in appearance and outlook. Even as children, Andonis had been the pragmatist, Salvo the visionary. When they played, Salvo made up dangerous, daring games, while Andonis was content with the tried and true. It was a shame that the attributes which kept them friends as children had driven a wedge between them as adults.

"Why are you staring?" Salvo demanded.

Andonis shrugged. "I was just wondering what became of the Salvo Gibrian who chased women and gambled at dominoes? I think I much preferred his company."

"He grew up. But unlike some I could mention, he did not lose his passion in the process. Little wonder Talia finds you boring these days."

"Is that how she describes me?"

"Among other things."

Andonis felt great affection for Salvo's younger sister. At one time, she'd imagined herself in love with her second cousin, but Andonis being older and wiser had assured Talia that the infatuation was temporary. Sure enough, she soon recovered. But her opinion still mattered to Andonis. To think that he might have somehow fallen short in Talia's eyes came as a blow.

"Don't take it too hard," Salvo said. "At seventeen, Talia suddenly has every young man in the country pining after her, and she's thriving on it. Not that any of the maggots are good enough for her." The two men laughed; for a short time, their differences forgotten.

"Look, Salvo, over there." Andonis pointed to a stand of stunted cypress at the cliff's edge. "Remember when the three of us used to play under those trees?"

"How could I forget? We called it the giant's cowlick and christened it with a gold coin. I wonder if it's still buried there."

"I don't remember a gold coin," Andonis said as they neared the trees. "Whose was it?"

"Your grandmother gave it to Talia on her birthday. She was warned to guard the coin carefully because money didn't grown on trees. So Talia buried it under the cypress, partly for safekeeping, and also to find out whether money would actually gro—"

Just then, Salvo stumbled on a root. A barrage of dew-slicked pebbles broke loose, and before Andonis could react, Salvo had slipped over the precipice.

With a shout, Andonis fell to his knees. He found his cousin clinging to the edge of the cliff by his fingertips. Far below, the surf roared, the weathered rocks protruded from the waves like stumps of old teeth.

"Help!" Salvo cried.

"Hold on!" Lying on his stomach, Andonis pushed away debris that threatened to carry him over with his friend, then reached out and grabbed Salvo's wrists.

Erosion had scooped away the rock beneath the cliff's edge. There was no place for Salvo to get a foothold. His legs flailed helplessly.

"Stay still," Andonis ordered, "or you'll drag us both down. Now, listen! Release your hold—one hand at a time—and take my wrists. If you don't, I can only hang on. I won't be able to pull you."

Salvo's nails were turning blue. "I can't let go! I'll fall!"

"Do as I say!"

Horror filled his cousin's eyes. "Why? Do you want me to die?"

The notion could not have been further from Andonis's thoughts. But suddenly an image flashed through his mind, a shadow of things he couldn't comprehend. Rearing from deep within his subconscious, Andonis glimpsed terror, chaos, and agony far beyond human endurance.

Then, just as unexpectedly, Andonis thought of his grandmother. She would have called it a sign. She would have told him to heed it. All he'd have to do was cling to his cousin's wrists until his own strength depleted. Salvo would plummet to the rocks below, and this portent—if that's what it was—would never come to pass.

Senses numbed, Andonis loosened his hold. But the yank of icy flesh jolted him to reality, and he tightened his grip on Salvo once more.

"For the love of God, Donis, what are you doing?"

Their eyes locked, Salvo's dark and pleading, Andonis's gray and swirling like the mist around them. Gravity was already taking its course. In a matter of minutes, they could both meet their death on the rocks below....

But despite his grandmother's counsel, Andonis had never believed in omens. Ignoring his cousin's desperate cries, he let go with one hand to grab Salvo's forearm with two. Then, with strength born of loyalty and love, Andonis pulled Salvo to safety.

CHAPTER ONE

"MORNING, KAREN."

Plop.

A pile of manila landed foursquare on Karen Miller's morning paper. "You did it again, Molly," Karen cried. "You missed the In basket."

The receptionist peeped around Karen's partition and grinned. "You looked like you needed a good jolt. Besides, it's eight-thirty, and the waiting room's packed."

Karen finished her coffee and put the newspaper away in a drawer. "It's just as well. I need something to keep me awake. Someone should have warned me not to order pay TV until I could afford a VCR. Do you know what ungodly hour the James Dean movie finally finished?"

"I could guess by looking at you," Molly said with a giggle. "Nah, just kidding. You look fine."

"Thanks," Karen mumbled as the redhead bounded off. And now, to face the files. Their dog-eared condition was not encouraging. Karen opened the top folder, groaned, tossed it aside, opened the second and groaned again. Every Immigration counselor had a batch of problem cases that never went away. From all appearances, it looked as though Karen's had conspired to show up on the same day.

First was the family who wanted to sponsor their best friend from southern Europe. He was forty-three, illiterate and earned his living by tending other people's goats. After three intensive counseling sessions, she still hadn't been able to make them understand that "best friends" could not be considered relatives, no matter how great the affection, nor did Canada have a large demand for goatherds. The family was scheduled to come in again this afternoon, bringing along the "best damned immigration lawyer in the city." Their choice of words, not hers.

Then there were the Garcias, the latest case of newlyweds. Estelle was a large, pasty-faced Canadian of thirty-eight who until this year had never had a boyfriend, let alone come close to matrimony. The groom was a twenty-year-old Mexican—short, dark and silver-tongued.

Estelle made ketchup on the assembly line of a local cannery. Miguel had entered Canada with a group of farm laborers to pick tomatoes. The couple apparently met at a company picnic and fell in love at first sight. The following weekend, they were married, and the Monday after that, came in to Immigration to apply for Miguel's permanent residence.

In a private interview with Karen, the groom reluctantly admitted that he'd sired two children in his home town. But as he enthusiastically explained, the woman wasn't his legal wife. Her real husband was serving ten years for manslaughter. Miguel had simply been trying to keep her cheerful.

He hadn't told Estelle about the children because he was afraid of her reaction. Miguel swore to Karen that he adored his wife and wanted nothing more than to make her happy. Yet in the next breath, he was asking Karen how one applied for Unemployment Insurance benefits.

A week ago, Karen had placed a memo in the file saying that the Garcias failed to show for their interview. She'd scheduled a new appointment for this morning, and this time she was leaving nothing to chance. Picking up the phone, Karen dialed their number.

"Hello, Estelle, this is Karen Miller from the Immigration office."

Estelle sounded as though she'd been sleeping. "Wha...who? Oh, yeah, you."

Despite the less than effusive greeting, Karen remained courteous. "I'm phoning to remind you of your eleven-o'clock appointment. Your husband is supposed to bring in the results of his medical."

There was a pause. "You mean, like, today?"

"That's right."

"Do both of us have to be there?"

Karen sighed. "Yes, I would like to see both of you. Weren't you able to switch shifts? You told me last time that you could."

"I don't have to switch shifts. I been laid off."

"Oh, I'm sorry to hear that. What about Miguel? Is he still working?"

"Uh...nope, he quit."

Karen gritted her teeth. "Why?"

"Couldn't hack the work, I guess."

"What are you living on?"

"I'll be getting pogy soon, and Miguel's got a couple of job interviews lined up."

Sure he does, Karen thought, making a note in the file. Of all Miguel's dubious attributes, ambition did not seem to be among them. "Do you know if he's had his medical yet?"

"I'm not sure. I think, maybe."

"Could I speak to him, please?"

The bride made a choking sound, as though she found it difficult to fib while groggy. "Uh...well, he's uh... sleeping right now."

"Tell him it's important."

"Oh. Okay...I'll see what I can do." Estelle pretended to leave the phone, but Karen could still hear her breathing into the receiver. After a minute or so, Miguel's bride spoke up again. "He's in the shower, but I'll tell him you called. You said eleven o'clock, right?"

"Yes. And please remind your husband that if he doesn't show up today, I'll have to turn the file over to enforcement."

"Why would you do that?" Now Estelle sounded panicky. "I mean, we're doing everything legal, aren't we?"

"Well, yes, but it looks to me like Miguel is only—oh, never mind." There might come a time when Karen was obliged to be blunt with the Garcias, but until then, she would give them the benefit of her considerable doubt. "Listen, Estelle, if you can't get Miguel to come in, I would still like to see you."

"I don't know why. I'm Canadian. It's not like you can deport me or anything."

"I didn't say anything about deportation."

"Maybe not, but it's what you guys do, isn't it?"

Karen shut her eyes. "Not if we can help it, Estelle. And as you say, not to Canadians."

Mrs. Garcia mumbled a halfhearted promise to be there at eleven, but Karen wasn't counting on it. Miguel was probably long gone by now, and Estelle was simply too ashamed to admit it.

While Karen entered the details of her conversation in Miguel's file, Molly popped around the partition. "Hey, Karen, there's a client out there that I'm saving for you."

She looked up. "Why am I the lucky one?"

"Because," Molly whispered with a conspiratorial hand to her mouth, "he's absolutely too incredible to be believed. I mean this guy'll knock the panty hose right off your feet. Even if he is kind of...old looking."

One of the tasks Molly took seriously was screening clients. If there was an exotic dancer in need of a work permit, she would promptly inform the male counselors. On one such occasion, Karen had been standing in the wrong spot and was nearly trampled in the rush. Interesting male clients, however, were rarer, and since there were only two female counselors—one of whom Molly didn't care for—Karen always got first dibs.

"What do you mean by old looking?" Karen asked suspiciously.

"Well, he looks like forty going on seventy-five. Know what I mean?"

"Good grief, I'm thirty-one. Does that mean I only have nine good years left?"

Molly grinned. "Heck, no. As long as you keep coloring your hair, no one will ever suspect—"

"I do not color my hair!" Karen threatened to hurl a stapler at Molly. "Where's the client from?"

"I don't know. Some weird place I never heard of."

Geography was the one area where Molly could use a little polishing. It didn't help the Immigration Commission's image when the receptionist couldn't differentiate between Argentina and Arkansas.

"I'll be out in a minute. And thanks for, uh...saving him for me."

Karen set aside Miguel Garcia's file. It would be nice if, just once, she could be proven wrong. Maybe Estelle and Miguel would actually show up this afternoon. Maybe they were really in love and would stay together even after Miguel got his permanent residence. *Sure, Karen, and there really is a Santa Claus.*

She felt around under the desk for her shoes and slipped them on before heading for the front counter. Molly handed Karen an info slip with the client's name, his date of birth and citizenship. Attached to the slip was a black passport, somewhat the worse for wear. There was no record of a previous file, meaning this was the client's first visit to the office.

He was from Sanvito. Unlike Molly, Karen did know that Sanvito was a small independent island in the Mediterranean. A few years ago, the country was in the news constantly because of political upheaval. Now little was heard about the place, except from the occasional plucky travel writer bemoaning what a lovely sunspot Sanvito might have been.

Karen looked up at the waiting room half full of clients. A Mennonite family with eight children comprised the majority, but off to one side sat a man, alone. There could be no doubt he was the one over whom Molly gushed.

He was staring off into the distance, arms folded across his chest, apparently unaware of Karen's perusal. His features were lean, enhanced by a deep olive complexion and the defined shadow of whiskers. Straight black hair touched his collar and fell across his forehead. He was dressed in a white shirt and gray slacks; his shoes were carefully polished.

A refined man, Karen thought, and certainly handsome. But she couldn't understand why Molly had pronounced him "old looking." His face was craggy like one might expect of a forty-year-old, but his lean hard body could have been that of a man much younger.

Glancing down at the memo, Karen read his name aloud. "Andonis Sotera."

When he turned to look at her, she understood.

It was his eyes that were old, both haunted and haunting. Even more remarkable, they were a shade of gray so pale, so misty, they were almost no color at all.

DONIS TOOK ONE LOOK at the official and cursed his luck.

A woman.

He didn't need this added aggravation. Donis had learned from experience that women had a talent for hearing more than what was said, comprehending more than was meant to be revealed. He admired their instincts; at times, he even envied them. But this morning, he simply wished this one had been a man.

"Would you come with me?" she said.

Donis stood up and followed her through a corridor of cloth partitions in nondescript pastels. He was relieved to note that she wore no uniform to indicate her rank. All too often, brass buttons and epaulets brought out arrogance in the wearer, eliminating any chance of reasoning with them.

Not that a man could actually warm up to this woman's choice of attire. Her severely tailored camel suit could only be described as prim.

The officials had no offices as such, merely separate cubicles divided by the cloth partitions. The woman ushered him into the fifth cubicle and invited him to take a seat. She sat behind the desk, placed the passport in front of her and folded her hands neatly, precisely.

Donis took the opportunity to size up his surroundings. Two chairs for clients, a desk, and by the window a credenza lined with vinyl-covered binders. There were no silly ceramic pencil holders, no funny notes pinned to the walls, nothing to provide a clue to the woman's personality. So far, she struck him as prim... and dull.

He read the name plaque. K. L. Miller. Anglo-Saxon. Was the surname hers or her husband's? Donis glanced at her hands. No rings. She looked about thirty. Probably divorced. No, take that back. Never married.

"What can I do for you, Mr. Sotera?"

Carefully he formed a smile and motioned toward his passport. "As you can see, the document I was issued at the Toronto airport is valid only for a week. I would like more time to visit, please."

She picked up the document and examined it. Donis, in turn, examined K. L. Miller further, to determine whether she might prove adversary or ally.

She was slightly taller than average and of slender build. Her hair was a becoming shade of ash blond, curled under smoothly at the shoulders like a bell and pulled back at one side by a comb to reveal a tiny pearl stud on her earlobe. Except for a purely functional watch, the earrings were her only jewelry.

Donis's personal preference ran to women with gold bangles and flowing skirts. He believed women ought to celebrate their femininity, make the most of their capacity to entice. Judging from what he'd seen of this one, he concluded that K. L. Miller, in gold bangles and flowing skirts, would look ridiculous.

"I see that you were issued a visa in our Vienna office," she remarked. "Is that where you reside?"

"No, I simply happened to be in Austria at the time and was able to arrange a convenient flight. I travel quite a bit—for the Sanvitan government—but have never had the opportunity to visit your country. I would have flown from Sanvito, but as you are undoubtedly aware, Canada no longer has consular representation in my country."

"We used to," she observed, "until your country cut off diplomatic ties."

Was that reproach he heard in her voice? Sarcasm? Or were paranoia and fatigue getting the better of him? There was no reason why a Canadian should care one way or the other.

"Unfortunately, that is so," he admitted. "We are, however, reexamining our alignment with western nations. Once our domestic stability is restored, I am certain we will open our doors again."

Officer Miller was regarding him intently, but Donis was accustomed to the attentions of women. It didn't always mean they were paying attention to what he said.

After a short time she pulled her gaze away. "Uh... please excuse me for staring. It's just that we don't get many Sanvitans in southwestern Ontario. In fact, you're the first one I've ever met."

He indulged himself in a rare smile. "That is understandable. Few Sanvitans have the opportunity to travel." He turned the pages of his passport, and his fingers brushed Miss Miller's—by sheer accident, of course. "As you can see, I have diplomatic status, which affords me certain . . . privileges."

She moved her hand a safe distance from his. "Yes, I—I noticed the seal and gold ribbon, but I wasn't sure what it meant. What exactly do you do for the government?"

"I am chief economic advisor."

She tipped her head, as though she was impressed. "Is that so?"

"To the president," he added for good measure. The muscles in his stomach tightened, a defensive reaction Andonis had learned to control, but not eradicate. "Are you familiar with the workings of the Sanvitan government?"

"Only from what the press says occasionally."

A tactful answer, he thought, and one which admitted absolutely nothing. "Our head of state," he explained, "is the self-appointed president for life, a concept alien to your part of the world, is it not?"

Karen smiled. "In Canada, we have prime ministers. At times, it only seems as though they're in power for life."

"I see. Perhaps our governments then are not so different." Her wit surprised him. Government lackeys were usually such humorless types.

"Why did the Immigration officer at the airport give you only a week's entry?" she asked.

"I had no intention of staying longer." His tone was smooth, well rehearsed. "I made arrangements to call on several corporate headquarters in Toronto. With that out of the way, I was so intrigued by your country, I decided to take an extended holiday. It's been too many years since I traveled solely for pleasure."

"Do you have friends or relatives in southwestern Ontario?"

"None."

She looked up, startled. He must have answered too sharply. Andonis reminded himself to exercise more care.

"I'm only asking because London isn't usually part of a tourist's itinerary."

"It should be," he said. "London appears to be a charming city."

She laughed as though he'd paid a compliment to her. In an oblique way perhaps he had. Her cheeks blooming with color, Donis was forced to reconsider his opinion. Perhaps Miss Miller was not the cold flounder he'd first imagined her to be.

"How long would you like to stay?" she asked, opening a desk drawer.

"A month . . . six weeks."

"I do have to ask certain routine questions."

"But of course."

"Do you have a round-trip air ticket?"

"Yes." He paused. "Do you wish to see it?"

"If you have it with you."

"It's in my valise at the train station. I could fetch it and bring it in later if you like."

"No, don't bother. I'm sure, since you were issued a visa and an entry permit, everything is in order."

Donis leaned back in his chair. "Thank you."

To his relief, K. L. Miller retrieved a document from the drawer and picked up a pen. It looked as though the first step, the worst step, was over. She would likely believe anything he told her now.

"Have you lived in London all your life?" Donis asked as she copied details from his passport onto the visitor's permit.

"I grew up on a farm about thirty miles outside of London."

"Ah, that would account for your complexion. Milk and honey, we would call it in Sanvito."

She colored again. "Thank you."

From her discomfiture, Donis surmised that Officer Miller was not accustomed to turning pink on the job. Pity, he thought; she wore the hue well.

"Where will you be staying while you're in London?" she asked, once again a paragon of efficiency.

"I have not decided. Could you recommend a decent hotel, some place central where I can take advantage of the sights?"

"We have a convention center with an excellent hotel a few blocks from here."

"Perfect. When we have dispensed with this paper work, perhaps you could give me directions."

"I'd be happy to."

He hadn't given her appearance enough credit, he realized now. The prospect of dealing with a female must have clouded his perception, but she really was quite pleasing to the eye. When she tipped her head a certain way, her hair swung out like burnished gold. Her wide-set eyes were green—not a murky half-hearted shade, but a rich hue, like the leaves of a sycamore in midsummer. K. L. Miller, he decided, might not be devoid of passion, after all. She could simply be a woman who concealed her passion well.

"There you are," she said, stapling the pink document into his passport. "You may remain in Canada as a visitor until the sixteenth of August. If you wish to stay longer, just drop in to the nearest Immigration office."

"Very good."

"I am required to advise you that you're not allowed to accept employment while visiting in Canada."

His smile was the essence of charm. "Believe me, Miss Miller, nothing could appeal to me less than the prospect of employment."

Karen handed him the document, relieved that the interview was over. She hadn't felt this nervous since Michael Caine came in for a work permit. But on that occasion her attack of nerves was understandable. Andonis Sotera, for all his exotic good looks, was hardly a celebrity.

"Thank you," he said, taking the passport. "Now about the directions to that hotel..."

"Oh, yes, I almost forgot." Karen's fingers scrambled across the desk for a pen. Maybe she was just overtired. Staying up until three wasn't conducive to a good day's work. "It's the Holiday Inn," she said, "and it's not hard to find." Karen sketched an abysmal map of downtown London and pushed it across the desk. "I've marked the location of our office on Talbot Street. If you turn left here at Dundas and keep walking, you can't miss the hotel. There's a pedestrian walkway over the street."

Leaning over to study the drawing, Donis lay his hand on the desk. That's when Karen saw the ring. She assumed right away it was a wedding band. Of course, a man as appealing as Mr. Sotera would be married. He would have a loyal Sanvitan wife waiting at home with a brood of well-mannered children, the picture-perfect Mediterranean family.

But taking a closer look at the ring, she was puzzled to see a medieval-style cross engraved in the gold. Karen had read enough about Sanvito to know that most civil liberties, including freedom of religion, had been abolished after the presidential election. It struck her as odd that the president's economic advisor would openly wear a symbol of his faith.

She decided to risk a comment. "I couldn't help noticing your ring. Is it an antique?"

Donis Sotera's fingers tensed briefly. "I have no idea of its age. It is a gold band, nothing more."

"But isn't the expression of religion forbidden in Sanvito?"

He sat up and slowly tucked the map into his pocket. "I must say, Miss Miller, you are a knowledgeable civil servant, not to mention observant."

Karen sensed at once that she'd overstepped her bounds. While Andonis Sotera did not seem offended, he did look clearly uncomfortable. From the corner of her eye, she could see that he was twisting the ring so the cross no longer showed.

"I read *Time* every week," she said, hoping to make light of the issue. "It keeps me informed."

"I see. Well, you are correct. The practice of religion is officially banned in Sanvito, but we are not fanatics. I wear the ring for sentimental reasons. The original owner was a . . . person whom I admired very much."

"I'm sorry if I seem to be prying." Karen's face was burning with embarrassment. She hadn't made a professional gaffe like this in years.

"There's no need to apologize. As I said, your knowledge impressed me." He took his passport and stood up. "Now then, are we finished?"

"Yes, we are."

"Then, once again, I thank you." Taking her right hand in his, Andonis Sotera inclined his head. For an instant, Karen actually thought he was going to kiss her hand. But he only shook it briefly and left.

For the longest time Karen sat at her desk, feeling a mixture of relief and disappointment. Thank heavens not every client had this debilitating effect. She wondered what it was that unnerved her. Maybe it was the startling combination of his olive skin and pale eyes—no, it was something more subtle than that.

He had an aura, a way about him, one of tightly coiled watchfulness. Andonis Sotera was the kind of man one might meet in a Moroccan café after dark, or on the deck of an exclusive luxury cruise ship. In short, he was the kind of man most women never met.

WORKING IN THE SUMMER ought to be illegal, Karen thought at the end of the day, stepping from the air-

conditioned Federal Building into the sweltering afternoon sun. As if the temperature wasn't unbearable
enough, cars were bumper-to-bumper, belching exhaust
while ill-tempered office workers elbowed their way to bus
stops and parking lots. It was enough to make a person
contemplate early retirement.

But as soon as she reached the shady expanse of Victoria Park, Karen relaxed. She removed the pumps that
spent most of their day beside her and crossed the park
barefoot. Her panty hose were in her purse, part of a daily
summer ritual that bordered on rebellion. Mr. Rathbone,
the office manager, preferred that ladies wear stockings on
the job. Karen complied grudgingly, but at 4:00 p.m. every
day, she happily ducked into the ladies' room and peeled
off the lower half of her civil servant trappings.

Home for Karen was a gracious, red-brick apartment
building that had overlooked Victoria Park since the days
Victoria herself ruled the empire. She paid dearly for the
mullioned windows and high ornate ceilings, but considered the money well spent. The apartment stayed cool,
even during London's raging summers, and in winter the
fireplace was a godsend. But the feature that had won
Karen over was the cushioned window seat where she could
curl up for hours and daydream.

Karen, who opted for the stairs instead of the brass elevator that sometimes got stuck between floors, was slightly
out of breath when she stepped inside the apartment and
heard the phone ringing.

"Hi, Karen, where've you been? I've been trying to call
you for an hour."

It was her baby brother, Tim. At twenty-five, he was
hardly a baby, but Karen, who'd been a terribly mature six
when he was born, still liked to think of him that way.

"I was doing some window shopping. Could you hold
on a second?" Karen dropped her purse and shoes, then

crossed the oak floor to the window seat, trailing the phone cord behind her. "Okay, now we can talk."

"Well, I'm glad I caught you. How would you like to come over for dinner?"

"I'd love to. When?"

"Tonight."

"Oh, no, not tonight, I'm exhausted. I had a fight with an immigration lawyer over a goatherd, and I—"

"Dad's coming too."

Karen's excuses skidded to a halt. "Why? Is something wrong?" Given the relationship between father and son, it was not a ridiculous assumption.

"No, nothing's wrong. It was Sue's idea. Ever since we bought this house, she's wanted to invite him. I guess it wouldn't hurt to give in just once."

How like a Miller male, Karen thought, to give in for the first time after five years of marriage. "I think it's wonderful that Dad's going to be there, but why such short notice?"

"I only found out myself an hour ago," Tim said with a chuckle. "When I got home from work, Sue had a roast in the oven. She'd phoned Dad herself, figuring if I had time to think, I'd talk her out of it . . . again."

Karen admired her sister-in-law's perseverance. She'd accomplished more with Tim in a few short years than his own family had done in a lifetime. "Okay, let me have a shower and a few minutes to unwind."

"Dinner's at seven. Don't be late. Sue's gone to a lot of trouble."

Karen wasn't fooled by his cavalier tone. What Tim really meant was, *Please get here before Dad does.* "I'll be there as soon as I can," she promised.

With the windows of her trusty old Honda rolled down, Karen drove down Springbank Drive along the banks of the Thames River. The Canadian London was surprisingly similar to its English namesake, a picturesque city of parks, gardens and meandering waterways. But they shared idiosyncrasies, as well. Streets were laid out with no apparent logic, they changed names at the most unlikely places and were the cause of horrendous traffic snarls. Even the weather was notably similar. Ontario's London was known for periods of incessant rain, while the rest of the province basked in sunshine.

Tim and Sue's latest home was in an affluent subdivision of colonial two-story houses. A reflection of Tim's business acumen was that his neighbors were at least fifteen years older than he. During his last year of high school, he'd landed a tidy profit in penny stocks and used the money for his first down payment. He'd been buying up houses ever since, renovating and selling them within the year.

Karen had lost track of how many places her brother and his wife had lived. Once, she'd had a nightmare about tossing out the wrong change-of-address card and losing Tim and Sue altogether. Now, she had a street map open on the seat beside her and still got lost twice before finding the place.

When Karen saw her father's red pickup in the driveway, her stomach knotted. She had tried to get here quickly. Hopefully it wasn't too late.

Sue answered the door right away. A dark-haired little dynamo, Sue Miller had what Karen called perpetual energy—an absolute requisite for living with a man like Tim. "Thank heavens, you made it," Sue said. "I was beginning to worry."

"I tried to get here sooner. How are things going?"

"Not bad, so far. Your dad's only been here a few minutes. He and Tim are in the living room, talking."

Karen gave her a dubious look. "Talking?"

"Well, you know what I mean. At least, they aren't shouting—yet. I've got to check on dinner. Would you join the men and see if you can keep them unarmed?"

"Okay, but give me a shout if you need help in the kitchen."

Sue had done a remarkable job of making the house feel like home, despite walls stripped of paper, bare plywood floors and a Scarlett O'Hara staircase that was minus a railing. Occasional tables held vases of fresh-cut flowers, and cheery curtains hung from all the windows.

Karen found father and son seated, predictably enough, in opposite corners of the room. William Miller was butting out a cigarette and clutching a bottle of beer to his ample stomach. A glum-faced Tim was slouched on the sofa, nursing a rye and ginger. Both men perked up when they saw Karen, as if she were the floor show they'd been waiting for all evening.

"Hello there," her father said.

"What took you so long?" was Tim's greeting.

"A locomotive with sixty-four cars," Karen answered, taking no offense. Tim only behaved like this when their father was around. She crossed the room to kiss her Dad and would have liked to kiss her brother, too, but he'd nixed that custom sometime around his eighth birthday.

"How are you?" her father asked.

"Fine, thanks. How are you?"

"Not bad."

The greetings were a reflex of sounds that had little to do with feelings or concern. Not that real feelings weren't there; it was just that . . . well, that was the way Millers got through occasions of togetherness—as noncommittally as possible.

"How's work?" was her father's second question.

"Same as usual," Karen replied, knowing that no further embellishment was expected or desired. She sat beside Tim on the sofa. "Looks like you're hard at it again, little brother. You've only been here, what, two weeks?"

Little brother, who towered over Karen's five-foot-six, grinned proudly. "No point in wasting time, is there? I like this house. Should look pretty good when it's finished."

"It's a gorgeous home. Are you planning to lay hardwood in the foyer?"

"We're doing the whole main floor in oak parquet. We laid some in the last place, and buyers loved it. The stair rail's going to be hand-turned oak."

"Sounds lovely. Can't wait to see it."

There was a moment of awkward silence. But before Karen could think of a way to fill it, her father's voice boomed across the room. "Looks like the crop might be coming off early this year."

Tim and Karen turned in unison to stare at their dad. He usually waited until everyone was enjoying dinner before he launched into "the topic."

"Uh...what crop is that, Dad?" Tim asked, glowering.

Karen poked her brother in the ribs. Not that it was going to do a damned bit of good.

William Miller's combative expression matched his son's. "Tobacco. What'd you think I meant?"

"But you grow hay. You haven't grown tobacco in four years."

As if in defiance, his father reached into his shirt for a crumpled pack of cigarettes and lit one. "It's what I done for thirty-five years. I still got a right to talk about it."

"Go ahead, if it makes you feel good," his son remarked with a shrug. "Go ahead and smoke, too. We don't mind, do we, Karen? We've been breathing it in all our lives."

"Tim, stop it," Karen begged. "So, tell me, Dad. How do tobacco prices look this year?" Heaven knew, her true feelings were not much different from Tim's, but she was willing to accept that tobacco had fed and clothed the Miller family.

The frown lines on her father's face eased, as they did whenever someone showed an interest in his former occupation. "Hal Martin figures they'll stay about the same. Prices have held pretty steady since the time we lost the European market."

Karen hadn't seen the Martins, their neighbors on the farm, since high school graduation, yet not a single occasion went by that Dad didn't mention them. Given what happened between the two families, Karen was amazed that her father didn't despise them. Instead, he had adopted a pathetic sort of hero worship. Sometimes, Karen wondered which was the healthier attitude.

Sue outdid herself that night with a veal roast Orloff and chocolate torte. Nor did she seem to mind when Dad used the occasion to reminisce about Mom's wholesome, no-fuss cooking. Tim seethed through dinner, but at least he stayed quiet. It was the closest to an amicable evening that the Millers had had in months.

"I'm sorry about Tim," Sue said to Karen as they loaded the dishwasher. "I know he really wanted things to go smoothly tonight."

"No reason for you to apologize," Karen said. "Tim should know better by now. He's a grown man. But then, so is Dad, and look at the way he behaved."

"Don't be too hard on Dad. He misses your mom badly."

"We all do, Sue. But one of these days, he's got to realize that dumping on his kids is not the proper way to grieve."

"He doesn't dump on you. He just ... he doesn't know how to express his feelings."

Karen gave a short laugh. "No kidding. That's a Miller trademark. Mom was the one who kept the family together, and now that she's gone ... I don't know, Sue. Sometimes, I wonder if it's worth the trouble."

Sue's pixie face fell. "Don't say that, Karen. I know it's frustrating, but there's nothing more important than your family, no matter how rough things get."

"I know, but—"

"And don't even *think* about giving up on those two men in the other room. Tim and Dad may not realize it, but they need you. So do I." Sue grinned. "You're the only reasonable in-law I have."

KAREN WAS GLAD TO GET HOME. She knew that Sue was right about the things she'd said, but it didn't make things any easier. Whenever Karen came away from an evening like this, her one overriding emotion was relief that it was over. Surely there was more to family togetherness than that.

She put on her nightgown and, too overwrought to sleep, turned on the small TV in her bedroom. The eleven-o'clock news was almost over when the phone rang.

"Damn! Not again," Karen muttered, as though her brother's call had come five minutes, and not five hours, earlier.

"Miss Miller?" said a man with an accent.

"Speaking."

"This is Andonis Sotera. We met at the Immigration office this morning. Do you remember?"

Who could forget Andonis Sotera, Karen thought wryly. He'd been the high point of an otherwise dreary day. "Of course I remember. How did you find my number?"

There was a pause. "You are the only K. L. Miller in the directory."

"So I am. What can I do for you?"

"I have found myself in an awkward situation, what you would call in English a pickle, I believe."

His choice of words made her smile. "What kind of pickle?"

"I am in jail."

CHAPTER TWO

"YOU'RE IN JAIL? Why? What happened?"

"It was an unfortunate misunderstanding, but I am having trouble convincing the authorities."

"What have you been charged with?"

"Let me think. Assault causing ... what did they call it now?"

"Assault causing bodily harm?"

"Yes, that was it."

Karen's shock turned to alarm. Given Mr. Sotera's status with the Sanvitan government, and that Canada did not officially recognize Sanvito, this could turn into a bureaucratic nightmare. Karen could see herself writing memos to the Minister of Immigration until doomsday.

"Miss Miller, are you still there?"

Karen shook loose her self-pity. "Yes, I'm still here. Would you—that is, do you want me to come down to the jail and see if I can straighten things out?"

"Would you, please? I would be forever indebted."

"I'll be right down—" Karen stopped herself. "Oh gosh, I'm sorry, Mr. Sotera, I wasn't thinking. I can't actually go to the jail myself."

"Why not?"

"You see, we take turns as duty officer after hours, and I finished my shift last week. I'm supposed to phone the one on call if something comes up."

"Could you not make an exception in this case?"

"I wouldn't mind, but I don't have the authority to make that decision. I'll call the duty officer right away, though. I'm sure he won't be long in getting there."

"Who is the duty officer? What is he like?"

"Barney? He's..." Karen cleared her throat, trying to think of a way to describe Barney Coxwell that would not distress Mr. Sotera more than he already was. "He's, well...very experienced."

"I see."

She must not have sounded very reassuring.

"You must do what is right, of course," he said. "But, Miss Miller, if you would, please tell your colleague that I must get out of this place. Do not let them keep me here behind bars."

The desperation in his voice seemed way out of proportion under the circumstances. It wasn't as though detainees were mistreated in the London Jail. Karen clutched the receiver as though it might somehow comfort Mr. Sotera. "I'll do everything I can. Try not to worry."

Overtired and worried for her client, Karen's fingers shook when she dialed Barney's number. Why did he, of all people, have to be on call this week? If, as Andonis Sotera claimed, it was a misunderstanding, there should be no problem getting him released. But with the exuberant Coxwell on the case, Karen's client would be lucky if further charges weren't added.

Barney's wife answered the phone.

"Mrs. Coxwell, this is Karen Miller. Sorry to be calling so late, but we have a client at the London Jail. Is Barney there?"

"No, I'm sorry, he's already out on a call. He left about half an hour ago."

"Do you expect him back soon?"

"He told me not to expect him home before dawn. He got a tip about some illegal mushroom pickers in Aylmer."

Karen turned her face so that Mrs. Coxwell wouldn't overhear the sigh of relief. At least Andonis Sotera would be spared one indignity tonight. Thanking Mrs. Coxwell, Karen hung up and called the office manager.

"Rathbone here."

He sounded as though he'd been sitting by the phone waiting to answer it. But that was how dedicated civil servants like her boss sounded at all hours.

Karen explained her client's predicament, irritated to hear that her voice took on the slight breathlessness it always did in Mr. Rathbone's presence. Try as she might, she'd never been able to break the infuriating habit. Mr. Rathbone had never said or done anything, but he'd always made Karen feel that her promotion from file clerk to counselor was a token gesture to appease Regional Headquarters. Even though she'd won the competition six years ago and countless other women had moved further up the Immigration ranks, Karen still struggled with that insecurity. It was, she supposed, a simple clash of personalities.

The manager listened patiently to her story. When she finished, he said, "Call another counselor. Evans should be home."

"But, Mr. Rathbone, I'd really like to handle this case myself."

"I was given to believe that you didn't like working after hours." Mr. Rathbone had a voice that sounded like dry leaves being crushed.

"I don't usually, but well . . ."

"You haven't done enforcement work for some time, Miller. Are you sure you could handle this one?"

"I can, Mr. Rathbone. I'm sure I can." If she'd had a tail, it would be wagging right now.

"All right, then. Go ahead. I'll expect a full report in the morning."

Elated, Karen phoned the London Jail to confirm that Andonis was there and not at the detention center on the outskirts of town. That done, she threw off her night-gown, climbed into jeans and grabbed her car keys from the top of the fridge.

The police station was only a few minutes' drive from Karen's apartment. She parked behind the building and went around to the glass doors in front. The desk sergeant, who'd been expecting her, held the door open.

"Haven't seen you in a while," he said. "How's it going?"

During her six years as a counselor, Karen had met or worked with most of the veteran officers on the London Police Force. "Same old thing. How's the prisoner? Is he behaving himself?"

"Oh, he's all right. Seems a little nervous."

"You would be, too, if you were visiting a foreign country and suddenly found yourself behind bars."

"Yeah, I guess I would," the sergeant said. "I'll call one of the guys to take you down."

Karen was soon following a uniformed lieutenant down a set of stairs and through a corridor punctuated by a se-ries of metal doors. Every time one of them clanged shut behind her, Karen jumped.

She'd conducted dozens of interviews in these holding cells, but had never gotten used to the atmosphere. The cement walls were painted a nauseating yellow, and the lights were so bright they made her eyes ache. She could understand why Andonis or anyone would be reluctant to spend the night.

Karen was taken to the last cell where Mr. Sotera sat on a narrow cot in the corner. His head was downcast, el-bows on knees. There was a rip across the front of his white shirt and an angry bruise on his cheekbone.

At the sound of the door being opened he looked up with a haggard expression. Though he tried to smile, he couldn't quite manage it. "You came after all, Miss Miller."

She smiled for both of them. "Call me Karen. Most of my clients do."

The lieutenant held the cell door open, and Karen stepped inside, unconcerned when the bars were locked behind her. Even if her client were dangerous, which she very much doubted, Karen knew the police officer would remain nearby.

Andonis Sotera's eyes warmed like liquid pewter. "I would be honored to call you Karen. And please, you must call me Donis."

"Donis," she said softly, sampling the texture of his name on her tongue. She nearly touched the bruise on his cheek until she realized the gesture might be misconstrued. She limited herself to asking, "Does it hurt?"

"Only when I wink." He motioned toward the narrow cot. "Please sit down. I regret my hospitality cannot extend further."

"Thank you."

Over the years, Karen had arrested, escorted and deported all manner of clients—prostitutes, thieves, runaway kids, even a convicted murderer. There was no reason to feel as though this was her first day on the job. Yet that was precisely how she felt, and with all the classic symptoms—clammy palms, dry throat, pounding pulse.

"What happened?" she asked, willing herself to calm down.

"Have the police not told you?"

"I'd like to hear your side of the story first."

"Very well. It was such a foolish thing, my fault entirely. I checked into the hotel you recommended, relaxed for a while, then went out for something to eat. By the time I came out of the restaurant, it was dark and I had lost my bearings. So I took out the map you gave me and was studying it when someone approached from behind and placed a hand on my shoulder.''

''Did you think it was a mugger?''

He stared at her blankly.

''Did you think you were being robbed?''

''Oh, yes, mugger, I have heard the word, but in connection with places like New York City. No, I had no fear of muggers since I seldom carry anything of value. My reaction was purely instinctive. I thought I was being followed because of... well, who I am.'' He pushed a tense hand through his hair.

''What do you mean, who you are?''

''I have told you that I advise the president on matters of economic policy. Unfortunately, Sanvito's economy is in a state of flux. It is only natural that a man in my position would attract enemies.''

''But you're in Canada. Surely you wouldn't expect to be followed all the way here.''

Donis shrugged. ''I do not claim to have behaved rationally. Perhaps it was fatigue, preoccupation, whatever. I merely reacted.''

''So what did the man want? Did you ever find out?''

''He had intended apparently to offer assistance, but before he could speak, I had driven my elbow into his stomach and thrown him to the ground.''

Donis, though he stood an inch or two under six feet, was not a physically imposing man. His body suggested agility and quick reflexes rather than brute strength, the kind of man who might excel in the martial arts.

''What happened then?''

''We struggled. He managed to tear my shirt and hit me in the face once, but I think he got the worst of it. After a few minutes, he surrendered. From the way he was moaning, I thought he was badly injured. But when a policeman appeared, my assailant practically leaped to his feet, demanding my arrest.''

Donis's situation so far did not look promising, but it wasn't Karen's place to counsel him on the law, except as it pertained to his visitor's status. Taking a notepad from her purse, she jotted down details.

"Have the police told you when you will appear in court?" she asked.

"Tomorrow morning. But at the risk of repeating myself, I do not wish to spend the night here. I will sign a bond, I will offer my personal guarantee—whatever is required, but please, for a man of my position to spend time behind bars..." He left the sentence unfinished, at an apparent loss for words.

Outwardly Donis was the quintessence of composure. But Karen sensed something deeper in his words, something like desperation.

"I'm not sure I can—" she began.

Donis seized her arm. "I beg of you—"

The lieutenant lunged at the cell, hand poised at his holster. "Let go of her."

"Forgive me," he whispered, abruptly releasing Karen's arm.

"It's all right," she said, a little shaken. She nodded her reassurances to the policeman. Turning to Donis, she was struck again by the look in his eyes. For reasons she couldn't understand, it was obvious that Andonis Sotera was living on the ragged edge of terror.

As acutely as she sensed his fear, however, Karen was aware of his reticence. She would give anything to know what lay behind the mask, but was certain Donis would evade the question, as a politician evades a contentious issue.

"Have you made arrangements for counsel?" she asked.

"I beg your pardon?" He shook his head briefly, as though returning from a daydream.

"Legal counsel. Have you requested a lawyer to appear with you in court?"

He shook his head. "The officer mentioned it when I was arrested, but I assumed that right was limited to Canadian citizens."

"No, everyone is entitled to legal representation. Would you like me to arrange it for you?"

He considered this a moment. "I think not. Having no defense for what I did, I will simply appeal to the court's mercy."

"If that's your decision, fine, but I must warn you, Donis, that if you're convicted as charged, there will have to be an Immigration inquiry to review your status."

"You are saying I could be deported."

"Either that, or asked to leave voluntarily. It depends on the nature of the conviction."

"Would I be obliged to return to Sanvito?"

"Not necessarily."

"In that case, what happens, happens."

Karen was putting away her notebook when an idea struck. "I don't want to get your hopes up, Donis, but I may be able to get you released tonight."

His eyes flooded with gratitude. "By all means, do what you can."

At Karen's request, the lieutenant unlocked the cell door and let her out. Donis watched her leave. K. L. Miller, he had to admit, was a different person away from the office. Her briskness was not so evident, her femininity allowed to emerge.

She seemed more at ease with Donis which pleased him, but not for the usual reasons. He wanted no woman's syrupy affections seeping through his defenses. God knew his life was volatile enough these days. But if Karen was attracted to him, then it was likely that, so far, she suspected nothing.

And *that* was good. Turning his face from the blinding light, Donis lay down on the cot to await her return.

Upstairs, Karen approached the desk sergeant. "Is the arresting officer for the Sotera case still here?"

"No, he went off duty a while ago. Want me to pull the file for you?"

"Please."

The sergeant went into a back office and returned a minute later with the report.

Karen read it through. "Charges laid by Dominic Scapiletti. Richmond Street address, sells furniture at White Oaks Mall. Did you get a look at the man?" she asked the sergeant.

"Just for a second."

"What did he look like?"

"Medium build, dark hair, about five seven. He was wearing a cheap gray suit—or what was left of one. Poor guy'd been roughed up pretty good. That's what a person gets for trying to do his civic duty."

Karen refrained from making a reply. "Listen, if I could make suitable arrangements for Mr. Sotera tonight, would you consider releasing him to my custody?"

The sergeant gave her a wink and a nudge. "Your custody, Ms. Miller, or Immigration's?"

Going along with his joke, she laughed. "Good question. I haven't exactly decided yet."

"Ha, I'll bet you haven't. It's okay with me to release him. We just kept him here so you guys could talk to him."

"We appreciate that." Karen handed back the file.

Although he appeared to be sleeping, Donis sat up the instant Karen returned to the holding cell.

"Everything's been taken care of," she said as the lieutenant let her in.

Donis looked at Karen and then at the unlocked bars behind her. "You have secured my release?" he asked, disbelieving. She'd been gone scarcely fifteen minutes.

"You're free to go, as long as you promise to show up for court in the morning."

Abandoning his usual caution, Donis flung his arms around his liberator. "You, Karen, are wonderful. A miracle worker! I don't know how you did it, but I thank you."

Karen, pressed stiffly against his chest, mumbled into his shirt. "I'm afraid you won't be staying at the Holiday Inn, though. I took the liberty of making other arrangements. Of course, you're under no obligation..."

Donis was surprised to feel Karen's heart pounding as rapidly as his. She was so cool on the outside.

"Where I stay makes no difference," he said, reluctant to loosen his arm from her waist, "as long as there are no bars on the windows." Donis let his fingers idle through her hair. He felt an inexplicable urge to calm her, as though Karen were the one who'd undergone the ordeal tonight.

"There won't be any bars," she said, "but, Donis, uh...do you think you could, maybe, let me breathe again?"

His lips were touching her hair. He could smell the apricot essence of her shampoo. Then her softly uttered request filtered through, and Donis sprung his arms. "Forgive me, Karen, I did not intend to—that is, I..."

"It's all right." When Karen stepped back, Donis saw the heightened flush of her cheeks. He tried to ignore the stirrings of pleasure deep inside him.

"It's nice to be appreciated," she continued, patting her hair self-consciously. "But as I was saying, your accommodations for tonight won't be luxurious, though I think you'll be comfortable."

Donis cleared his throat. "Where will I be staying?"

"At a Jesuit seminary here in London. The priests have guest quarters and quite often help us out when our clients require emergency shelter."

His vague stirrings of lust scattered. "What did you say? That I would be staying with priests?"

"Yes. Does that bother you?" As she phrased the question, Karen realized what she had done. Now it was her turn to blanch. She'd placed the representative of an atheist country into a seminary. Not one of her more diplomatic moves.

"Do not misunderstand," Donis said hurriedly. "I have no objection to the arrangements. I was merely... surprised, that is all."

His fingers were linked together as he spoke. From the corner of her eye, Karen noticed Donis groping for the ring finger of his right hand. He looked down then as if surprised to discover it was bare.

Karen recalled the ring Donis had worn that morning, but was careful to avoid mentioning it. She'd committed more than her share of faux pas today. "The police will return your possessions to you as soon as we go upstairs," she said discreetly.

He nodded. "Yes. Thank you."

Outwardly Donis was once again in control. The wariness Karen had sensed that morning was even more fixedly in place, but this time she was not so easily persuaded. When Donis held her so intensely a moment ago, she had caught a glimpse, however brief, of the man inside. She had felt his turbulence, passion—perhaps even fear. But control? No.

The realization disturbed her, and Karen felt herself retreating behind professional brusqueness as they dispensed with the red tape of Donis's release. She was probably overreacting anyway, caught up in the drama of freeing this handsome Sanvitan. Next she'd be expecting him to pledge his eternal gratitude, for heaven's sake.

After signing the last of the forms, Karen and Donis waited in the station foyer for Father Peter who arrived within minutes. Karen was delighted and relieved to see the priest. A solid man with a broad smile and wavy dark hair, Father Peter had a marvelous way with people. He'd come to Canada from Hungary in 1957 after the Soviet invasion. In all these years, his compassion for the needy and displaced had never diminished.

"I hope I haven't kept you waiting too long." The priest shook Karen's hand warmly. "Sancho was giving me trouble again." Sancho was the priest's ancient, wood-paneled station wagon, named after Don Quixote's loyal squire.

Karen laughed. "What's ailing him now?" She'd once had the dubious pleasure of driving Sancho from the office to the seminary. It had taken her half an hour to start the blamed thing, only to have it belch and bunny-hop the entire way.

"The carburetor... again."

She couldn't resist teasing him. "Why don't you bring Sancho to a garage? I'm sure they could fix whatever you did to the carburetor last time."

Father Peter clenched a hand to his heart. "My dear child, how could you even suggest such a thing? I would never abandon Sancho to the ministrations of mechanics. They're usurers, even the Catholic ones. All I need to repair the car is faith...and the proper tools." He turned to Donis who'd been watching the exchange quietly. "How do you do? I'm Father Peter."

Donis shook his hand. "Father."

Karen had half expected to find condescension or animosity in Donis's expression, yet what she saw closely resembled awe.

"You must be tired, son," Father Peter said. "I'll take you home, and tomorrow, when you are rested, we will become better acquainted. What time should we be in court?" he asked Karen.

"Nine."

Donis turned to her. "Will you be there?"

She looked up and felt the strong pull of his gaze, as potent and inexorable as his embrace. It would have been simpler, she realized, to call another counselor tonight instead of coming to the jail herself. To say yes to Donis again would be just as effortless. But there were guidelines to follow, chains of command. This was Karen's job, not some self-proclaimed quest for fulfillment. "I'm sorry," she said. "There's another counselor who's assigned to court duty."

"Of course," Donis replied. He dropped his gaze. Karen felt herself plummet.

The three of them walked outside to the parking lot. It had been a long day. Karen was glad to hand over the responsibility of Donis to Father Peter for the night.

"I understand you are from Sanvito," the priest said to his guest.

"That is correct."

"Years ago, when I was studying in Rome, I became acquainted with a young priest from your country. I know it's most unlikely, even foolish of me to ask, but perhaps you have heard of him..." Father Peter scratched his head. "Now, what was his name again?"

Hiding a grin, Karen dug through her purse for the car keys. Father Peter was not nearly as forgetful as he pretended to be; it was a tactic he employed to put people at ease.

"If he is still a priest, he would likely not be in Sanvito anymore," Donis observed.

"No, I suppose not. But I wish I could remember his name. Ah, well, it will probably come to me at three in the morning."

While Father Peter struggled with Sancho's crotchety lock, Karen was struggling with an irritating case of self-indulgence. Her responsibility toward Donis Sotera was over. She'd given him his visitor's extension, she'd done what was necessary to effect his release. Tomorrow, his case would be handled by others. There was no reason to see him again, no reason to wish that she would.

Donis, as if to make things worse, walked over to Karen. She looked up reluctantly. His eyes matched the silver of the moon behind them. "I hope I have not inconvenienced you too much this evening," he said.

"Not at all. I was just...doing my job."

"If everyone is as compassionate as you, then Canada is truly a remarkable country."

She brushed aside the unsettling praise. The man could obviously turn the charm on and off at will. "I'm sure you'll be comfortable at the seminary, but if there's anything I can do..." *Don't you just wish...*

Her chastisement trailed off when she realized that Donis was lowering his face to hers. Cradling her cheeks in his hands, he kissed her forehead, then smiled. "In my country, it is customary to reward kindness with a kiss. And you, Karen, have been most kind." He didn't linger. He turned and walked over to Father Peter's car as casually as if they'd spent the evening playing bridge.

Karen, dazed, got into her own car. She could still hear Father Peter chatting through the open window. "He was a bookish sort of fellow, that priest..."

THE NEXT MORNING Karen went into her supervisor's office. Liz O'Connell was on the phone, but she waved Karen to a chair, inviting her to wait. Karen sat down, the Sotera file in hand, and tried not to eavesdrop. It was impossible.

Liz, who'd been married and divorced three times, had a social life that put women half her age to shame. Karen couldn't understand where Liz found the energy—or the men.

"I know it seems like I've been avoiding you," Liz was saying, "but my mother really is sick. I told you... bronchitis, a dreadful case, with all sorts of complications. She's almost ninety, and I am her only child...I knew you'd understand. Okay, talk to you later." Liz dropped the receiver as if it were a dead rat. "What's wrong with women?" she said to Karen. "We meet a jerk, we practically throw ourselves in his path. Then a nice guy comes along, and what do we do? We treat him like garbage."

"I assume from what you're saying, that was a nice guy on the phone?"

Liz ran her hand through short, frosted hair. "Yeah, he's no looker, mind you, but he's nice. Fifty-three, widowed, no kids."

"What's wrong with him?"

"His clothes are falling apart."

"What?"

"I'm serious. This guy's got plenty of money, but he keeps things forever. We were at the Grand Theater a few weeks ago, and during intermission, the entire lining of his jacket fell out and landed on the floor."

Karen bit her cheek to keep from guffawing. "No kidding? What did you do?"

"With all the dignity I could muster, I walked away and called a cab. That's when I decided my mother was too ill for me to date, anymore."

"Is she ill?"

"No, she's dead. But it *was* bronchitis with complications that killed her."

"Oh, I guess that's okay then."

"No, it's not. It's dreadful having to lie to avoid hurting someone—but never mind that. What can I do for you?"

"I went out on a call last night."

"Oh, yes. Mr. Rathbone mentioned something about it this morning. Anything exciting?"

"It's all here," Karen said, handing her the file. "I thought you might want to read the report before you turn it over to management."

"Good, thanks." Liz perused the memo. "High up in the government, eh? Not the kind of guy you'd expect to get into trouble."

"That's what I thought. I have a favor to ask you, Liz." If the supervisor had been anyone but Liz O'Connell, Karen wouldn't have even broached the topic.

"What is it?"

"Could I sit in on the court hearing this morning?"

"Why? We already have a court officer."

"I know, but I guess I've sort of taken Mr. Sotera's case under my wing."

Liz flipped through the file until she came to the photocopy of Andonis Sotera's passport picture. "Aha! So that explains this sudden interest. He's gorgeous."

"Come on, Liz, it's nothing like that."

"Like what? No need to play coy with me. If I had a client who looked like him, I'd no doubt react the same way."

It was probably easier, Karen decided, to concur with Liz than to come up with an excuse of her own. "Okay, what can I say? You're right. The man's a veritable feast for the eyes."

"I knew it."

"So may I go?"

"I'm afraid not. Jim Evans phoned in sick this morning, so we're a counselor short. Besides, the court officer has to be there anyway to cover the break-and-enter trial of those foreign students. We'd just be duplicating our efforts."

Karen swallowed her disappointment. "Oh, well, thought I'd ask anyway."

"If it's any consolation, I'll let you know as soon as I hear what happens to your client, okay?"

"I'd appreciate that."

During lunch hour, Karen was in no mood for company. It was impossible to be alone in the Federal Building's cafeteria, so she went outside for a walk. It was driving her crazy, but all of her thoughts were taken up with Donis. She hadn't heard from Liz, but it was possible that his case hadn't even come up yet.

Karen did not consciously set out to visit the public library. But when she saw the building, a thought popped into her head. She felt a little guilty walking in, as though her motives were less than honorable.

But Karen could think of no better way to learn more about Donis. Squaring her shoulders, she approached a librarian and requested her assistance in looking up articles on Sanvito. Soon Karen was seated at a microfiche viewer, totally absorbed by what she was reading.

Sanvito was little more than a speck on the map, about the size of Malta, midway between Sardinia and the northeastern coast of Spain. Its strategic location in the Mediterranean had made the island vulnerable to seafaring conquerors. Over the centuries, Sanvito had been ruled by Phoenicians, Romans, Greeks, Byzantines and Spaniards. Hard-won independence from Spain came shortly after World War I.

Now, it seemed, the island grappled with a new brand of domination. The current president of Sanvito—elected, it was said, by rigged ballots—ruled with a totalitarian hand. Land was confiscated in the name of progress, censorship imposed, and severe taxes levied to support the evergrowing military budget.

The Sanvitans, proud of their civil liberties, did not take these sanctions lightly. Soon after the dictator took office, the Sanvitans began to assemble in the haven of their churches to debate ways of bringing down the government.

The head of state retaliated swiftly. Churches were burned or boarded up and all forms of religious observance banned. Worse, great numbers of clerics and traitors were executed, further inflaming the Sanvitans' terror and zeal. Finally, in another attempt to maintain control, the president declared the island to be in a state of siege and closed her borders to the world.

When Karen checked her watch, she was amazed to discover her lunch hour was over. There were still more articles to read, but Karen had seen enough. She switched off the microfiche and left the building.

No wonder Donis was wary of men who approached him after dark. As Sanvito's chief economic advisor, he had every reason to fear reprisal. Donis would surely have been responsible for the tax system and even for the flagrant expropriation of land. No doubt he was as despised by the Sanvitan populace as the leader he worked for.

To think how easily Karen had been taken in by his charm. She'd blithely given him six weeks to stay in Canada, then pulled every string to get him out of jail. Andonis Sotera was no tourist, that much was certain. But what was he really doing here? And why was he so desperate to be released from detention?

By the time she reached the office, Karen wished she had left well enough alone. If she hadn't gone to the library. If she hadn't been so damned curious...

But it was too late for regrets. There was a very real possibility that Canada was harboring an undesirable, and something would have to be done.

Not that it was entirely Karen's fault. The Canadian visa officer in Vienna had issued Donis a visa, and the airport examining officer gave him a week's entry. They should have exercised more caution, they should have questioned him more thoroughly. But Karen shook her head, disgusted with herself for passing the buck. She was every bit as accountable as the others.

What she needed now was time to consider the evidence against him. Conjecturing about a client's background was one thing. Accusing him of political crimes, or heaven knows what, was something else entirely.

First Karen called the police station and requested information about Mr. Scapiletti. A few minutes later, a constable called her back with the address and phone numbers.

Karen tried Mr. Scapiletti's home number first.

"You got the wrong number," a man said.

She repeated the number she'd been given.

"Yeah, that's it, but there's no one living here by that name."

Next Karen called the furniture store at White Oaks Mall and asked to speak to the manager. "I've never heard of Dominic Scapiletti," the manager said.

Karen hung up, her suspicions confounded.

A moment later the intercom buzzed. It was Liz. "Thought you'd like to know, the charges against Andonis Sotera have been dropped."

"Dropped?" Karen said. "What happened?"

"The plaintiff, Scapiletti, didn't show up."

"Oh my God," Karen said, stunned. "Liz, I've got to talk to you right away. I think I've made a terrible mistake."

CHAPTER THREE

KAREN SPENT THE NEXT half hour telling Liz what she'd found out about Sanvito. Liz listened carefully, as she always did. But her response was not what Karen had anticipated.

"I think you're overreacting," Liz said.

"After what happened in court, how can you say that? I mean, no one's even heard of this Scapiletti person. He could very easily be a Sanvitan."

"Oh, come on, you've been watching too many espionage movies. So the plaintiff used an alias and a false address. Maybe he's got a record with the London PD, maybe he really intended to mug your client. Who knows? That's still no reason to assume the worst about Donis."

Karen leaned back and tried to regroup her thoughts. "Okay, let's assume the assault charge was just a coincidence. What about Donis's occupation? He's come right out and admitted he works for the Sanvitan president. Anyone who works willingly for a tyrant has got to be one himself."

"Hold on a minute, Karen. I appreciate your disapproval of the things that are happening in Sanvito, but imposing your personal prejudices on others is not part of the job."

"That's not what I'm doing," Karen protested halfheartedly.

"Aren't you? Then you know as well as I do that in order for us to take action against Sotera, he has to be convicted of a criminal offense, not merely suspected of doing what you think are unpleasant things."

"But, Liz, the Sanvitan government has arbitrarily wiped out private ownership of land. There's widespread corruption—"

"According to what source?" Liz cut in. "What appears as corruption to you may be necessary economic reform to someone else."

"What about the execution of innocent people? Priests, students... I suppose we have a nice diplomatic term for that too."

"Are you accusing your client of pulling the trigger at these executions?"

"Well, no, but he would obviously have a hand in some of the decision making."

"He probably does, but you're still missing my point. I know you have to make value judgments as an Immigration counselor, but you also have to know where to draw the line. All you have are a bunch of old newspaper articles and an assault charge that's been dismissed for lack of evidence. Do you get what I'm saying?"

An hour ago Karen had been so sure of her feelings. Now she felt like the perpetrator of a witch hunt. "I guess I understand."

"I knew you would. Hey, chin up, okay? In case I haven't mentioned it lately, you're one of the best counselors in this office. Dedicated, bright, terrific with the public. But you take things too seriously. If you don't learn to ease up, you'll make yourself crazy."

"Are you suggesting I should just put Donis's file away and forget about it?"

"Yes. Put it away for a month, and we'll see if anything happens in the meantime. If it makes you feel better, I'll talk to enforcement and have them investigate this Scapiletti thing."

"Thanks, and I appreciate your listening."

Liz smiled. "That's what I'm here for."

Karen returned to her desk to find a staggering new pile of files. Molly had obviously been around again.

WILLIAM MILLER sat nursing his coffee at the kitchen table. "I got twelve quarts of strawberries in the cold cellar from Gladys Martin's garden," he said.

"That's nice," Karen replied, staring idly outside.

The Saturday morning sun called attention to a build-up of grime on the windows. Karen made a mental note to wash them as soon as she finished her coffee. The windows would never have been allowed to reach this state if Mom were still alive. In fact, Dad would have been the first to complain.

"I figured since we got the berries," her father went on, "you might want to put up a few jars of preserves. You could take some home with you, bring a jar over to Tim and Sue's."

Karen placed her empty cup in the sink. "It's too hot to make jam today, and anyway, you can freeze strawberries. There's nothing to it."

"I wouldn't know the first thing about that."

"I gave you a freezer cookbook last Christmas, remember? Where did you put it?"

He scratched his thinning hair and affected a look of helplessness. "Can't say as I recall."

Karen held her tongue until the wave of frustration passed. "More coffee?"

"Nope, that's fine for me, thanks. Think I'll stretch out for a while. You'll be staying the night, won't you?"

"Not this time. I'll have lunch with you, but after that I have to get back to London."

Her father didn't ask why she had to get back, and normally Karen would have volunteered the information, but today she felt like assuming her brother's role for a change.

If Dad was interested in her life, he could darned well ask about it.

But he didn't. Her father got up from the large table and shuffled off to the bedroom as though he was on his last legs instead of a hale and hearty sixty-nine. Karen cleared the rest of the dishes, then got out a bottle of ammonia and a bucket for the windows.

The kitchen was part of the original farmhouse that her father and mother had moved into as newlyweds nearly fifty years before. As the Millers could afford it, new wings and additions had been built to accommodate their six growing children.

The house sat on the tobacco farm that William Miller used to own. But a few years ago, when tobacco prices dropped, he found himself overextended with the bank and was forced to sell. Now the land belonged to their neighbors, Hal and Gladys Martin, and Karen's father paid them rent to live in the house he'd built himself.

All the Miller children were grown now, living in places as diverse as California, Florida and New Brunswick. When Mom was alive, all the kids and grandkids used to come home for Christmas. Not anymore. Now only Karen and Tim included Dad in their plans, and Tim did so with the greatest reluctance. It was sad what had happened to their family, Karen thought as she buffed the picture window. But considering the way they had been brought up, it was also inevitable.

She finished the first floor in an hour and decided to leave the rest for another day. She was tempted to leave her father a note and go home before he woke up, but that would have been unkind. He was alone all week. Karen knew how much he appreciated her visits.

The only reading material in the house was an old set of encyclopedias and the latest issue of *Farmers' Almanac*. So to pass the time until lunch, Karen went into the cold cellar and brought up the twelve quarts of strawberries. By the time her father awoke, the berries were simmering in a huge pot on the stove, and jars were sterilizing in the dishwasher.

"Hi, Dad, did you have a nice rest?"

His eyes flickered with pleasure at the sight of the simmering cauldron. "Not great. I'm gonna have to see the chiropractor about my neck again."

"It's still bothering you?"

"Yeah. Hal Martin's had the same problem for years. Happens to farmers all the time. Stress, you know."

Karen turned away and continued stirring. There were days when she empathized with her father's loneliness and loved him so much it hurt. But there were other times, like today, when everything he said and did were irritating. His helplessness around the house, his moaning and groaning, his ever-narrowing scope on life. If that was what growing old was like, Karen dreaded it.

"I might be going on a training course next month," she ventured for the sake of conversation.

"Is that so?" Peering outside, her dad checked the thermometer and entered his findings on the calendar by the chair. He didn't mention a thing about the clean windows.

"It's going to be in Hamilton," Karen pressed on, determined to pique his interest. "An enforcement course."

"Enforcement? I don't care much for the sound of that."

"It's not police work, Dad, you know that. I've explained it to you before."

"What's it about then?"

Maybe this hadn't been such a great topic to bring up after all. "Uh...it's on terrorism."

Her father's face grew ruddy. "What the blinkin' hell do you need to know about that for?"

"Well, it's...it's something we should all be aware of. I mean, no country is exempt from—"

"I'd say it's a damned fool thing for people to be learning. And to think taxpayers are footing the bill for that nonsense. What would your mother say if she were alive?"

Sighing, Karen dropped the sticky spoon onto the counter. "I don't know. Probably the same thing as you."

"Damned right she would. I can't understand young women these days. When you started with Immigration, you had a perfectly good job in the file room. You could've taken that promotion to clerk supervisor and be getting the same salary and benefits without worrying about some hotheaded fool blowing your head off."

Karen slapped a pair of oven mitts against the counter. "Dad, you know how much I hated that file room. I worked really hard to get out of that job and refuse to feel guilty for showing some ambition. Besides, no one gets their head blown off, for Pete's sake."

"What are you getting so worked up for?"

"I'm *not* getting worked up! But just because you and your friends can't fathom what I do for a living, doesn't mean it's wrong for me to do it."

Her father took out a cigarette and tapped it methodically on the table. "You must be coming down with something. Your mother always used to get testy before she caught a bug."

THE UNIVERSITY of Western Ontario often held film festivals, and this weekend they were featuring movies with Grace Kelly. That was why Karen couldn't spend the night at her father's, had he cared enough to ask.

She met two of her girlfriends at a campus pub for a drink, then armed with a box of hankies, sat through six hours of Grace and Bing, Grace and Jimmy, Grace and Cary.

The women parted company outside the screening room, promising to get together again soon. Karen walked alone across the gently rolling campus to the parking lot. It was a perfect summer night—starry, clear with just the whisper of a breeze.

It was a funny thing about movies, Karen thought. A person was never quite the same after seeing one. Maybe that's why she enjoyed them so much. There were movies that inspired, ones that exaggerated life's absurdities and movies that could turn an ordinary bedroom into a ghastly place of creaks and shadows. Unfortunately an evening with Grace Kelly had done none of those things. What Karen felt most was restless.

Not that she resented the actress's achievements. And not that she expected glamour in her own life. But surely there was something more to look forward to than what she'd experienced so far.

Granted, she had a secure job, friends, family, good health. And while there was still the attainment of husband and children, Karen had witnessed enough crumbling marriages among her friends to know it was no solution for tedium.

In twenty-six years, if she was lucky, she could look forward to an honorary dinner and a pension from the civil service. And if her colleagues chipped in generously enough, she might even get a nice gold brooch. Good grief, that was a depressing thought.

As she drove home, Karen tried to shake her mood. When the car radio played a schmaltzy ballad, she switched it off. If she saw a happy young couple on the street, she looked away. It amazed Karen to discover that a state of nothingness could hurt so much.

Next, she tried reason. A good night's sleep was all she needed. Sleep, plus a long abstinence from old romantic movies. Having come up with a remedy of sorts, Karen began to feel better.

When she stopped for a red light, her gaze slid idly to the bus shelter on the corner. It was lit up, so she could see the man waiting by the entrance. He looked familiar. Karen leaned closer and saw that it was Andonis Sotera.

Impulsively she leaned across the seat and rolled down the window. "Need a ride, stranger?" she said, grinning.

Donis jerked his head toward the voice and squinted suspiciously. "Who are you?" he called out.

"It's Karen, from Immigration."

The light had turned green by this time, and cars behind her were honking. Karen turned into the side street, parked and stepped outside.

She hadn't forgotten her misgivings about Donis, but her talk with Liz had helped put things in perspective. Karen knew that when a case aroused her interest, she was often her own worst enemy. So when she'd put the Sotera file away a few days ago, she'd nearly succeeded in forgetting all about him.

"What are you doing out at this hour?" Donis asked in his delectable Sanvitan accent.

Karen took in the unruly black hair and the lean, shadowed contours of his face. The combination of her mood and the nighttime made her feel dangerously reckless. Maybe she shouldn't have stopped, but it was too late to change that.

"I was seeing a movie with friends, three of them actually—movies, that is." *You're babbling, Karen.*

Donis, who until now had been visibly wary, broke into a smile. The tension fell from his shoulders as if he had dropped a cloak. Karen was the tense one as she watched Donis approach. He was wearing faded jeans snug against his thighs and a white shirt with the sleeves rolled to his elbows.

"What are you up to tonight?" she asked.

"I'm waiting for a bus."

It occurred to Karen that his answer was really no answer at all, but she refused to follow it up with a second question. This was a social meeting, not an interrogation.

If Karen hoped to follow Liz's advice, she had to remember that Immigration was a job, not a state of mind.

"If you're heading into town," she said, "I can give you a lift. Did you go back to the Holiday Inn?"

"No. Father Peter invited me to stay at the seminary for the duration of my visit, which suited my purposes nicely. The hotel rates were somewhat beyond my budget."

Maybe she was rationalizing, but Karen felt better knowing that Father Peter had extended an invitation to Donis. The priest was a consummate judge of character. If he could accept Donis's background such as it was, then so could she.

"I'm glad you like it there," she said. "The seminary is in a beautiful section of the city."

"I agree," Donis replied. "I have spent many peaceful hours wandering the grounds. It is reassuring to know there are still such places in the world."

His remark jarred her. Unlike Sanvito, she thought, then promptly dismissed it as unjustified. "Would you like to join me for coffee?" she asked, partly to make up for her earlier attitude and partly because she wanted to. "I know a little shop downtown that serves great cappuccino."

He didn't even pause to consider the invitation. "I would like to, but I have other plans. Another time, perhaps."

Karen swallowed a lump of humiliation. So the attraction wasn't mutual. What did she expect? If she hadn't seen six hours' worth of men falling for Grace Kelly, Karen wouldn't have even stopped the car.

"If your offer of a ride is still open, however..." Donis ventured.

The impulsive magic was gone, but Karen had made the offer, after all. "By all means," she said. "Hop in."

The car was small and with Donis as a passenger, it seemed even smaller. No matter how hard Karen tried to concentrate on driving, she could not ignore his nearness.

She caught the scent of his soap, and from the corner of her eye, she could see Donis clearly. The black tangle of hair on his forearms, the taut muscles of his thighs were enough to make Karen's palms grow slick on the steering wheel.

"Where are you headed?" she asked, clearing her throat once or twice.

"To Oxford Street. I don't recall the exact address, but I'll show you where to let me off."

"Are you going to a restaurant?"

"Yes. I am meeting friends—well, acquaintances, actually."

"That's nice," she murmured, wondering who these people were and where he had met them. If she weren't the mature woman she prided herself on being, Karen would have resented that Donis was getting along nicely without her. "You haven't been approached by any more strange men after dark?" The instant she asked the question, Karen could have kicked herself. What a snippety, stupid thing to say.

She could see Donis recoil, but he quickly regained his composure. "Thankfully, no. That reminds me, I meant to thank you for coming to my rescue at the London Jail. I must admit, it did—how do you say—rankle my masculine pride, but I am no less grateful for your help."

"Don't mention it," she said, rewarding him with a few points because he had.

"Perhaps you would restore my dignity by joining me for a drink some evening?"

The invitation came as a complete surprise. Karen turned to look at Donis. His smile would have caused a woman from another era to swoon. Karen somehow managed to limit her physical response to an outbreak of sweat along her hairline. "I'd like that," she replied.

"Wonderful. We shall make arrangements soon. Ah, the traffic light is about to change. You can let me off right here."

"Are you sure? I'd be happy to—"

"No, I insist, this is fine." Donis's behavior had suddenly changed, as though he found Karen an unwelcome distraction. "Thank you for the ride. Good night."

The light was green. Karen had no choice but to drive on. Through the rearview mirror, she tried to see which way Donis headed from the intersection. The neighborhood boasted a number of restaurants, some neon-lit and trendy, others housed in elegant old mansions. Which one, she wondered, would appeal to Donis and his new-found friends?

But her curiosity was to remain unsatisfied. Donis stood at the corner, hands in pockets, and waited while Karen drove away. She might have been imagining things, but she could have sworn that Donis didn't want her to see where he was going.

DURING THE NEXT FEW DAYS, Karen plunged herself anew into work. Anything was better than sitting around fantasizing about mysterious, foreign men. She had a fascinating career and ought to be grateful that she was no longer sorting files alphabetically. If excitement was what she craved, well, there were plenty of other cases to choose from.

Karen picked up the Garcia file and took it to her supervisor. "I'd like to pay a visit to my newlyweds."

Liz looked up from her stats sheets. "Which newlyweds are we talking about?"

"Miguel and Estelle Garcia."

"Oh, yes, the ketchup lady and the tomato picker. Talk about your match made in heaven. Are they having problems already?"

"They've had problems since the beginning. I can't process the application until Miguel brings in medicals, and I haven't seen him for a month. Estelle keeps making excuses, but I'm convinced Miguel has left her."

"Then go ahead and check it out. I take it you want to be part of the investigation?"

"I'd like to. Estelle seems to feel comfortable with me. Or at least, I'm the only one she knows."

"Okay, but be careful. These cases can get sticky sometimes."

"I know. I hate poking around in people's private lives, but it really bothers me to see women like Estelle get burned."

"Too bad the rest of us don't have an agency to screen men for us. We just have to take our chances. I'll see who I can drum up to go with you from enforcement." She picked up the phone and dialed an extension. "Hi, Barney. Which of you fellas wants to go out with a ravishing blonde? No, not the lady from Income Tax, you dope. Karen. She's in my office."

Liz had barely hung up when Barney Coxwell appeared at the door. Karen looked up at him drolly. "What took you so long?"

"Hiya, kiddo, it's been a while since you and I went out bagging turkeys together."

Karen shot Liz a look of frustration. "Can't you make him stop saying that?"

"Stop saying that, Barney," Liz said without enthusiasm, as if knowing her reproach wouldn't do any good.

"Whatever you say, boss." Barney, a man in his midfifties, had a myopic, mama's boy image that fooled illegal immigrants every time. Only his colleagues knew the truth, that Barney's personality bordered on the sociopathic. "Who're we checking out this time?" he asked.

Karen got up. "I'll tell you all about it in the car. Let's go."

They rode the elevator to the basement garage where the government vehicle was parked. Barney held out his hand when they reached the car. "Keys?"

Karen folded her fingers around them. "It's okay, I'll drive."

"Hey, loosen up, Miller. If we're gonna look like a happily married couple, you gotta let me sit behind the wheel."

For two cents, she'd have slugged him. "No one in their right mind would ever think we're married, Barney."

"Maybe not, but lemme drive anyway."

They could have spent the next hour arguing, but Karen was anxious to get this investigation over with. Knowing she would soon regret it, she surrendered the keys. "I'm warning you, the first time I hear so much as a single tire squeal, I'm out. Got that?"

He grinned and slid into the driver's seat. "Got it, baby."

When they were on the road, Karen filled Barney in on the details of the Garcia marriage.

"Sounds like a live pair, all right," he said. "By the way, I checked out Dominic Scapiletti, the guy who messed with your client, Sotera."

Her interest piqued, Karen turned to him. "What did you find out?"

"The address he gave, there's no such place."

"Really? Has he made any contact with the police or anything?"

"Not a word. Funny, eh? As for Sotera, he checked out of the Holiday Inn and left no forwarding address. I don't know where he ended up."

"I do. He's staying at the seminary."

"Is that right? Were you talking to the priests?"

"No, I gave Donis a ride into town on the weekend."

"Oh yeah? Cozying up to the customers, are you?"

"Get off it, Barney. He was waiting for a bus, and offering him a ride seemed like the polite thing to do."

"Whereabouts was he headed?"

"He was meeting friends at an Oxford Street restaurant."

"Friends? Who were they?" If Barney had had antennae, they'd be standing straight up and quivering.

"Calm down," Karen chided. "How should I know? This may come as a surprise to you, Barney, but visitors are not prohibited from mingling with the natives. Besides, Donis is not under investigation. Liz only asked you to keep an eye open."

"As far as I'm concerned, baby, everyone is under investigation."

Karen looked away with a huff. She should have known better than to reason with a man who jotted down license plate numbers of people who didn't look Canadian.

They drove in silence for a while until Barney said, "Remember my mushroom pickers?"

"The ones in Aylmer? I remember."

"Got all nine written up and deported."

"Congratulations," she said dryly. "Your stats will be impressive this month."

"My stats are always impressive. I only need one more Section 18 before the end of the week, and I'll have an even ten arrests this month."

"Tell you what," Karen offered. "If it turns out that Miguel Garcia has left his wife, I'll let you write him up."

"Hey, no kidding? You'd really let me do that?"

Karen couldn't help but laugh at his heartfelt expression. Although admittedly one of the most irritating people in the office, Barney was top-notch at enforcement. He was tireless, uncomplaining and ready at all hours to "bag turkeys."

Karen's major complaint against Barney was his treatment of clients; it was deplorable. Remarkably enough, however, the office had yet to receive a single complaint about him from the Human Rights Commission. Karen attributed this to the inexorable laws of Murphy. There were people forever destined to get away with illegal parking and cheating on their income tax. Barney Coxwell was one of those people.

Estelle and Miguel Garcia lived near the Armed Forces base. Their bungalow, along with dozens of identical matchbox neighbors, had once belonged to the Department of National Defense. They were a grim reminder of days when the demand for army contingents was high. Some of the homes had a shabby, neglected look to them; the Garcias' was one of the shabbiest.

Karen and Barney walked past scraggly shrubs to the front door. The screen was torn, and Barney seemed to take perverse delight in knocking on the inner door through the hole.

From inside the house they could hear the pulsing rhythms of rock music, too loud for anyone to hear a knock. This time, Barney opened the screen door and, to Karen's horror, pounded with both fists.

"Stop it, Barney, you're making the whole house shake."

His boorish method worked. The music stopped, and someone inside swore in Spanish. "I'm coming, I'm coming. Hold on!"

Karen glanced at Barney in astonishment. "That's Miguel. I can't believe it."

The door opened to reveal all five feet two inches of Miguel Garcia in a pair of track shorts. His glower suggested a man for whom stature was not an impediment. "What you want?" he barked.

Barney presented his badge with a well-practiced whoosh and clap. "Coxwell, Immigration. This here's Miller—"

"I know who she is."

Karen did her best not to hide behind her partner. She never shirked while doing investigations, but she never cared for them either. They made her feel unwelcome, like a door-to-door salesman.

"Are you Miguel Garcia?" Barney asked.

"I might be."

Karen rolled her eyes. "It's him," she said. "Barney and I would like to talk to you, Miguel."

"What for?"

"We want to discuss your application to remain in Canada."

He lifted his palms in a gesture of apathy. "So, go ahead, man, talk."

"Could we go inside?" Karen asked, trying to balance Barney's antagonism with courtesy.

Miguel gave her partner an icy glare, which Barney returned with one of his own. "You come in," he said to Karen. "Coxwell here can wait outside."

Leaving Barney on the front steps was tempting, but Karen needed him as a witness. "Mr. Coxwell is my partner. You're not required to let us inside, but we are within our rights to question you."

"Okay, what the hell. I got nothin' to hide."

They stepped into a dismal living room. The walls were painted a hospital green, and the place reeked of kitty litter. Karen looked around and decided the aluminum dinette chair was the least likely to be contaminated. Barney didn't take a seat. He wandered around the room, hands behind his back.

"The reason we're here," Karen said, "is that you've failed to appear for three interviews and still haven't brought in your medicals."

Miguel ogled her briefly, then sauntered out of the room without reply. He returned a minute later carrying a can of beer and flopped onto the sofa.

"Ms Miller asked you a question," Barney pointed out. "Why haven't you shown up at the office?"

The young man stared insolently at the ceiling. "I don't know, man. Maybe I keep forgetting."

"Your application can't be processed until we get your medicals," Karen said.

"What do I care 'bout your stupid forms? I got working papers, I got my woman, I don't need another stamp in my passport to tell me I can stay."

Barney took a step toward him. "Wanna bet? Keep that up, and you won't be staying."

Miguel laughed. "Oh, yeah? Gonna kick me out cause you don't like my face? Look, man, I'll get the medicals done, one of these days. But right now I got other things on my mind, know what I mean?"

"Where's Estelle?" Karen asked.

"At work."

"I thought she was laid off."

He didn't answer right away. "She was. She got called back yesterday."

"I understand you quit your job," Karen said.

"That's right."

"Why?" Barney cut in. "Picking tomatoes too good for the likes of you?"

Karen cringed. Mercifully Miguel seemed to take no more offense than he already had.

"The job was okay. I done worse things for a living." Miguel held out his arm. "This is why I quit." His skin was dark, but scarred with purplish welts. "I'm allergic to tomato plants."

"Aw, you poor boy—" Barney began.

"It's true, man. Something on the leaves does this to me."

"Have you seen a doctor about it?" Karen asked.

"No, but I showed it to the nurse where Estelle works. She gave me some lotion and told me it would go away if I stayed away from tomatoes."

Miguel looked genuinely worried, which surprised Karen. There was so little about the man that seemed genuine. "Why didn't you go to a doctor?"

"I didn't want to, in case it was something serious. You might send me back home to Mexico, and I didn't want to leave Estelle."

"People very seldom get deported for medical reasons," Karen said. "You should've let me know what the problem was."

"You're from the Immigration. I sure as hell wouldn't trust you with my problems."

Barney, meanwhile, had wandered into the kitchen, leaving Karen to continue the interview. Technically Miguel could have stopped him and demanded a search warrant, but unless they had something to hide, clients seldom objected to a search. Karen always asked a client's permission before she searched; Barney usually did it the other way around.

"Hey, Garcia, your wife allergic to doing dishes?" Barney called out.

Miguel rolled lazily off the sofa. "What you talking about?"

"Come here and take a look." Barney motioned to Karen. "This place is a pigsty."

Karen turned to her client. "May I?"

"Who cares?"

The kitchen was a disaster. Both sinks overflowed with dirty dishes, while a mangy tabby cat tiptoed through the refuse on the counter. Karen didn't know Estelle that well, but she found it hard to believe that the woman would leave her kitchen in a state like this.

"I'm going to ask you a question," Karen said to Miguel, "and I want you to answer truthfully. Are you and Estelle still living together as husband and wife?"

Miguel's jaw pulsed, but he met her stare head-on. "Like I said before, she's at work. When she comes home, she'll clean this mess up."

"Would you show me some evidence that Estelle still lives here?" Karen tried to keep her tone nonthreatening; she could only hope Barney would stay quiet in the meantime.

"Why should I show you anything?" Miguel retorted. "I already told you to look where you want."

"Show us your closet," Barney ordered.

"My what?"

"Your bedroom, where you keep your clothes."

Karen was expecting a scene any minute. To her amazement, Miguel gestured toward the bedroom, and they followed him. The double bed was unmade, with the sheets thrown back as if only one person had slept there last.

Barney threw open the closet doors. One half was filled with men's clothes—suits, shirts and pants—most of which looked new. The other half was empty. "Looks mighty bare in here, Garcia. Your wife keep her clothes someplace else?"

"They're at the cleaners."

Karen was sickened by the discovery. Bad enough that Estelle had been duped into marriage by this creep, but to lose her home to him as well. How much better it would be if Miguel had been the missing party.

Karen was standing by the bureau and began to open the drawers. It was the same situation as the closet—half the drawers filled with men's things, the other half, except for an abandoned sachet, bare.

"No one sends all their clothes to the cleaners at once," Karen said. "Why don't you tell us the truth this time."

"Okay, okay, have it your way. Estelle isn't here. She's visiting her parents."

Karen recalled a detail from her interview with Estelle. "Both her parents are dead. She inherited this house from them."

Miguel was clearly getting nervous. He was hopping from one foot to the other and looking around as though he might yank an explanation from thin air. "I'll tell you what you want to hear, okay? She's gone. We had a fight on the weekend, and she packed up her things. I dunno where she is."

Barney lived for moments like these. His face took on a glow that was almost rapturous. "Well, well, well. So you and your wife split up."

"No!" Miguel shouted. "We're still married. She's still my wife. Everybody's got troubles when they first get together. You understand that, don't you, Miss Miller? That don't mean the marriage is over. And it don't mean Immigration's got the right to poke its big nose into my affairs either."

"It does give us the right," Karen pointed out, "if we are of the opinion that you married Estelle solely to remain in Canada."

Miguel's dark eyes flashed with anger and challenge. "Where do you get off making opinions, Miss Miller? Where does it say in the law that we're not allowed to have problems, like any other couple? I love my wife. I loved her from the day we met, and I want her back. That's why I'm staying right here in this house. If I wanted to go, I'd just go, wouldn't I?"

Karen could think of no reply. She looked at Barney, whose expression suggested that he'd love to slap a pair of handcuffs on Miguel and drag him to the office.

But Miguel had made a valid point. If he had intended to renege on his marriage vows, it wouldn't make sense for him to stay here. He would more likely skip town and blend into the vast illegal networks of Toronto, Montreal or Vancouver.

"Let's go, Barney." Karen still had the feeling that something wasn't right, but there wasn't enough evidence for a Section 18 report. They had no choice but to wait and see what happened.

"Yeah, all right," Barney muttered.

On their way out, Karen handed Miguel a business card. "If you find out where your wife is, I want you to call Mr. Coxwell or me. Do you understand?"

"Yeah, sure."

"And I want you to make a doctor's appointment right away."

Miguel said he would, then kicked open the front door with his foot, a clear indication they had overstayed their welcome.

THE KITCHEN of the Trattoria Palermo was a far cry from the air-conditioned comfort of the dining room where patrons daintily twirled their linguine and sipped their chianti. Steam billowed from pots of boiling pasta; the ovens were filled with huge pans of cacciatore and lasagna in preparation for the dinner hour.

Donis no longer found the aromas suffocating as he had the first few days on the job. He no longer noticed the aromas at all. Who could notice anything while up to his elbows in hot soapy water?

There was a time when Donis would have been appalled at the very thought of washing dishes for a living. He was no blue blood—few Sanvitans were—but he'd been raised with a sense of self-worth. He'd worked hard to put himself through school. Later he'd proven himself to be a first-rate economist. He had discerning friends, an endless supply of admiring women—everything an ambitious man could possibly want.

Now look at him. Who would have believed he would end up like this? With his thumbnail, Donis flicked a piece of burnt noodle from a plate before rinsing it under the sprayer.

Things, however, could be worse. Canada wasn't such a bad place if a person used his head. And the people weren't as frosty and unapproachable as he'd imagined they would be.

Take Karen Miller, for example. At the start, he'd been fooled by that cool, seamless image she presented. Had she held her chin a fraction of an inch higher during that first interview, he'd have passed her off as a mindless snob. Passed her off—and promptly forgotten all about her.

But at the London Jail, Karen had displayed other colors—warm hues he hadn't seen or felt in a woman for a long time. Compassion, sincerity, thoughtfulness. Some women would have flaunted their position, but Karen didn't. Donis respected her professionalism. More importantly, he took comfort in knowing that professionalism would never lure him to a woman's bed.

Then, dammit, there was the other night. Of all the needless complications—to have Karen show up out of nowhere and offer him a ride into town. Until then, he'd considered K. L. Miller nothing more than an attractive, pleasant lady who was worthwhile knowing in case of an emergency.

But there'd been something about Karen that night. Some captivating spark he'd never noticed before. He saw it in the dazzle of her smile, in the daring way she swung her hair when she leaned out the car window. If they'd been strangers meeting somewhere else—Athens, Cairo, Rome—he'd have hopped into the car at once and directed her to the nearest steamy nightclub. And she would have gone, laughingly, without the slightest hesitation.

But this wasn't Athens or any other lusty European city. This was London, Ontario—staid, conservative, Canadian. Karen was not a free spirit looking for a good time, and Donis was no longer a carefree young man with money and time to spare. Those days were long gone—

"Andonis Sotera?"

Donis stiffened, not only at the sound of his name but at the hand that had clamped rudely onto his shoulder. "Who are you?" he asked without turning or lifting his hands from the dishwater.

"Coxwell, Immigration. I wanna see your documents."

A short while later, Coxwell ushered Donis, handcuffed, into the Immigration office. And curse his luck, the first person Donis saw walking through the reception area was Karen. She saw—or appeared to see—Coxwell first. She looked at him curiously, then turned to Donis. All at once, the color drained from Karen's face, and he heard her murmur, "Oh, no..."

Donis returned her stare with eyes as cold as his heart. "You must be proud of yourself, Miss Miller, having done your job so well."

CHAPTER FOUR

"WHAT'S GOING ON, BARNEY?" Karen glared at her colleague, mindless of the clients curiously watching their exchange. There had to be some mistake, arresting Donis, and if there was, Coxwell would never hear the end of it.

"Thanks to your timely tip, the afternoon wasn't a total waste after all."

"My tip? What are you talking about?"

Barney gloated at Donis who, except for the tight clench of his jaw, was expressionless. "After I dropped you off, I decided to check out a few places on Oxford Street where you dropped Sotera off. Sure enough, there was your friend, bright as day, scrubbing dishes in the Palermo. And not a work permit to be found."

Karen dropped her face in her hands, wishing she could simply dissolve from view. There was no way to make Donis understand. She should have known that even the most casual of remarks were grist for Barney Coxwell's mill.

When she looked up, tears were beading at the corners of her eyes—tears that had no place on the job, but were there nonetheless. "I'm sorry," she said to Donis.

He wouldn't even look at her.

"What's there to be sorry for?" Barney cut in. "You were only doing your job." He tugged at Donis's arm. "Come on, Sotera. We got a report to write."

THAT AFTERNOON, Karen met her sister-in-law after work. Sue was a nurse and worked shifts. Whenever she did have free evenings, Tim expected her to stay home with him. But tonight he was working late, so the two women intended to make the most of the occasion and go shopping.

But after they'd visited their eighth shoe store, Sue Miller fell onto a bench, shopping bags beside her. "That's it for me. If I try on one more pair of shoes, I'll collapse and so will my arches."

"Sue, what's wrong? You usually have ten times more energy than I have."

"Nothing's wrong with me. I've just never been on a suicidal shopping spree before. I was about to ask you what's going on."

"Nothing, nothing at all." Karen knelt down to readjust the packages spilling out of her shopping bag. Funny, she couldn't remember half the things she'd bought. Whatever happened to the emotional release she always derived from spending money?

"Is work getting to you?" Sue asked.

"No... well, maybe a little."

Karen knew that Sue wouldn't press for details. Her sister-in-law understood that Karen was sworn to secrecy in her job. It was just as well that they couldn't talk about it. Karen didn't want to think about Donis. She didn't want to think about the look in his eyes when Barney dragged him in.

Donis was in the wrong for working illegally, not her. If her inadvertent slip of the tongue brought about his arrest, there was no reason for Karen to feel guilty. None whatsoever.

Ignoring a pang in the pit of her stomach, Karen pointed to a jewelry store in the center of the Arcade. "Let's go in there."

"Why? You never wear jewelry."

Karen looked at her petite sister-in-law who favored large, colorful costume jewelry and managed to get away with it. "I'm thinking of changing my image," she said. *Not to mention my line of work.*

"All right, if you insist," Sue replied, sighing, "but promise we'll go to Say Cheese afterward. I'm famished."

"Promise."

Karen pored over every display case in the store, but nothing caught her eye. Even the expensive jewelry looked cheap, maybe because that's the way she was feeling. *Damn.* If only she could learn to leave her work at the office, instead of dragging it around inside all the time.

"Haven't you seen a single thing you like?" Sue pleaded.

Karen glanced around hopelessly, then pointed to a display of gold chains. "That's what I want."

"What? Plain old chains? We've been here nearly half an hour. Surely you could come up with something a little more imaginative."

"But I want to wear one...here." Karen held out her ankle.

Sue burst out laughing. "You with an ankle bracelet? I'll believe that when I see it."

"I've always wanted one, really. I've just never had the nerve." Karen frowned. "But do you think it'd be too much? I mean, I don't want to go overboard."

"I can understand your worrying," Sue said with a smirk. "Put a chain on ankles like yours, and men will be dropping dead on the street. I don't think you should risk it."

Karen had to laugh. "Come on, Sue, I want your honest opinion."

"You'll look great. Try one on."

Feeling wanton was better than feeling guilty, Karen discovered, even if it was a temporary respite. She selected a chain with a tiny gold heart and wrapped it around her bare ankle. The chain looked good, even a little provocative, against her lightly tanned skin. Karen held out her leg in a Betty Grable pose. "Well, what do you think?"

To Karen's horror, Sue didn't answer. Instead, a familiar male voice rumbled from behind. "Hardly your style, is it, Miss Miller?"

Karen whirled around. It was Mr. Rathbone, her boss, a man notorious for showing up at the most inopportune times. "What a surprise... Sir."

Mr. Rathbone was a tall, angular man with a serious face and a serious outlook. Except for his silly policy on panty hose, he wasn't bad to work for, but he always made Karen feel uncomfortable.

"Spending all your hard-earned money, are you?" he said.

It was a cliché, a sincere attempt at humor. There was no reason for Karen to reply with, "Yes, but—" She stopped herself and tried again. "It's a gift... for a friend."

"I see." A familiar silence fell between them. Mr. Rathbone refolded the newspaper that was under his arm and saluted. "Well, see you Monday."

"Yes," she said in the perky tone she hated. "Have a nice weekend."

When Mr. Rathbone was out of sight, Karen looked at Sue. Sue looked at Karen. The release of tension made them burst into giggles like a pair of naughty school girls.

Sue regained her composure first. "So, *Miss Miller*, now that you know how your boss feels about the chain, are you still going to buy it?"

Feeling purged by the attack of hysterics, Karen picked up her purse and pulled out a credit card. "Darned right. Not only that, I intend to spend this weekend perfecting my tan. Next time Mr. Rathbone mutters, 'No stockings, Miss Miller?', I'll flash him my ankle and say, 'Guess.'"

DONIS HEARD THE STEEL DOORS clang shut. The sound, cold and immutable, echoed through his body. His back was to the jailer, but he could hear the key grinding in the lock, the key ring jingle as the guard walked away. The stripping of one's freedom, Donis had learned, was an audible, rhythmic thing, the sequence of sounds never varying.

But familiarity didn't make things any easier. Sanity, once it was threatened, could never again be taken for granted. Each time, one's hold on reality became more tenuous, one's need to escape—by whatever means—more desperate than before.

The only reason Donis had clung to reality two years ago was because he'd resigned himself to death. Death was the only option, and he'd come to accept it. But to have this happen again, now, when the worst finally seemed to be over...

Donis sank wearily to the cot, bleary eyes taking in his surroundings. This wasn't the London Jail, so it lacked even the small comfort of familiarity. This place was on the outskirts of town. What had they called it? The Detention Center, that was it. Donis lay down and closed his eyes.

Detention. Being held captive against one's will. The very name evoked memories, demanded comparisons. Granted, here the cot was softer, the cell cleaner, but other than that everything was the same.

Without freedom, time became an alien word. It twisted and warped like a phonograph in a fire. Darkness and sunlight became memories, interchangeable and irrelevant. Days were notches carved into a wall, nights defined by the rare and blessed snatch of sleep.

As time melted, solitude, so treasured in the real world, rose up and festered like a leprous monster. There were two things a man could do to combat the fear of solitude. He could ignore it, recede into the furthest depths of his mind and asphyxiate from the lack of fresh thoughts. Alternatively he could multiply into a dozen selves, hoping to fight off the monster, but in reality depleting his sanity twelve-fold. Donis had tried both methods. One was as bad as the other.

And then there was the physical starvation, the slow, agonizing breakdown of one's body. First the fat, then the lean. There is no sensation more hideous than that of one's muscles dying, one's bones crumbling....

"Hey, Sotera, wake up! Your dinner's getting cold."

His eyes flew open, and he sat up. There was a tray of food in front of him. The guard was standing in the cell with the door open behind him. Donis could not understand. Guards never entered the cell.

It had to be some kind of torture. Either the food was poisoned, or they didn't intend to let him eat it. He would pick up a fork, his mouth would water, and the guard would kick the food away.

But the heavyset man sauntered out of the cell, leaving the tray. "Eat up," he said, locking the door. "It'll have to hold you till breakfast."

Donis watched the guard retreat down the corridor. The smell of seasoned meat wafted through the air. He couldn't bear it. Donis grabbed hold of the bars and shouted, "Take the food away!"

The man turned around. "What's your problem? Got something against shepherd's pie?"

"Listen to me. I am not a criminal. This is all a mistake. I cannot survive another two years."

The guard chuckled. "Two years? You haven't even been here two hours."

The temperature in the cell block was temperate, but Donis shivered. His shirt was wringing wet. When he thought about the food, his stomach cramped as though he hadn't eaten in a week. In part of his mind, he hadn't.

"If I must stay, then g-get me a priest," he said, repeating a plea he'd once uttered half a world away.

"What's that?" the guard asked.

"A priest. I have money. I can make it worth your while."

"Hey, would you mind speaking English?"

Donis shook his head in confusion. Why didn't the guard understand? He had asked for a priest, a simple request.

"Hey, are you all right?" The guard was coming toward the cell. "You're not looking so great."

Donis was confused by the man's language. It wasn't Sanvitan. It was something else—French? No, English.

"Hey, Sotera, listen to me." The guard was slapping him on the face through the bars, but lightly, as if reviving him. "You'll be all right. Just hang on, and I'll get you a glass of water."

Donis again watched the guard leave, and slowly, painfully, he returned to his senses. This wasn't Sanvito; it was Canada. The hunger, the deprivation were from another place. By the time the guard returned, Donis, for the most part, had recovered. He thanked the man and accepted the water.

"You're looking better now," the guard said. "Got some color back in your face anyway. Is there anything I can do?"

There was so much about this country Donis didn't understand, so many contradictions that perplexed him. "Why do you treat prisoners so kindly?"

The guard seemed relieved to be dealing with a rational man once again. "I wouldn't call you a prisoner, Mr. Sotera. Like Mr. Coxwell said, you're just being detained until the Immigration inquiry."

"Ah, yes, when was it again?"

"They said it'd be Monday."

"But today is only Friday."

"Yeah, well, they can't always schedule those hearings as quickly as they'd like to."

Three days. Donis knew that every hour of those three days would be an eternity. He felt the panic rising once again, but this time, he fought it successfully. "Am I allowed to make a phone call?"

"Depends on who it's to."

Inexplicably, his first thought was of Karen. It was her voice he'd like to hear, her face he wanted to envision at the other end of the line. But the compassion he'd once imagined in Karen Miller was an artifice. He knew that now. It was thanks to Karen that he was locked away like some common thief.

"I'd like to call a priest," he said at last. "Father Peter at the seminary."

"No problem. I know the fellow."

"Am I . . . allowed visitors?"

"One a day, just like the vitamin. Let's go make the call now, then you might feel up to eating." The guard unlocked the door and escorted Donis to a room with a telephone.

As he watched Father Peter come down the corridor a short while later, Donis realized, not for the first time, how life resembled a spiral. One seemed to travel ever forward, yet so often situations would repeat themselves, altered only slightly by time and circumstance.

"How are you, son?" The priest entered the cell and shook Donis's hand. "You look pale."

"I am tired, but well."

Father Peter sat down and continued the conversation they'd begun on the phone. "You should have told me you needed money. We have resources at the seminary. You wouldn't have had to take a job."

Donis shook his head. "It's not as simple as that."

"Isn't it? You must have known the foolish risk you were taking."

"For heaven's sake, Father, I was washing dishes, not performing appendectomies. From what I can gather, most

Canadians wouldn't think of accepting such employment.''

"That's true, but it does not excuse what you've done.''

"Perhaps not, but I swear to you, I did not come to Canada to make money. I came because—well, there are reasons far beyond what seems obvious.''

"Do you trust me enough to tell me those reasons?''

Donis pushed a hand through his disheveled hair. Father Peter's question was difficult to answer. The capacity for trust had eroded in Donis over the years. When he first came to this country, this town, he'd hoped that things might be different. But now...

Father Peter seemed to understand. "Don't force the issue, son. Say only what you feel comfortable saying.''

The compassion, the release of pressure was almost palpable. Donis took a deep breath and said the first thing that came to mind. "All I did was take a temporary job, and for this I am detained. As an economist, I am aware of what developed countries spend in the care and feeding of prisoners. It seems to me the taxpayers would be better off letting me wash dishes, as I am not a criminal.''

"You're misreading the situation, Donis. I have dealt with many similar cases over the years. You're not being held for criminal charges.''

"So I was told. Nor am I being held for political reasons. Coxwell told me I was being detained for insufficient funds, no proof of return transportation to Europe and a previous brush with the law—as if the assault was something I could have foreseen and prevented. These details apparently were enough for Coxwell to believe that I would not appear for an Immigration inquiry.''

"Would you appear for the inquiry, knowing you might be deported back to Sanvito?''

Donis appreciated Father Peter's frankness. His response was equally candid. "No.''

"I thought as much. What became of your airline ticket? You must have had one when you entered Canada."

"I did. I cashed in the return portion."

"How much money do you have now?"

"Two hundred dollars, more or less."

"Then you haven't enough to leave Canada on your own. It's unfortunate, but not surprising that you've been detained."

"What if I said I don't want to leave Canada?"

"You've gone about it the wrong way. You would have had to apply for permanent residence at a Canadian consulate outside the country."

"I made inquiries at the consulate in Vienna. They advised me that Canada had little demand for economists in my area of expertise, and that if I were to make application, the processing could take a year or more."

"That is true."

"But I couldn't wait a year. It was dangerous enough to wait until the end of the day."

Father Peter frowned. "I don't understand. Why was it dangerous?"

Here they were again, Donis thought, completing another revolution on the spiral, back to the priest's earlier question. As he did so often during times of indecision, Donis thought of his grandmother. If she were here, she'd be telling him Father Peter came into his life for a reason. It was up to Donis to use the opportunity wisely.

What would Grandmother have to say about Karen, he wondered, irrelevantly? Something about a wolf in sheep's clothing, perhaps. The notion stung, far more than it should have.

Donis tried to console himself. *You've been deceived far worse in your day. Why can't you keep it in perspective?*

"Donis, are you still with me?" Father Peter asked.

He shook himself free of Karen's image. "I'm sorry. My mind was wandering. If I tell you about my past, you must promise to hold it in the strictest confidence. Lives other than mine are at stake."

The older man smiled patiently. "I am a priest, remember? Confidence is my specialty."

"And what about your friends?"

"My friends? I don't understand."

"People like Karen Miller." Donis probed the priest's face for some reaction; he found none.

"Karen and I respect each other's confidentiality. What you say to me will go no further. I can promise you that."

Donis believed, and so he confided. For well over an hour, he talked and Father Peter listened, asking only the occasional question. When it was over, Donis felt absolved, as though this had been a confession of another kind.

"If you will allow me," the priest said, "I can help."

"How can you be so certain? You should know from what I've told you that another man, more or less, will not make any difference."

"I wasn't referring to the problems you left behind. I meant that I can help you stay in Canada if that's what you want. I can act as your counsel at the inquiry."

"You would do that? Why?"

The man folded his hands around a knee. "Because I know how it feels to escape from something with no thought except to keep running. But sooner or later, one must stop running and that's when the real fear sets in."

Donis's first instinct was to turn down the priest's offer. In Sanvito, to accept help was considered a sign of weakness in a man. Perhaps that was why Sanvitans had accomplished so little through the years.

Adversity had taught Donis a different truth. He'd seen it time and time again among the exiles he'd worked with.

To accept the aid of others was a sign of courage. To do so graciously and humbly was the greatest challenge of all.

Donis looked up with all the courage he could muster and said, "I would be most grateful for your help, Father."

CHAPTER FIVE

ON MONDAY AFTERNOON Barney Coxwell came into Karen's office grinning broadly. "Boy, is your client up a creek without a you-know-what," he blustered.

Karen put her pen down. "I can think of several clients in that predicament. Who are you referring to?"

"Sotera, the sexy Sanvitan, as Molly calls him."

Donis's inquiry had commenced that morning at the District Office. Karen had been on pins and needles all day, waiting to hear the outcome, but she'd hoped to hear it from someone other than Barney. "All right, since you're obviously dying to tell me, what happened?"

"The hearing's adjourned till this afternoon, but the CP figures he'll get deportation, no problem."

Karen knew the case presenter was a fair man. Although his job was to represent the Immigration Commission at the inquiry, he only recommended deportation when it seemed justified. He did not share Barney Coxwell's need to draw blood.

"Why wouldn't he recommend voluntary departure?" Karen asked. "There's no criminal activity involved."

"Ha, that's what you think. District Office telexed the authorities in Sanvito to check out Sotera's story. There's no record of his passport number—"

"Maybe there was some kind of mix-up."

"Hey, you didn't let me finish. There was no mix-up. Not only does Sotera not work for the president, he's not even Sanvitan anymore."

"What is he?"

"Zip. He's stateless. Two years ago, the president publicly stripped him of his citizenship."

Karen felt a rush of conflicting emotions. "Where did he get the passport?"

"It's a fake."

"Oh, my God."

Barney rubbed his hands with glee. "Can't you just see the Section 18 Report? By the time they finish writing the damned thing up, it'll be an inch thick."

"Barney, would you just shut up for once?" Karen was trying to think, an activity that was almost impossible in Coxwell's presence.

"Hey, no point in getting steamed at me, baby. Tall, dark and handsome did it all himself." With that, Barney shambled off, leaving Karen sorely tempted to hurl a manual at the back of his head.

Instead she marched straight over to Liz who was pulling the latest issue of *Cosmopolitan* out of her desk.

"Could I talk to you a minute?" Karen asked.

"Sure, I was just on my way down for coffee. Want to join me?"

"I can't. I've got a client coming in ten minutes."

Liz sat down on the corner of her desk. "Go ahead. I'm listening."

Karen's intention had been to gripe to Liz about Barney. He was so ignorant, so damned impossible. But Karen knew that nothing anyone said or did would change the man's personality. And squealing on him would only diminish her own professionalism. So for the umpteenth time, Karen bit her tongue about Barney Coxwell.

"Did you forget what you wanted to say?" Liz asked.

"No, I . . . I just wanted to ask you a favor. When you find out the results of the Sotera inquiry, would you mind letting me know?"

Liz gave her a look of empathy. "I can tell by the look on your face that Barney's already filled you in."

"In his inimitable way, yes."

"I hope you're not feeling guilty about how you handled the case."

Until Liz put the truth into words, Karen hadn't realized it. When it came to Donis, she did feel guilty and foolish. She shrugged. "I don't know how I'm feeling."

"You did your job as well as anyone could have. There was no way you could have guessed that he was lying about his passport and everything else."

"But I'm not talking about the passport, don't you see? All those horrible things I accused Donis of after I read up on Sanvito. I was wrong. He doesn't work for the president. The president hates him. So Donis couldn't be responsible for the atrocities in his country."

Liz took a minute to consider Karen's remarks. "I hadn't thought of it that way, to tell you the truth. But don't be too quick to exonerate the guy. He may not be the dictator's henchman, but his record is far from spotless."

"I know, but forging a passport or lying about his citizenship—that's something a person does to survive. It's not cruel or inhumane or...any of those things." Karen sank into a chair, feeling helpless.

"You could be right. I imagine everything will sort itself out in the inquiry. But why are you telling me this, Karen? It's not like you owe me an apology or anything."

"I know. I just...needed to talk to someone."

Liz laughed. "Barney really gets to you, doesn't he?"

Karen shook her head ruefully. "When he gets within ten feet of my office, I see red."

"Of course you do. It's the reflection off his red neck. Listen, Karen, for what it's worth, I've seen Donis. I can understand why you've taken him under your wing. I wouldn't mind tucking him under mine, either. But you don't know anything about him, other than what District Office has dredged up."

"Yes. So?"

"So normal, everyday people do not trot around the globe on forged passports. They do not lie to government officials, and they don't lose their citizenship unless they've done something pretty serious."

"You're saying I'm being too easy on him."

"All I'm saying is to keep an open mind, unlike a colleague we could mention. It's the most important thing you can do right now."

Liz's words were slow to sink in, but they did finally. "Okay," Karen promised. "I'll work on it."

"Good. I'll let you know how the inquiry turns out, but meanwhile, I'm going downstairs. *Cosmo*'s got a new quiz I'm dying to try out."

"What's it called?"

"How to assess your MQ, your Marriage Quotient. Want to try it after me?"

"Good heavens, no," Karen said, laughing halfheartedly. "I've had enough bad news for one day."

IT WAS NEARLY CLOSING TIME when Karen saw Liz again. "I just heard from District," her supervisor said.

Karen drew in a deep breath. "What did they say?"

"Donis has been ordered deported."

"Oh, no—"

"Hang on. The order's been stayed, and he's been released from detention."

Relief flooded through her. "Really? Why?"

"He's made a claim for refugee status. Father Peter was his counsel."

For the first time, Karen felt gratified. She'd been responsible for introducing Donis to Father Peter. At least she'd done something right. "That means Donis won't have to leave Canada until the committee has reviewed his case. With their backlog, it could take months.''

"That's right," Liz agreed.

"Who's going to conduct the refugee hearing?''

"Actually, that's what I wanted to talk to you about. I was thinking maybe you could.''

Karen couldn't believe her ears. "Me?''

"You've done them before. Do you think you can handle this one?''

"Are you kidding?'' Joy bubbled through her, and she laughed. "This refugee hearing will go down in Immigration history as the greatest ever conducted.''

"My goodness. I can't wait to read it.''

"In fact, if you weren't my supervisor, I'd give you a great big hug.''

Liz O'Connell threw out her arms. "Aw, what the heck? Give me one anyway.''

THE BOARDROOM WAS AS READY as it could ever be, if Karen would just leave it alone. She had rearranged the writing pads, pencils, water pitcher and glasses so many times she was ready to scream. The outcome of the hearing did not depend on whether writing tools were laid out symmetrically, asymmetrically or tossed at random. Karen knew that, even while ensuring that the writing pads were perpendicular to the table's edge.

A Bible was out of sight on a chair beside her. She'd found that clients were sometimes uncomfortable when the Book was on the table. The tape recorder was ready, a fresh cassette ready to roll.

All that was missing was Donis.

At precisely one o'clock, there was a knock on the door. Karen stood. "Come in.''

Donis entered alone, looking pale and drawn. He wore a suit of gray linen, tailored in European style.

"Good morning," Karen said, trying to sound both professional and reassuring.

He seemed to be weighing the import of her greeting. "Nice to see you," he said. "Isn't it curious how our paths keep crossing?"

"Does that bother you?"

"I must admit it did when Father Peter first told me who was conducting the hearing."

The rebuke, though gently uttered, stung. "And now?"

Donis managed a grim laugh. "If I hadn't developed a craving for Mediterranean-style sausages, my opinion might have remained unaltered."

"I beg your pardon?"

"I went to a Portuguese market yesterday afternoon to buy *chorizo* and was chatting with the proprietor about Canada. He told he that he'd come here with his family five years ago."

Karen smiled. "That must have been Mr. Medeiros."

"You have quite a reputation, it seems, for being—how shall I put it—*simpatica*."

"So you've changed your opinion of me because of a shopkeeper?"

His expression eased. "And from what he said about Coxwell. The man, it seems, has a ruthless reputation among immigrants."

Karen felt the tension between her shoulder blades melt. "Barney is...thorough," she admitted, motioning for Donis to take a seat. "Isn't Father Peter going to be here?"

"No. I decided to proceed with this hearing alone. He has done more than enough for me already."

Another positive sign, Karen thought, feeling self-confidence return in small measures. For Donis to trust her was important. For him to like her mattered, also, although that was something she chose not to probe too deeply.

"Before we begin," she said, "I would just like to point out that the purpose of this hearing is solely to gather information. I won't be making any recommendations for or against your claim, and there will be no editing of this interview. The tape along with a typed transcript will be sent to the Refugee Status Advisory Committee in Ottawa, and they will make the decision as to whether or not you are a refugee as defined by the United Nations Convention."

"I understand."

"Do you have any questions before we begin?"

"None."

She pressed the Play button and ignored the flutters in her stomach. These were normal, a variation of stage fright. But once the hearing got underway, Karen was certain she'd relax.

"This is an examination under oath," she began, addressing the machine, "held at the London Immigration Centre on July 24 in London, Ontario, to determine whether the claimant is a convention refugee pursuant to Section 45.1 of the Act." She looked up at Donis. "What is your full name, please?"

"Andonis Miliano Sotera."

"Mr. Sotera, it is required that you be under oath during this interview. Do you have any objection to swearing an oath on the Bible?" She watched for signs of hesitation or offense and saw none.

"I have no objection."

Karen held out the Bible and asked Donis to place his right hand on the cover. He was wearing the ring, the cross plainly visible. When his fingers touched the Book, they were trembling. Karen felt a respondent tremor through her arm as she recited the oath.

Donis answered in the affirmative, adding without hesitation, "So help me, God."

Karen put the Bible away. "What is your date of birth?"

"July 27, 1948."

Three days from now, Karen noticed, glancing at her notes. Irrelevant questions rose in her mind. Did anyone know it was nearly his birthday? Was there anyone who cared? She put the thoughts aside and asked instead. "Where were you born?"

"Muniz, Sanvito."

"What is your marital status?"

"Single."

His answer came as a shock. All this time, Karen had been convinced he was married. Not that Donis had given any indication, but somehow, imagining a Mrs. Sotera in the background had helped Karen maintain a certain perspective.

She cleared her throat. "Any dependents?"

"No."

"Do you have living relatives?"

"As far as I know, my grandmother is still alive, and I have two cousins—distant cousins."

"Where do they live?"

"My grandmother and one cousin are in Sanvito. The other, I believe, is in Spain."

Karen jotted his answers down as a backup to the recording. She was grateful for something to do with her hands.

"I think this would be a good time," she said, "for me to stop asking questions and let you talk. What the committee wants to know is why you feel you cannot return to Sanvito or the country—in this case, Austria—from which you embarked to Canada. Feel free to tell your story however you feel comfortable. Begin with your childhood, if you like, or start at the present and work back. If I do interrupt, it will be solely for clarifications."

She suspected that Donis would prefer an open-ended interview. There were clients who were too nervous to talk without prompting, but Karen preferred to stay in the background. This was the claimant's story, not hers.

Donis picked up a pencil and kept his eyes focused on it when he spoke. "I suppose my childhood does play a role in later events, although I don't intend to dwell on the early years. My father was editor in chief of the Sanvitan national newspaper, and my mother stayed home to raise their only child. At age eighteen, I went to Barcelona to study economics, then returned to Sanvito and accepted a clerk's position with the government. Fortunately there was a shortage of qualified economists, and I moved up the ranks quickly. By the time I was thirty, I was in charge of reviewing and developing economic policies for Sanvito."

"Who appointed you to that position?" Karen asked.

"The president." He met her eyes squarely. "The previous one, that is."

Karen was relieved. His answer was crucial in assuring her that this would be a truthful interview. No more evasions, no more half truths.

"I held that position for six years," he went on to say. "Then after the last election, I was asked to resign. Or to be more precise, my offices were ransacked and the locks changed."

Karen caught the irony in his voice and was grateful for the recorder. The committee couldn't fail to hear it as well.

"I did financial consulting for a time, but the country was in a turmoil. Clients were busy liquidating assets while my services, thanks to radical economic reforms, became obsolete. I joined my father's newspaper as a business columnist."

"For the record, what's the name of the newspaper?" Karen asked.

"In English, it is called the *Observer*." He gave her the Sanvitan name and spelled it for her.

"Please go on," she said.

"My father was always vocal when it came to politics, and he made no exception for the new regime. Everyone knew the ballots had been rigged, but he was the only one brave enough to speak the truth. He gave me free reign to assess land and tax reforms in my column. Needless to say, the *Observer* was soon censored by the head of state, but we were prepared for that eventuality."

"What did you do?"

"We created an underground communications network, a way for people to learn what was happening. Much of the groundwork was done by my mother who, although she seemed the typical Sanvitan housewife, was a keen observer of people. She was what you might call a grass roots political analyst. She'd predicted what would happen to Sanvito years before this last election."

"How did the network operate?"

"It was a simple concept, really. A code was established to describe certain government actions. It was further refined to describe precise locations, dates and times. For example, if a journalist learned that a certain parcel of land was to be confiscated within a week, an article would appear in the newspaper—seemingly unrelated—such as 'U.S. Breakthrough in Artificial Heart Implant.' People who belonged to the network could interpret the article and know exactly what was going to happen."

"But knowing ahead of time, they still couldn't prevent expropriation, could they?"

"No, they could not. But Sanvitans are tenacious. They would sooner trample a crop or burn it to the ground than give the land away. And that is what they did. The president, of course, was outraged by these acts and ordered the arrest of anyone who resisted—even the women and children."

"Didn't the government catch on to what the newspaper was doing?"

"They did, but not as quickly as one might expect. There was fierce loyalty among the government's opponents. While our system lasted, it was effective."

Karen was moved by the pride in Donis's voice, the fire in his eyes when he spoke of his homeland. Now suddenly, the fire dimmed. She sensed a turning point in his story.

"At my father's insistence, I flew to Geneva to cover an economic conference. I tried to tell him it was an unnecessary extravagance, but he wouldn't listen. While I was gone, my father and mother were arrested. The news reached me by the—how do you put it—grapevine, and when I tried to return home, I discovered that all travel routes to Sanvito had been canceled. No planes, no ships, nothing was moving in or out of the country."

"What did you do?"

"I flew to Barcelona, the nearest European port, and bribed the captain of a Spanish freighter to take me to Sanvito."

"Were your parents arrested because of their newspaper?"

"For no other reason. I also know that the president had been waiting for me to turn my back, that is, to leave the country before arresting my parents."

"Wouldn't it have made more sense to arrest all three of you? He must have known you were actively involved."

"There is no doubt that he knew, but three Soteras in custody would have been too contentious. My parents and I were well respected. We knew many people, inside the government and out. The president took great pleasure in separating me from my parents and preventing my return."

"Do you know for certain those were his motives or are you speculating?" Karen asked.

"The president admitted it to me himself."

A shiver ran along Karen's spine, as though she'd been touched by something evil.

"Are you cold?" Donis asked. "Would you like my jacket?"

Karen smiled. What would the committee think of this recorded display of chivalry, she wondered. "I'm fine, thanks."

Donis continued. "Discontent among the people was growing daily. They began to hold political assemblies in the churches, the only place they felt safe from the Military Police. The government responded by closing the churches and executing the clergy for inciting treason."

"Were they given trials?"

"Certainly, and everyone was found guilty."

"What did you do when you got back to Sanvito?"

"I went to the most influential person I knew in Sanvito, my grandmother. My mother's mother was an innocuous little woman dressed in black, but she was an important link in the resistance movement that the soldiers had foolishly overlooked. I hid in her home and assisted her in the clandestine movement of exiles out of Sanvito. A few weeks after my return, we heard that my parents had also fallen victim to the firing squad."

"Oh, my God," Karen said.

Donis, utterly composed, pointed to the machine. "The tape is about to run out."

She hastily turned it over, wondering how a person adjusted to the execution of his parents. She couldn't even begin to imagine.

"By this time," Donis went on, "the country was falling apart. Businesses were closing, inflation was rampant. With crops destroyed or poorly managed, people were going hungry. We did what we could to distribute food and clothing, but it was a losing battle. The island could not sustain the population, and people were escaping by the hundreds."

"How did they get away?"

"Mostly by sea. Naturally these operations had to take place at night, and we had to change the point of embarkation regularly to stay one step ahead of the police. It was risky, but looking back, it was the only thing that kept my grandmother and me sane after what happened to my parents.''

Donis poured himself a glass of water and sipped it slowly. Karen did not hurry him.

Over the years, she had conducted refugee hearings for Cambodians, Lebanese, Palestinians, Nicaraguans. There was a common element that always hit her the hardest. It was the imbalance, the inexplicable disparity between her life and the person's across the table.

They were the same in so many ways; they ate, slept, laughed, cried. But while Karen agonized over a two-dollar error in her phone bill, people elsewhere lost their entire life savings to five hundred percent inflation. While Karen bemoaned the lack of clothes in her closet, people were escaping with the shirts on their backs. Her mother had died of natural causes; Donis's had been killed for a cause.

She felt ashamed. Ashamed for her discontent, ashamed for the accident of her birth. It was a feeling that often came over her in these hearings, and one that stayed with her for days.

Donis pushed the glass away. ''One night, I was helping a relative escape, the cousin I mentioned earlier. She was a student of veterinary science in Barcelona and had been visiting Sanvito when the travel ban was imposed. Her boat had just pulled away when the Military Police arrived. They shot at the vessel, but it escaped unharmed. I was taken immediately to prison.''

''What did they charge you with?''

''The usual—insurrection, treason. I was, however, spared the mockery of a trial. Instead, the president took me to the town square and held a public ceremony—quite elaborate, actually—during which my Sanvitan citizenship was stripped.''

''Why would he do that?''

"I believe that the man was overcome by megalo-mania. He wanted so desperately to show his omnipotence, he had to prove he could even rescind people's birthrights."

"What happened after that?"

"I was taken back to prison and spent the next two years in solitary confinement."

The helplessness, the anguish rose again in Karen. How could people do that to others? How did others allow it to happen?

"Did you know that the sentence was two years?" she asked.

Donis laughed harshly. "My sentence was to have been the firing squad the morning after the ceremony. I will never forget that evening in prison. They brought me a feast, food such as I had not seen in Sanvito for months, and told me to eat hearty because in the morning I'd be dead. That morning never came. For two years, I never knew if the day would be my last. For two years, I saw no one, spoke to no one, except the guard who brought my food, and he never answered."

As Karen watched and listened, so much about Donis became clearer. The eyes, years older than the man, the self-control that crumpled at the mention of a cell.

She felt an odd pang, as if time had suddenly shifted to some other plane. How much poorer her own life would have been, Karen thought, had she not met Andonis Sotera.

If he was aware of his effect on her, Donis didn't show it. He continued to relate his story. "One day, I received an official announcement from the office of the president. Apparently the courts of appeal had been reviewing my case for two years and finally concluded that the death penalty was indeed appropriate. I remember reading the edict and laughing."

Donis looked at Karen as though they were having a private conversation. She tried to appear supportive but couldn't think of a thing to say. What was there to say?

"Can you imagine laughing at one's death sentence?" he remarked, expecting no reply. "But I had lived with the threat for so long, reality was like a farce. By evening other emotions began to take hold. I still had no fear of death, but felt a need to make contact with this world one more time. I desperately needed to talk to someone, anyone, before I died. I called for the guard, convinced he would ignore me as usual, and asked to speak with a clergyman."

"Were there any left in Sanvito?"

"I had no idea, nor did it occur to me that I might be offending the authorities further by making such a request. When one only has a few hours, such details pass unnoticed. To my amazement, a priest did appear very late that night. It was dark when the guard ushered him into the cell, leaving us with the lighted stub of a candle."

The ambience in the boardroom had changed again. Fury had given way to anguish, and now Donis spoke with quiet reverence. Karen recalled seeing that look of radiance on his face once before, but offhand she couldn't recall the occasion.

"He was wearing a hooded cowl," Donis explained, "so I could not see his face. But his voice? I will never forget the sound. It was as though all the richness of humanity, the pathos and the passion had been woven into a single tapestry. Perhaps his voice was quite ordinary, who knows, but not having heard another human speak for two years..."

"What did he say to you?"

"He asked me if I was Roman Catholic. I told him I was raised in the Eastern Orthodox faith. But he brushed that aside, saying we were children of the same God. He offered to hear my confession. I replied that I'd been confessing for two years and imagined that God had already heard the greater sum of my sins.''

The gentleness of his humor warmed Karen, and a tear slid unexpectedly down her cheek.

"I explained to the priest that all I really needed was to hear a human voice and to learn something of the outside world before I left it. So we spoke of the things that I had missed most—art, music, the changing of the seasons. He was a wonderful emissary. I asked him how he had managed to remain in Sanvito, and he admitted he was a token priest, allowed to wear a cassock for the sake of propaganda. I remember the sorrow in his voice when he said that, a sorrow so profound a man could drown in its depths.''

Donis poured himself more water, but stared at the tumbler without drinking. Karen held her breath.

"The priest leaned toward me. By this time, the candle was barely flickering. He said, 'I have been given permission to offer you Holy Communion. Will you accept the Sacrament?' I told him I would. He beckoned me closer and began to recite the liturgy. But as he made the sign of the cross, his wide sleeve swept over the flame and extinguished it. The guard at the end of the hall said something, but the priest told him not to worry about the candle, he was nearly finished anyway.

"He continued the blessing in utter darkness. But being deprived of light for so long, my senses were acute. I could hear the hurried rustle of cloth, though I could not understand what was happening. When the priest said, 'The Body of Christ,' he pressed something into my palm. A host...and a ring. 'Wear the ring,' he whispered. I put it on at once. Then he handed me a small flacon of wine. As I drank, he dropped his robe over my head. I was confused and frightened. He pressed his mouth to my ear and said, 'A boat waits to take you to Spain. It's moored on the eastern shore near the grotto.' ''

"He was helping you escape?" Karen asked, incredulous.

"He was exchanging places with me. When I asked why, he said hundreds of people were desperately waiting to escape Sanvito, but no one would risk helping them. They wanted me back. They were calling me The Deliverer."

"Good Lord," Karen murmured.

"I was not prepared for this turn of events. I couldn't handle the enormity of the priest's sacrifice. Those few moments in the cell were among the most agonizing. But the priest gave me no time to consider. He shook the cell door and called out for the guard. His last words before the guard arrived were, 'Beware of the Red Watch.' He had no time to explain further."

"Did the guard suspect anything?"

"I was certain he would shine his flashlight directly into my face, but the beam of light swung around to the ring and the empty flacon in my hand. That was apparently enough to satisfy him. Minutes later, I was a free man."

The boardroom fell silent.

"Did you ever find out what happened to the priest?"

Emotion blurred the edges of Donis's words. "H-he was shot the next morning. I—I never even found out his name."

CHAPTER SIX

"NOT...EVEN...HIS NAME." Donis fell silent, relinquishing his mind to the quagmire of his past. It sucked him in every time, so that he could scarcely move, scarcely think. And even more terrifying, it seemed harder each time to pull himself out, as though one day, his resistance would be so ineffectual that he'd never get out. He'd be forced to live in his past forever.

He heard some distant click, but the meaning of the sound didn't register.

"Donis, are you all right?"

His lips curved into a half smile. Such a nice voice, a kind voice.

"Donis?"

The voice touched his hand. Or rather, the person who owned it touched his hand.

He looked down. Her skin looked winter pale over his, the veins delicate and bluish along her palm. Donis turned his hand over, so that their inner palms met. Perhaps it was the warmth he found there, or the gentle pressure she exerted with her fingers. Whatever, it was enough to bring him back.

Donis lifted his gaze.

Karen.

He saw the turmoil, the fear in her eyes. "What's the matter?" His voice cracked, as though from disuse.

"I thought you were going to...I don't know...pass out or something. I was worried."

Angels must look like her, he thought. Fair and fine and sweet. Yet there was nothing ethereal about her presence. Her breasts rose and fell with each breath; her features had the translucence of maturity. Karen Miller was every bit a woman.

"I'm all right," he said, though it was only half true. What he needed from Karen more than anything was to be held, to be wrapped in her arms so tightly, so completely that he never need fear his past again. And of course, he could not ask for such a thing.

"Are you sure?"

He smiled at the inadvertent irony of her question. "Quite sure."

"We could take a break, if you like."

"No," he said, too quickly to convince even himself. "I would prefer to... to continue, please."

She held his gaze for some time. It was, in its way, an embrace, and he clung almost desperately to the welcoming sensation.

"Then we'll go on," she said, pressing the Record button. "You mentioned that the priest issued a warning before you left the cell."

"A warning." He thought for a moment, fearful once again of the quagmire. But this time, amazingly, it didn't pull him in. "Yes," he recalled. "The priest told me to beware of the Red Watch."

"What is the Red Watch?"

"The Sanvitan secret police, a powerful and deadly organization." His voice came out stronger now. He wondered if Karen noticed; he wondered if she sensed his gratitude. But then, why should she? "They... they came into existence while I was in prison, which is why I had not heard of them."

"What does the Red Watch do?"

"Their major function is to seek out Sanvitan exiles and either bring them home for trial or eliminate them. Elimination is the preferred method unless..."

"Unless?" she urged gently.

"Unless they are deemed to be of value to the state. Doctors, engineers, the country was desperately short of skilled people."

"How could they force an exile to return?"

"There are a number of effective methods. One of the most common was to kidnap the expatriate or, failing that, to abduct his family. The ransom, of course, would be that the exile return to Sanvito and resume his business."

"I see."

Donis saw Karen shudder, and he regretted being the cause of her distress. *If only I could hold you, the way I long for you to hold me...* But she didn't appear to be aware of his need. Thank God. What would she think of him if she knew?

"I assume the Red Watch would employ torture, harassment—whatever is required." She was taking notes as they spoke. His eyes were fixed on the firm grip of her pencil.

"Naturally."

She looked up. "You've implied that this secret police force operates outside of Sanvito. How do they elude the local authorities in other countries?"

Donis sighed deeply, forcing himself to concentrate on the questions. "They blend into their surroundings. Many of the operatives pose as exiles themselves, which of course further increases the risk of those who leave Sanvito. The Red Watch could be your best friend, your neighbor, the friendly grocer. The government managed to glean many of its members from the discontented masses."

Karen put the pencil down and folded her hands. "Could we go back to the night you escaped from prison? What happened after you were let out?"

"I walked to the eastern shore, a distance of several miles, certain with every step that I would be discovered. But no one followed me. I found the boat waiting where the priest had said it would be. Only one man was aboard, a retired Spanish captain. We set sail at once, reaching Barcelona by dawn."

"Was someone there to meet you?"

"Yes, my cousin, who'd escaped Sanvito two years earlier." Donis smiled at one of the rare pleasant memories. "She was waiting at the dock with a bottle of wine and a new passport."

"A real passport?"

"A real passport would have been impossible to obtain. This was a forgery, the same document I presented at this office. For me to travel and work effectively, I required convincing Sanvitan credentials. Fortunately those who arranged my escape had anticipated this and were thorough in their preparations."

"Who were these people?"

Donis took time to reply, hoping she wouldn't press for names. "Friends, associates. Enemies of the state."

"What did you do? Did you stay in Spain?"

"For a few weeks, yes. I helped to refine our system for bringing people out of Sanvito. Then I began to travel through Europe, assisting in resettlement and to warn expatriates of the Red Watch."

"Wouldn't that have been common knowledge by then?"

"No. Many believed the Red Watch was a rumor, started by the government. The international press had never reported a word about our secret police. To do so would be to admit the inefficiency of their own governments to prevent the Red Watch, something which does not sit well with most European nations."

"But you said that Sanvitans who were apprehended by the Red Watch were often killed. Wouldn't authorities eventually have noticed a pattern?"

Karen, he was beginning to discover, was an insightful woman. Insightful...and lovely. An irrelevant combination, but a blessed one. "You must remember that countries in Europe are small and numerous, while Sanvitans are a mere sprinkling among them. Also, the assassinations were made to look like accidents. A woman falls under the wheels of a bus. Is it murder? A drunken student topples from the balcony of his apartment. Was he pushed?"

"I understand. From what you've said, I can see why you couldn't return safely to Sanvito. But could you tell this hearing why you came to Canada, considering you were reasonably safe in Europe?"

"At the risk of sounding noble, my safety was not a primary concern in coming here. I am adaptable and could easily start a new life anywhere. But my reputation as The Deliverer, exaggerated though it was, had taken on almost fanatical proportions in Europe and in my country. Wherever there were Sanvitans, one found desperation, false hope. There was nothing I could do to convince them that my days as The Deliverer were finished. Permanently."

"Why were they finished?" Karen asked. "Wasn't that the reason they planned your escape?"

"It was, but unfortunately I eventually became more of a danger than a help. For a year or so after leaving prison, I managed to elude the Red Watch by constant travel, by backtracking and altering my itinerary at the last minute. Then I began to hear stories about Sanvitans I had recently visited. There was a man in Milan, for example. I helped him and his family establish a small business. Three months later after I saw him, he was bitten by a spider and died. Soon afterward I spent a few days with a young couple in Bonn, West Germany. A week after I left, they were killed in a moped accident. By then I was convinced that the Red Watch was closing in on me.''

"Did they apprehend you?"

"Not personally, but I do not believe this was their mission. It was the other exiles they wanted. Soon after the moped incident, I traveled by foot to an isolated farm outside of Vienna where I was scheduled to meet with a businessman. He'd owned a highly successful tannery in Sanvito, but after the election the government took over his business. We met in the middle of the forest to talk. I recommended that he and his family settle in a small community nearby. There were people willing to help him reestablish. He agreed to my suggestion, and we went our separate ways." Donis paused, waiting for the inevitable pull. It didn't happen. "I had not yet reached the edge of the forest . . . when I heard a gunshot."

"Your friend was shot?"

"Yes. I hurried back and found him lying face down. He'd been shot in the back. I rushed to the village and placed an anonymous call to the police. I wanted desperately to inform the man's family myself, but I knew the Red Watch were following me and would likely have killed them as well."

"Where did you go?"

"I took the back roads to Vienna, obtained a Canadian visa from the consulate and boarded the next available flight to Canada."

"Why Canada?"

He smiled, reflecting on his earlier naïvete. "It seemed a good choice at the time. I had heard that your country has a large arctic wilderness and a strong economic base. The former, I hoped, would discourage most Sanvitans from seeking refuge here, and the latter appealed to my professional interests."

She smiled with him, and he dared to believe his fortune might be changing. "Are you worried about the Red Watch tracing you here?" she asked.

"I doubt that the Red Watch find me worth their while anymore, now that I am no longer involved with the exiles."

An expression of relief seemed to cross her face. "Is there anything else you'd like to add?"

Donis shook his head. "No, nothing."

"Then this refugee hearing is concluded." Karen switched off the machine and removed the cassette.

"What happens now?" he asked.

"The transcript will be sent to Ottawa, and meanwhile, we wait for their decision."

"How long will that take?"

"I imagine several months, at least. The committee's being deluged with refugee claims. In the meantime, we'll issue you a Minister's permit that allows you to work."

The complexity of bureaucracy never ceased to amaze him. "Are you saying that now I shall be allowed to do something I was arrested for a week ago?"

Karen chuckled. "That's what I'm saying. The permit should be ready by tomorrow afternoon, if you'd like to come in and pick it up."

So I shall have the opportunity of seeing you again. It was disturbing to suddenly discover how much that mattered to him. "I will come in tomorrow," he said and got up from the chair.

"You did very well today," she said as she gathered her materials.

Standing at the door, he turned to her. "I could not have done so well without you.

A CHAMBER QUARTET was presenting an impromptu concert in Victoria Park. Karen, her workday finished, wandered over, drawn to the intertwining melodies of a cello, bass violin and two recorders. Judging by the players' ages, they were university students, supplementing their income with donations tossed into an instrument case.

Karen removed her shoes and stretched out on the grass to listen. Overhead the afternoon sun poured through towering maples. The music seemed to weave through the hushed murmurs of the audience, the vivid textures of flowers and ivy. This was London at its most glorious, Karen thought, closing her eyes to enhance the ambience.

For half an hour or so none of the tunes were familiar, but then the cellist and flutist began a duet. Karen sat up, enchanted by the classic, plaintive melody. Some long-ago memory filled in the lyrics. *Alas, my love, you do me wrong...*

"'Greensleeves', is it not?" said a voice behind her.

Karen whirled her head around, and pleasure sparkled through her. "Donis!"

He dropped a gym bag to the ground. He had changed into casual clothes since the hearing that afternoon. It pleased her to see that he looked utterly at ease. "I went to the YMCA after the hearing," he said, "taking advantage of their free introductory visit. When I came out, I heard the music."

"Have you been listening long?"

"Long enough to observe you are a closet romantic. Has anyone ever told you that?"

"Not that I can recall. But what makes you say that?"

"I saw the look on your face, faraway, dreamy. And I saw the way you touched the leaves of that clover."

Karen glanced down. Sure enough there was an uprooted clover in her hand. She hadn't been aware of doing it, but she must have been stroking the leaves as she listened. "Maybe you're right," she said. "There is a sentimental streak in me somewhere."

Donis stretched out beside her. "What does a fair-haired, green-eyed Canadian woman see when she gazes so far away?"

The music, the surroundings made the question perfectly credible. But when Karen tried to answer, her mind went blank. "I don't know. I don't form a definite image or anything. It's more like . . . this sounds so silly . . . a feeling. I feel as though I'm thousands of miles away, doing something wonderful, something adventurous . . ."

"You are."

Karen laughed. "Working for the federal government? Oh, sure, a regular wish come true."

"But look at the people you meet, the stories you've heard—not bad for a girl who was born and raised in rural Ontario."

"Funny, I'd never looked at it that way before, but you're right. And I do love my work most of the time."

Donis spread out his hands. "There, you see? It's all a matter of perspective, isn't it?"

They were sitting close; their knees were almost touching. The grass felt damp and musky beneath Karen's hand. What would it be like, she wondered, to make love on damp, musky grass?

Karen nearly gasped. Sex was not something she often contemplated, and certainly not in specific terms. But there was no denying it this time. She'd not only contemplated making love—she'd visualized her partner, as well.

"Would you like to go somewhere for a drink?" Donis asked.

For an instant she panicked, thinking he'd somehow read her thoughts. But the music had stopped. And even if Donis did have seduction on his mind, Karen could bring things under control long before they reached the rolling-in-the-grass stage.

"Yes," she replied. "I'd like that."

At Donis's insistence, Karen chose the place, a cozy Hungarian café not far from the office. Depending on one's mood, the decor of dark wood and muted florals was either somber or tranquil. Today Karen was aware of tranquility, seasoned with a sprinkling of nervousness and sexual fantasy.

They picked a quiet table near a window. When the waiter had taken their order, Donis leaned over to Karen. "You look uncomfortable. Does it bother you to be seen with a client?"

He didn't ask the question as though he was offended. It was just that he had a directness, an earnestness, about him that sometimes knocked Karen off balance.

"No, not at all," she said. She twisted the napkin on her lap. "I'm just...I guess I find it hard to know what to say all of a sudden."

"Are you intimidated by me?"

She looked at his lean, dark face, gazed into his misty eyes and felt like blurting out, *Who wouldn't be?*

"No, it's not exactly you," she hedged. "It's...well, I'm overwhelmed by what you said at the hearing today. After all the things you've gone through, I feel as though we couldn't possibly have anything in common." *Except perhaps a mutual curiosity about taking the other to bed.* She'd been very aware of the looks he'd given her during the hearing.

Donis held out his hands and glanced around the room. "We have this café in common. We had the music in the park...we have now."

Karen shook her head. "You're amazing."

"Why do you say that?"

"I mean, look at you. You've been to hell and back, and you still look as though you've stepped off the cover of *Esquire.* Do you always land on your feet like this?"

Donis stared at her blankly. "Land on my feet? What is that?"

"Oh, sorry, it's an expression we use in English, referring to the way cats fall. They always land on their feet and never seem to get hurt."

"Ah, I see. I have never thought of my life in those terms, but I am a firm believer in destiny allotting us only what we can endure and nothing more."

"That's a healthy way to look at things."

"Do not overestimate me, Karen. I am as susceptible to doubts and insecurities as everyone else. Actually it is you who inspires me with your cool, Canadian reserve."

"Oh, come on."

"It is true. When I am in your presence, I feel obligated to . . . land on my feet, as you say. Or at least to give the appearance of doing so."

Karen laughed, delighted by his charming way with words, by his refreshing sincerity. The waiter arrived with a carafe of wine and a platter of cheese and fruit. Donis's face lit up. It occurred to Karen that his appreciation of life's pleasures would naturally be more acute, being deprived of them for so long. That realization drew her just a little closer.

She watched him pop a grape into his mouth and shut his eyes in sheer ecstasy. "This is exquisite," he said. "You must try the grapes."

"They can't possibly be as good as you make them seem," she said, grinning.

He tipped his head quizzically. "But they are. You must understand, Karen, that Sanvitans are a—how would you say it—sensuous people. You will understand that about us with time."

With time. The phrase taunted and pleased her. But with firm resolve she pushed it from her mind. When it came to Donis, there could be no guarantee of time. They came from different worlds, from different ways of life. Even if they did find common ground, the real possibility loomed that Donis would be forced to leave Canada.

"Eat, please," he said, holding up the platter.

Karen nibbled at a piece of cheese. Then she tasted her wine. The dry crisp vintage was perfect.

"You've been listening to my life story all afternoon," Donis said, taking a break from the food. "Tell me about yourself. Brothers and sisters, husbands, lovers."

"Husbands and lovers, I have none," she said, matching his playful tone. "But I do have three brothers and two sisters. One brother lives in London. Everyone else is scattered all over the continent."

"Have you never been married?"

Karen took a healthy swallow of wine. "No, but I came close twice."

"What happened?"

"The first time, I was only nineteen. We became engaged just before my boyfriend went away to university. Halfway through the year, he wrote to tell me he'd met someone in his biology lab."

Donis brushed a hand through the air. "You were far too young anyway." He made the observation as though he were a doting uncle, entitled to offering unsolicited opinions. Funny, Karen thought, she rather liked his method of rationalizing.

"You're right," she said. "I shudder whenever I think I could have been stuck with that man for the past twelve years."

"What is he doing now?"

"He quit university and is managing an all-night video store."

Donis chuckled as he refilled their wineglasses. "You would have had an excellent choice of first-run movies. What about betrothal number two?"

"You are nosy, aren't you?"

"I could pretend not to be, but that seems rather foolish. Anyway you are not obliged to tell me anything if you don't wish to."

"I don't mind. It's just that I don't usually talk about these things. I got engaged a second time about four years ago. We'd been going together for a couple of years, and there are still times I wonder whether I did the right thing." Karen swirled the pale gold liquid in her glass. "After all, here I am, practically over the hill—"

"Over the hill? That is another of your English idioms?"

"It means...too old."

"Ah, similar to 'long in the tooth,' no?" he said, his eyes twinkling.

"I think I prefer my cliché, thanks," she retorted. "This fellow was very nice. My parents liked him, he got along well with people, he was a hard worker."

"Those are reasons for hiring a housekeeper. What does it have to do with a husband?"

"Well, compatibility is important—"

"Did you love him?"

Karen wondered whether the wine was to blame. Why else would she have to think so hard to answer? "Well, certainly, I must have."

"Then why did you not marry him?"

Now she remembered, and the recollection made her laugh, even though it hadn't seemed funny at the time. "My fiancé met me after work one day and said he had a surprise. He drove me to a new subdivision and showed me the house he'd bought."

"For whom?"

"For us."

"He bought it without consulting you?"

Karen nodded. "He'd even picked out the color scheme and a three-room grouping. That's when you buy all of your household furniture at one cheap price." She emphasized the word cheap. "We had a terrible row, and I returned his ring. He still works in the Federal Building, and he managed to find someone who appreciated the house. They've been married a couple of years now."

"What are you looking for, Karen?"

"I'm not looking," she said, meeting his gaze as directly as she could manage.

"We are all seeking something from life, though not necessarily marriage."

"Oh, I see what you mean. I don't know. I have thought about that a lot. I'd like to...make a difference. Does that sound silly?"

"Not at all."

"Nothing as calamitous as what you've done. But I do feel that there's something out there for me. I just don't know what it is yet." She fell silent, pleased that Donis was confident enough to let the silence run its course. "Have you ever been in love?" she asked, inspired by his directness.

"You mean the kind of love poets write about?"

She laughed. "I guess that's the kind I mean."

"Not really." He shrugged. "When I was younger, Sanvitan women placed little emphasis on stimulating their minds. It seemed the more beautiful they were, the more boring. I could never conceive of spending a lifetime with any of them."

"Is it still that way in Sanvito?"

"Women's attitudes were changing, especially among the younger generation. But along came the election, and suddenly men and women were caught up in a struggle for survival. I suspect there are quite a few of us who never had the opportunity to fall in love."

"I'm sorry," Karen said. "I didn't mean to..."

"Mean to what?"

"Bring up...unpleasant associations."

Donis took her hands across the table. "That's not what you did. You shared a portion of your past, and I shared mine. There's no need to apologize."

Still feeling guilty, she looked up. "Really?"

"Do you know how long it has been since I have enjoyed a conversation such as this?"

Karen shook her head.

"Years. While I was in prison, of course, conversation was impossible. Meanwhile, my reputation as The Deliverer vastly outgrew my true capabilities. Later, when I met up with old friends, they would treat me as if I'd suddenly descended from Mount Olympus."

"I can understand why they might have felt that way. You were . . . you are an incredibly courageous person."

He released her fingers abruptly. "That part of my life, Karen, is over. I am no one's Deliverer now, and I want nothing more to do with it. Ever."

Karen drew her hands to her lap, feeling strangely bereft. "Are you sure that's possible?"

"Why do you ask?"

"I mean that your past is an integral part of you. You can't just run away and ignore it, even if you want to."

"I'm not running, that's just it. I intend to do nothing but live my life as quietly as possible."

The tone of their conversation had changed, which was the only reason Karen dared to ask the next question. "Donis, that first night you were in London, when you were charged with assault. Do you think it's possible that Dominic Scapiletti was a member of the Red Watch?"

He registered no surprise, no fear. But Karen knew that Donis, when he put his mind to it, was the quintessence of composure. "Anything is possible, but I doubt it."

"Why? I mean, he never showed up in court, he used a false name and address and disappeared."

"Which is why I am doubtful. The Red Watch are relentless and far from careless. If they had intended to apprehend me that night, they would have employed a more sophisticated method. Failing that, they would have to keep trying until they succeeded. I have been walking these streets openly, and nothing has happened. I see no reason to believe anything will."

"I hope you're right."

He drew his fingers through her hair. "You are a gentle lady, aren't you? Beneath that cool, brisk efficiency, it torments you to see people—even total strangers—suffer."

"That's only natural, isn't it?" she asked, so tempted to lean into his touch.

"Believe me, Karen, I have seen enough of the human race to know that compassion is far from natural. What makes life worth living are the exceptions—the rare souls who care—like you."

Just as Karen was about to lose herself in the sweet flow of his words, she felt an undertow pulling her in the opposite direction. Compassion was part of her job, the stimulus that saw her through long nights with clients in jail and harrowing refugee hearings.

Compassion was not sufficient reason for sharing a bottle of wine with a man as appealing as Donis. Things were moving too quickly, when Karen wasn't sure they ought to be moving at all.

"I have to go," she said, suddenly flustered.

"So soon?"

"Yes, I'd...uh, I forgot I have to do some things at home tonight."

Donis looked far from convinced but was too much of a gentleman to press for an explanation. "I'll walk with you."

"That's not necessary."

"That's not why I offered."

There was no challenge in his voice, no masculine bluster that would have set Karen's teeth on edge. Walking home with Donis would be pleasant, as pleasant as sharing wine and listening to a chamber quartet. Why should she hurt his feelings and cheat herself of a few more minutes enjoyment?

Dusk had descended like teal-blue gauze over the city. The shop windows were lit, and the air was comfortably cool. Donis held Karen's arm lightly as they walked, and she did nothing to discourage it, even while resenting her own duplicity.

Why can't you admit the truth behind those quivering, bleeding-heart emotions? You love the way Donis confides in you. You adore being seen with him, and you melt when he touches you. Compassion aside, it's his maleness that's turned you into a one-woman crusade.

Karen's cheeks were flushed, despite the coolness of the evening. That small brutal voice was right. From the beginning, she'd taken on Donis Sotera's case for a lot of reasons, and not all of them were noble.

They came to her apartment building and stopped short of the entrance. It was nearly dark. For an instant, Karen dallied with the idea of inviting Donis in. But the invitation would have been a civility. *Like hell.* Inviting him in was exactly what Karen wanted to do, and couldn't.

While she silently fussed and fretted, Donis drew Karen into his arms. As she wondered how to gracefully pull herself away, Donis tangled her hair in his fingers and brought his mouth to hers. There was no hesitation and no holding back. The kiss was decisive, hungry, as direct as the man himself.

Karen arched back, rising up on her toes so that their bodies were fully aligned. It was a reckless move on her part, and Donis afforded no chance for retreat.

Yet, just as Karen realized she was no match for his intensity, something beyond her own experience took over. She caught up to his passion, caught up and ran ahead. Their worlds, so far apart, came together in the joining of two mouths, two bodies. They were nothing, more or less, than a man, a woman.

But the meeting, though exquisite, was brief. As Karen's passion began to crest, Donis pulled away. She looked up, saw the mercurial fire in his eyes and murmured inwardly, thank God. He was no less shaken than she.

"You are such a lovely woman," he murmured, his voice gruff and sexy.

She managed a tremulous, "Th-thank you."

His gaze moved over the contours of her face. "It is I who must thank you. You have given me something I thought no one ever could. You have given me hope."

As Donis retreated into the darkness, Karen reached up and touched her lips. *If only you knew, Donis, you've given me the same.*

THE NEXT MORNING she woke up mortified. After only two glasses of wine—well, maybe, three—and she let Donis kiss her like that! What the hell was she thinking? What the hell was *he* thinking?

As only Karen's luck would have it, she ended up riding the elevator to the office with Mr. Rathbone, the manager. She squeaked a good-morning and held her breath, thoroughly convinced that her boss saw her kissing Donis on the street last night.

Mr. Rathbone was silent all the way up, but that didn't mean anything. He was probably trying to intimidate her, a tactic he often resorted to, and one that never failed for Karen.

Finally they reached the ninth floor. That was when he said, "Could I see you in my office for a minute?"

Following her boss down the corridor, Karen died a thousand deaths. Then stubbornly she rallied. Dammit, anyway. She was a grown woman. What business was it of Mr. Rathbone's if she chose to kiss a client in a public place? The only oath she'd sworn was of secrecy, not propriety—

"Andonis Sotera's permit," Mr. Rathbone said, picking up a file as he walked behind the desk.

Karen cleared her throat. "I beg your pardon, sir?"

"The Minister's permit. You put in a requisition yesterday."

She took the manila folder and pressed it to her chest, hoping it might muffle the sound of her hammering heart. "Is that all?"

He looked down his nose at her which, to be fair, was the only way he ever looked at anyone. "I believe that's all. Why? Was there something else?"

"No, sir, nothing else. Nothing at all. Thank you for the permit."

So she'd gotten away with it after all. It was inane, Karen told herself, to feel naughty at the age of thirty-one. Giddiness over a stolen kiss was totally unbecoming for a woman of her position. But so help her, it was all Karen could do not to skip all the way to her office.

The rest of the day Karen rehearsed scenarios while keeping an eye out for Donis. How was a person supposed to behave with a client after... what they'd done? As far as she knew, it had never happened to anyone else in the London Immigration Office.

Should she act witty, blasé, suggestive? Good grief, not suggestive. Blasé might be difficult to pull off, too. Witty, that was it. Treat the whole thing as a merry little joke.

Karen tossed her pen into the air. This was never going to work. Maybe she ought to leave Donis's file with Molly and ask her to issue the permit.

It was too late.

Molly's animated face popped around the partition. "Guess who's here?"

"I give up," Karen said, trying to sound bored. "Who is it?"

"Come on, Karen, you don't fool me. I've seen that little spark in your eyes when you talk about him, and I don't blame you. He is so cute."

Cute. Karen sniffed. Cute didn't even begin to describe that . . . hunk. "Thanks, Molly," she said, doggedly clinging to her professional decorum. "I'll be right out."

It would have been too much to hope that Donis might be unnerved at seeing her. Their eyes met, and he grinned as boldly as if they'd spent the night together, which only infuriated Karen further.

If a kiss unraveled her this badly, how would she ever cope with making love? What a stupid question. It would never happen. She wouldn't have to cope.

Fortunately the waiting room was nearly empty, and the only person who'd witnessed the smoldering visual exchange between Donis and Karen was Molly. She'd already formed her opinions, so no harm done there.

"You seem nervous," Donis remarked when they were in her office.

"Do I?" Karen felt like a coat rack had been rammed up the back of her dress. "It's uh . . . it's been a long day."

"I see." He sat back and waited. No, *withdrew* was the word. He was trying not to make her squirm, and for that Karen was grateful.

She brought out the official-looking document with the red seal and explained the legal conditions. Donis could work anywhere as long as the permit was in force. If the Refugee Status Advisory Committee did not reach a decision within the validity of the permit, it would be extended. If his refugee claim was disallowed, the permit would be revoked and the deportation order effected.

Donis listened to Karen's robotic presentation with a patient smirk. "And if my claim is allowed?" he asked. "You left that one out."

"Then you can stay on the permit indefinitely, for as long as you wish to remain in Canada."

"Very good." He leaned over to sign the document.

As Karen watched, her eyes fell on the date of her permit. The twenty-fifth of July. "It's your birthday in two days, isn't it?" she piped up.

"Yes, now that you mention it. Why do you ask?"

Heaven knew, Karen was not normally an impulsive person. When it came to entertaining, her idea of spontaneity meant six weeks planning, minimum.

But she had to do something to redeem herself. She couldn't let Donis walk away thinking he'd kissed an ice princess last night. She couldn't let him walk away not knowing whether he would ever want to see her again.

"I was thinking of having a little party for you. Nothing elaborate. Just a few friends."

Donis looked up as though she had just handed him the moon on a platter. "You would do that . . . for me?"

Karen suddenly felt as though they were sharing the moon. "Well, you are far from home, and you don't know many people. I just thought it might be nice . . ."

"It would be very nice."

"Good. Let's make it Friday, two nights from now at my place. You know the building, and my name is on the buzzer. Eight o'clock okay?"

"Perfect." To her undeniable delight, Donis leaned over and kissed her cheek. "You never cease to amaze me, Karen. Thank you for the permit, and I will see you Friday."

As soon as he left, Karen folded her arms on her desk and rested her head against them. *I never cease to amaze me, either.*

CHAPTER SEVEN

"MOLLY, ARE YOU DOING anything Friday night?"

The receptionist looked up while sucking her Coke loudly through a straw. "Gee, Karen, I didn't think I was your type."

"Very funny. But I'm serious. On some crazy impulse, I promised Donis a birthday party, and now I need guests."

The two women were in the cafeteria of the Federal Building, sitting at a long table unofficially reserved for Immigration.

The younger one giggled. "Why ruin the evening with a bunch of other people? Just tell Donis your friends had other plans, then it'll just be you and him."

"It's tempting, believe me. But Donis is expecting a party, not a candlelight dinner for two. I don't want to scare him off. You know how men can be."

"Tell me about it. I haven't dared feed Mick anything, in case he gets the wrong idea. Anyway, in answer to your question, I already have a date Friday night."

"With Mick? Why not bring him to the party?"

"Are you sure?"

"Of course. The more, the merrier."

"Well, we were just going to a movie. I'm sure he wouldn't mind a slight change in plans."

"Great. Can I take that as a definite yes?"

"Yeah, sure. Donis is a neat guy." Molly brought a conspiratorial hand to her mouth. "Just between you and me, I always get the feeling he's going to kiss my hand when he comes to the reception desk.''

Karen laughed. "I know what you mean. I get the same feeling." *Not to mention a sinking sensation when he doesn't.*

"What should we bring for a present?"

"Oh, don't worry about that. Gifts aren't necessary."

"Sure they are. Like, nobody can have a birthday party without presents.''

"Who's having a birthday?" Liz O'Connell appeared at the table carrying a coffee and two butter tarts.

"The sexy Sanvitan," Molly promptly replied. Not that Karen minded; Liz would have been the next one cornered anyway.

"Is that right?" The supervisor turned to Karen with an all-knowing grin. "Are you actually throwing a party for him?"

Karen couldn't help squirming. "It won't be anything elaborate. Just a little ... get-together. That's okay, isn't it?"

"Why are you asking me that?"

"Well, Donis is a client, and I wouldn't want this to be misconstrued as, you know, inappropriate behavior or anything."

"Oh, hell, I assume you're just going to serve him a cake with candles, not marry him, for Pete's sake."

The innocuous remark landed like a bomb in Karen's conscience. If cake and candles were at one end of the spectrum and marriage at the other, just how far was one allowed to progress in between? Then, dismissing her concern as premature and probably unfounded, Karen shrugged. "You're right, Liz. It's just a party."

"So am I invited?"

"Certainly. Do you want to come?"

"I'd love to. When and where?"

"Friday, eight o'clock, my place."

"Do I have to bring a date?"

"Not unless you want to."

The older woman waved a hand through the air. "Want to? Are you kidding? I'm off men forever. Celibacy has got to be better than the aggravation they cause."

"Gee, I don't know about that," Molly said, chin propped on her hands. "I can't imagine life without the excitement of falling in and out of love."

Liz bit into a butter tart. "That's because you're still young. Your bones and your heart haven't gotten brittle yet."

"What about Karen?" Molly asked with a wink. "Do you suppose she's getting brittle?"

Liz glanced at Karen who was visibly flustered at the topic of conversation. "I don't know, but I wouldn't waste any more time if I were her."

"Well, there you go," pronounced Molly. "You'd better nab Donis while you still can."

"I don't know about Donis," Liz said. "He's a sweetheart, but considering his circumstances, things could get a little sticky. Speaking of sticky, does anybody want this second butter tart? I gotta lose five pounds before the party."

I AM NOT GOING to "nab" Donis, Karen told herself the next evening. Spray-polishing the furniture in her apartment, she felt pretty good about herself. Throwing a party for Donis was a kind and decent thing to do. No one should be alone on his birthday, especially not in a strange country miles away from family and friends.

The guest list turned out to be no problem at all. Including herself and Donis, there would be six people, a comfortable, manageable size. Even Father Peter was coming, which particularly pleased Karen. She knew he was the closest to a real friend that Donis had in London.

She was surprised to learn from the priest that Donis was no longer staying at the seminary. He was sharing an apartment with a machinist from Ireland whose wife and children weren't due to arrive for several months.

Truth be told, Karen's reaction wasn't exactly surprise; it bordered dangerously close to anticipation. Donis's new lodgings were downtown, only a few blocks from her place—unlike the seminary, which was clear across town and full of priests. Not that Karen actually visualized nocturnal visits, but it certainly made for a less awkward situation if and when such visits were to transpire.

Such overtly sexual fantasizing made Karen feel depraved, but what was a woman to do? She buffed the dining room table with frantic vigor. What, indeed? She had managed not to think about sex easily enough before Andonis Sotera came along.

A knock on the door made her jump, as if she'd been caught in some underhanded act. "Who is it?" she called out, wiping sweat from her forehead.

"It's me, Sue."

Relieved, Karen dropped her dust cloth and went to the door. "What a nice surprise."

Stepping inside, her sister-in-law took a deep breath. "Ah, the inspiring aroma of Lestoil. What's the occasion?"

"Just housecleaning," Karen said, not willing to launch into specifics of tomorrow night. She'd rather hear someone else's news and forget about the party. "Would you like coffee or something?"

Sue shook her head. "No, thanks. Do you have milk?"

"Milk?" Karen snickered. "Would you like cookies to go with it?"

"Ha, ha," Sue mimicked. "Just milk will be fine."

Karen went to the kitchen, took out a glass for Sue and plugged in the kettle for herself. "What are you doing out at this hour of the evening? I thought you had enough shopping after our last expedition.''

''I didn't come downtown to shop. I needed to talk to you, Karen.''

Karen brought the glass of milk to the table and noticed that Sue's complexion was nearly the same shade as the beverage. ''What's the matter? You look pale.''

''I'm all right, just a little . . . tired.''

''It's Tim, isn't it? What's my thick-headed, chauvinistic brother doing this time?''

''Oh, Karen, I shouldn't be dumping this on you, but Tim and I had such a big fight last night. I'm really scared.''

''What were you fighting about—does he want to move again?''

''No, it's not that. Something . . . important has come up, and I want us to share it with your dad. Tim and I talked about it last weekend, and he said to go ahead and make plans. So I phoned Dad and told him we'd drop around to see him tomorrow night—''

''At the farm?'' Karen asked.

''Yeah. Silly of me, eh? I should have realized. Anyway, I told Tim that we were seeing Dad on Friday and that we'd probably be spending the night at the farm. Tim hit the roof. He accused me of meddling, of always siding with your father and . . . well, a whole raft of nasty things.''

''One night at the farm isn't going to kill him.''

''That's what I tried to tell him, but Tim's afraid that Dad will come to expect regular visits again, and Tim has this phobia of things ending up the way they used to be.''

Karen remembered the way things used to be all too well. She, Tim and Sue used to visit their parents quite regularly, but after their father lost the farm, the visits became intolerable—endurance sessions, more than anything. Dad would sit around drinking beer and feeling sorry for himself. Mom would slave in the kitchen preparing feasts in the hopes that her children would be persuaded to stay over-night or for as long as she could possibly keep them there. Karen knew why Mom did that; anything was probably better than being left alone with her dejected husband.

In an effort to help out and alleviate the tedium, the young people would do chores. They mowed the lawn, chopped wood, weeded the flower beds. Not that any of them begrudged helping, but it was getting to the point of being expected.

Karen would pull up into the driveway, and Dad would be waiting with a list of things for her to buy at the store. He had all the time in the world to get them himself, but that never seemed to enter his mind. He saw himself as an authority figure again, the children expected to obey.

It was even worse for Tim who'd inherited his father's ambition and pride. Being newly married and committed to making profits in real estate, he didn't have the time or interest to devote to chores.

Fights between Tim and his father grew bitter and be-came more frequent. Then they learned that Mom was dying of cancer. What remained of the family shattered. Two years later, it seemed they were still picking up the pieces.

Shaking herself of the unpleasant memories, Karen fixed herself a cup of instant coffee. "What can I do to help, Sue?"

"Gosh, I don't know. I shouldn't have even bothered you, but I needed to talk to someone who understands Tim."

"Me?" Karen laughed. "I've never understood Tim. I just had to live with him."

"Most of the girls at work are single or divorced, and they figure I should just dump the neanderthal."

Karen grew serious. "I hope you're not seriously con-sidering that option."

"No, I'm not. In spite of the horrific fight we had, I still love Tim. He's not perfect, but heck, what man is?"

"True," Karen said and promptly thought of Donis. If a person could judge by appearances, he'd be as close to perfect as she'd encountered yet. Too bad appearances had so little to do with it.

"The one thing I've always admired about you, Karen, is that you've never given up on Tim."

"I've wanted to, plenty of times, but he'll always be my cute little baby brother. Besides, he's the only one I see anymore. To think we come from a family of six, and there's only two of us that still get together at Thanksgiving and Christmas."

"I know. It bothers Tim, too. Not that he'd actually admit it, but family occasions are important to him. What am I gonna do to get him and Dad together again?"

"Why don't I invite the three of you to my place?"

"Oh, would you?"

"Sure, no problem. I've been meaning to have Dad over for some time. What about Saturday?"

"Saturday won't work. I'm on afternoons at the hospital."

"How about Sunday brunch?"

"Tim's golfing Sunday with guys from the office. I work afternoons for the next two weeks, and...well, I'd really like to see Dad sooner than that. Would tomorrow night be okay?"

Karen's fingers tightened around the coffee cup. She should have seen it coming. The plans for Donis's party had fallen into place too nicely. What better way to upset them than with a Miller family crisis?

But Sue Miller was not a whiner. Karen couldn't remember the last time Sue had asked outright for help. She had cried on Karen's shoulder now and then, but when it came to solving problems, Sue hated depending on anyone but herself. Knowing that, Karen realised there was only one alternative.

"I'm having a small party tomorrow evening for a client. Would you like to come?"

Sue's face lit up, then fell again. "Oh no, a party. We wouldn't dream of imposing..."

"Nonsense," Karen insisted. "You wouldn't be imposing." *Only destroying any chance of my getting to know Donis.* Having him meet her family, God love them, was the last thing she needed.

"Well, if you're sure that we won't be in the way."

Karen kept a smile pinned to her face. Thank goodness she was learning the fine art of diplomacy in her job. "You'll be a wonderful addition to the party," she said. "I've always wanted you to meet some of my colleagues, and this'll be the perfect opportunity."

Sue got up from the table and hugged her. "You are the greatest sister a girl could have. And a party is the perfect atmosphere for us to share our news with you and Dad."

"That's good," Karen said, feeling the heavy burden of martyrdom. Whoever was keeping tally of good deeds for Judgment Day ought to award her bonus points for this one.

MOLLY AND MICK were the first guests to arrive. Molly, in a thigh-high skirt and tousled hair, looked every bit the trendy ingenue. But one look at Molly's date, and Karen's trepidation doubled.

Nick was small and wiry with pale skin and wispy black hair to his shoulders. He wore a black leather biker's jacket over his T-shirt and jeans, and silver studs outlined his ears. Karen was painfully aware of the generation gap as she held out her hand and said, "Hi, I'm Karen."

He shook her hand. "How ya doin', I'm Mick."

"Mick's a drummer," Molly said proudly.

"Is that so?" Karen replied, ushering them into the living room. "That's sort of every parent's nightmare, isn't it?"

"What is?" Mick asked.

"Nothing. It was a lousy joke anyway. Where do you play?"

"Uh... well, I'm not actually playing right now. I'm between bands, so I work in a car wash."

"Oh, how nice." Karen wasn't a snob. Truly, she wasn't. But how on earth was anyone going to get through this evening? "Have a seat, guys, and help yourself to the munchies."

"Where do you want me to put this?" Molly held out a flat, square package that could only be a record album.

Karen chided herself for thinking like an old-maid aunt. Molly and Mick were young and entitled to be radical, or whatever it was kids wanted to be these days. "That was really sweet of you to bring a gift. You can put it on the dining room table."

Karen offered them drinks. Mick turned her down, but Molly took a glass of sangria. Karen poured herself one as well and, taking a seat across from them, tried not to stare at Mick eating peanuts. He jiggled them in his palm with intense concentration, then whapped them into his mouth all at once. The effect was something like slapping the lid on a jar full of flies.

Finally there was a knock on the door. Karen fairly leaped off her chair. "Oh, excuse me, someone's here!"

She could've hugged Tim and Sue out of sheer gratitude. Never mind that until now their coming had been a sore point with Karen. Tim, for all his shortcomings, was a natural with people; so was his wife. If anyone could talk to Molly and Mick, they could. Then, as if to further tweak Karen's conscience, they came in laden with platters of hors d'oeuvres—a shameful contrast to Karen's chip dip and pretzels.

"I didn't bring a cake," Sue said, bustling the food into the kitchen. "I ran out of time and figured you'd be looking after that anyway."

Karen thought of the store-bought cake with icing roses she'd picked up on her way home tonight. "Oh, yes, the cake's taken care of. But, Sue, when did you ever get time to make this stuff?" She lifted foil wrappings to find stuffed mushrooms, cheese puffs, crab balls artfully arranged on oven-proof plates.

"I got up a few hours before work this morning."

Tim draped an arm around his tiny wife. "A couple of hours, listen to her. She was up at three o'clock. Some kind of amazing lady, eh?"

Karen flashed her brother what she hoped was a stern look. *Darned right she's amazing, Timothy, and you'd better appreciate her.*

But Tim, who'd never been much for telepathy, loped into the living room to greet the other guests. While Karen tried to absorb Sue's instructions for heating and serving the hors d'oeuvres, Tim effortlessly struck up a conversation with Molly's date. Karen had forgotten that Tim used to work in a car wash. Maybe there was hope for this evening yet.

Father Peter and Liz arrived together, an unlikely match if ever there was. The priest, as always, was wearing his collar and looking properly clerical. By contrast Liz looked like the star performer in a flamenco show, complete with a tight ruffled dress and enormous gold earrings.

Molly let out a playful whoop when she saw them. "Hey, I didn't know you two were an item."

Father Peter laughed. "We've been trying to keep it a secret."

Liz reached over and pinched Molly's cheek. "That's what I love about you. Just when I think I'm making headway with a guy, you go and open your cute little mouth."

Mick wore the expression of one who thought he'd come to a masquerade party by mistake. Father Peter, scooping up a handful of chips, sat beside him. "We're not really together, she and I," he explained, "just friends."

So far, all the guests, bless their hearts, had brought gifts, and conversation in the living room was surprisingly animated. Karen was mixing another batch of sangria when she heard the final knock on the door.

There was her father, clutching a six-pack of beer to his chest, wearing a decidedly concerned expression. Karen looked over his shoulder and determined at once the cause of his concern.

Donis was standing a few feet behind, looking around as though he wasn't sure of the right apartment. And if Karen knew anything about her father, she suspected that he was the source of Donis's doubts.

"Hi, there," William Miller said. "How are you?"

"Fine, Dad," Karen said. "I see you brought the guest of honor with you."

Her father glanced down in confusion at his case of beer. Then, catching on, he gestured over his shoulder. "Oh, you mean him? We rode up in the elevator together, but I didn't know he was coming here."

"Hello, Donis," she said, smiling determinedly. "I'm so glad you could make it."

Donis handed her a bottle of French wine, a vintage he'd taken great care in selecting. He'd hoped to impress her with his discerning taste, but wine was now the furthest thing from his mind.

Karen looked ravishing. Her dress was silk with a straight skirt and belted at the waist. Tailored, but exquisitely feminine in a deep shade of emerald green to match her eyes. She wore little make-up, as usual, but her eyes glistened and her cheeks bloomed with color. How could he ever have thought of her as prim and dull?

"You look lovely, Karen." The word fell far short of what he wanted to say, but her father, after all, was standing right there.

"Thank you. Dad, I'd like you to meet Donis Sotera. Donis, this is my father, William Miller."

Donis inclined his head politely as he shook hands. When he looked up, William Miller was eyeing him suspiciously. Donis had seen that look before, usually from middle-aged American tourists on European motor coach tours. The look was usually followed by patting whichever pocket held their wallets.

"It's a pleasure to meet you," Donis said, trying not to smirk at the way William Miller clutched his beer.

"Likewise," Karen's father muttered.

Donis was relieved to see several familiar faces. The young girl from the Immigration reception desk, an older woman who often smiled at him in the office and Father Peter.

Karen appeared nervous as she introduced the others. Donis thought at first he was the cause of her nervousness, but then decided, probably not. More than likely, it was the hostility in her family. Donis had sensed it as soon as William Miller saw his son. A shame, he thought. People's lives were so tranquil here, compared to what he had left in Sanvito. One would think that getting along would come easily.

"Tim, would you like to offer these gentlemen a drink?" Karen said. She was fluttering around like a wild bird in a cage. Donis wished he could take her aside to calm her— to calm himself—but it was much too early in the evening to hope for privacy. Assuming the opportunity would come at all. Why were there always so many people around when all he wanted was to be with Karen?

Donis chided himself for his ingratitude. There was a time when he would have given his left arm to have so many people around. Besides, Karen had gone to a great deal of trouble to organize this gathering at short notice. The least he could do was to give the appearance of enjoying himself. Donis accepted a glass of wine from Tim and, smiling politely, took a seat beside the young man with the riveted ears.

Karen couldn't believe how well the party was going. Liz was getting a little tipsy, Father Peter and Tim were talking politics, but other than that, the mood was quite pleasant.

Donis was a natural with people. He seemed to blend with the other guests almost effortlessly, drawing them out with questions and thoughtful remarks. With Mick, he talked drums; with Tim, he talked money. With Molly, he pored through Karen's record collection to find suitable music for dancing.

Still, gratifying though it was, Karen wished she and Donis had been alone for this occasion. She would have loved to be the sole focus of his attention, instead of sharing it with a roomful of people. Selfish, maybe, but she couldn't help the way she felt.

Suddenly anxious to get on with things, Karen gestured to Sue who got up and disappeared into the kitchen. Karen called the other guests into the dining room. She held Donis back until last, then watched his reaction as he entered the room and saw the table full of presents.

He didn't disappoint her. His eyes widened, and he looked for all the world like an enraptured little boy.

Donis turned to Karen. "Surely this is not all for me?"

Choked up, she barely trusted herself to speak. "You're the birthday boy. But first you have to sit here at the head of the table."

That was Sue's cue to march in with the cake while everyone joined in on the familiar chorus. Karen, teary-eyed, glanced at Molly who was wiping the corners of her eyes, too. Liz was the soppiest of all of them, trying to sing while blowing her nose.

For a minute or two, the expression on Donis's face was so intense, Karen was afraid she'd done the wrong thing. Sue placed the lighted cake before him, and he looked as though he wanted to bolt. Good grief, Karen thought, maybe birthday cakes were a sign of bad luck in Sanvito. How on earth was she supposed to know these things?

"Make a wish *before* you blow out the candles," Father Peter reminded him. "Otherwise the wish won't come true."

Karen glanced at the priest with renewed admiration. Quite an enlightened remark from a man who dealt only in prayer.

"A wish," Donis said, as though he were taking the matter seriously. "Any wish?"

"Absolutely," Father Peter assured him. "Such opportunities only come once a year."

Just then Donis turned and looked at Karen. Their gazes locked, and for a timeless instant, the two of them were alone in the room. Alone in the world. Then Molly or somebody started to cheer, and the touch of magic vanished. Later Karen would even wonder if she'd imagined it.

Liz handed him the gifts. To Karen's amazement, everyone except her dad had brought one. Tim and Sue gave Donis a Toronto Blue Jays T-shirt, which he loved. Sanvitans were baseball fanatics, he claimed, and this shirt would be the undisputed envy of all his friends.

No one else paid much attention to the remark, but it touched Karen deeply. Did Donis actually hope to return to Sanvito someday? Did he believe there would come a time when he and his boyhood friends could enjoy simple pleasures like baseball again?

Karen pushed aside her reflections. Donis was probably speaking figuratively, and she couldn't blame him. Birthdays were meant to be nostalgic occasions.

Liz gave him a guide book entitled *Things to Do and Places to See in London*. Along with the book she gave him a kiss on the cheek and a less than subtle hint, "There's a marvelous little bistro on page forty-three. If you're ever in the mood..."

Everyone in the room, including Donis, broke up, which was exactly what Liz was aiming for. Karen was thinking how Liz made the ideal party guest when she noticed her father slouched in a corner of the dining room.

It didn't surprise her that he was quiet. Even when Mom was alive, he'd never been much of a social animal. What shocked Karen was his expression. He was scowling at Liz as though she were the most disreputable strumpet he'd ever laid eyes on. Of all the uptight, narrow-minded...

Liz might be a little snookered, but she was still Karen's supervisor. All they needed was for William Miller to begin expounding on what a saint he'd been married to for forty-odd years.

Karen glanced at Tim and Sue, hoping to solicit their help if need be. But they were too busy enjoying themselves. Apparently no one except Karen had noticed Dad.

Donis opened her gift next. The box was deceptively huge, but the contents consisted of a business-size envelope tucked in one corner. Donis opened the envelope. "What a thoughtful gift, Karen. How did you think of it?"

"Just a hunch," she said, smiling.

His reaction pleased her. After a long restless night, Karen had finally decided to get him a three-month membership at the YMCA. It cost a bit more than she'd intended to spend, but heaven knew, Donis had had precious few luxuries in recent years. It might be nice for him to enjoy the weight room and spa while awaiting the decision from the RSAC.

Father Peter gave him a pair of tickets to the Grand Theater's performance of *Carousel*. Molly and Mick's present was last. Molly was so excited she was practically bobbing up and down as Donis opened the package.

"An album," he exclaimed, remarkably straight-faced. "I am very fond of music."

Karen had to bite her lower lip and didn't dare look at anyone. Molly was sweet, but it wouldn't occur to her that a refugee was not likely to have a turntable and speakers among his limited possessions.

"I don't believe I'm familiar with this group," Donis turned over the cover, which featured four young men painted green.

"Jiminy Crud," Molly explained. "They're terrific. They've redone a whole pile of sixties stuff in heavy metal. Could we listen to it, please, Karen?"

A pregnant pause descended on the room. Everyone turned to the hostess, anxiously awaiting her reply. Karen cleared her throat and swallowed. "How about just one cut? My, uh...my needle's not in very good shape. I wouldn't want to ruin Donis's new album."

So everyone dutifully sat through Jiminy Crud's murderous rendition of "Walk Like a Man," formerly done by Frankie Valli and The Four Seasons. Karen leaped up to turn the stereo off before they could hear "By the Time I Get to Phoenix."

"How about cake?" Sue chirped in. After she helped Karen serve the guests, she said, "Dad, Karen, would you two come into the kitchen for a minute?"

Tim came with them, obviously mellowed by the sangria and the mood of the party. He was almost grinning at his father who responded with a guarded look of his own.

"What's this, a powwow?" the eldest Miller asked.

"Sort of," Sue said, eyes twinkling. "Go ahead, Tim. You tell him."

His lanky frame slouched against the counter, Tim looked as awkward as a teenager grappling with puberty.

"Sue and I have something to tell you. We thought this time you might actually be interested."

"Tim!" Karen chided. Sue's response of a swift poke in the ribs was equally furious.

"Sorry," Tim mumbled, rubbing the injured spot on his side. "I didn't mean for it to come out like that. I just, uh—aw, hell, we're gonna have a baby, all right?"

Karen shrieked. "A baby! When?"

"January," Sue said.

"Oh, wow, I was hoping that's what the news was. Now I understand why you've been so peaked lately. Congratulations, guys!"

William Miller put down his bottle of beer. Humbly, beseechingly, he held out his arms. "That's great, kids. Really great."

Tim drew back at first, but only because he was his father's son, and affection did not come easily. The two men embraced at last, slapping each other's backs. "Thanks, Dad."

Karen would have sworn Tim was snuffling. Then, as if he'd suddenly caught on to affection, William lifted Sue right off the floor when he hugged her.

"Hey, take it easy with my wife," Tim teased. "She's delicate."

"I am not," Sue argued. "I'm just pregnant."

William set her down and wiped the corner of his eye. "When my son first brought you home," he said, "I figured such a tiny mite could never put up with us Millers. I don't know how or why you do it, but I'm awfully glad you do."

"Aw, Dad, somebody has to," Sue replied, laughing and crying.

Just then, Father Peter stuck his head into the kitchen. "I'm interrupting, aren't I?"

Karen's dad turned around, his face beaming. "Hey, guess what? I'm gonna be a grandfather!"

"Congratulations, William. Is this the first one?"

"Nope, seventh. Or is it eighth? Aw, what difference does it make? This one's gonna grow up right here in London. I'll be able to visit him and teach the kid everything I know."

Karen and Tim exchanged glances, but for once there was no hostility or rebuke in the exchange. Just a touch of exasperation and lots of love.

The time came for dancing. Molly's generation was apparently enjoying a revival of early Beatles, which suited everyone else in the room as well. Even Karen's dad recognized the tunes from the 1001 Strings versions his wife used to buy.

The coffee table was moved from the middle of the living room, providing an ideal hardwood dance floor. The party had turned genuinely festive, so much more than Karen had expected.

At first Mick danced only with Molly, and Tim danced only with Sue, but it wasn't long before others stepped in and the partners changed. Liz alternated between the two older men, but Father Peter eventually begged off from exhaustion. The sight of a rejuvenated William Miller wiggling his rear to "Twist and Shout" was enough to make Karen split her sides, but she was delighted. She hadn't seen her father this happy since—well, she couldn't remember ever seeing him this happy.

While others danced, Karen used the opportunity to clear the dining room, but what she really wanted was a few minutes alone. She had been reluctant to let her family join this celebration, and her reasons had been so selfish. She'd worried that her father would embarrass her with his narrow-minded ways. She'd been afraid that Tim would be his usual surly self with Dad there. They had proven her wrong, and Karen felt ashamed for not giving her family more credit.

"Here you are." Donis had come up from behind and slipped his arms around her waist. "Why aren't you enjoying the party with the rest of us?"

The taut contours of his body pressed against hers sent perilous sensations through Karen. She leaned back, her breath suddenly shallow. "I am enjoying it," she insisted. "I just thought I'd clear up a few of these dishes..."

"Leave them. I'll help you clean up later." His lips at the base of her neck felt like molten silk. He turned her around effortlessly until she was facing him. Their bodies were a mere whisper apart. "Dance with me," he murmured.

With another man, Karen might have been put off by the peremptory remark. She might have admonished him teasingly for not saying please.

But Karen saw the white-hot fire in Donis's eyes and felt the entreaty of his body holding hers. What she heard was not a command, but a softly spoken plea. It was as though Donis were saying, "Love me."

CHAPTER EIGHT

THE SONG WAS AN OLD FAVORITE, a song of people and places, of remembering. Yet as the lyrics drifted through Karen's mind, she didn't go back to earlier times. She was wrapped in Donis's arms, wrapped in the here and now. If there could be such a thing as nostalgia in the making, this was it.

And the mood was so right, so pervasive, Karen allowed herself to believe that Donis might be hearing the song the same way. He was with her, wasn't he? He'd sought her out to dance. And not so long ago, he'd kissed her.

"You are so special, Karen...so gentle," he said, confirming her secret feelings.

She smiled, nestling her head closer. Dancing, they were a perfect fit. Cheek to cheek, thigh to thigh. "So are you, Donis," she murmured. "So are you."

The song came to an end. Karen braced herself for the inevitable letting go of their bodies. But Donis held on, his hands moving along her back, his lips on her neck. Karen felt as though the music had woven a net with threads too delicate to see.

"So this is where the two of you have been hiding out!" The thread snapped at the sound of Liz's boisterous voice. Karen and Donis, equally startled, leaped back a step.

Liz wore a lopsided grin and her nose was a shade of garnet, not unlike the insidious sangria she'd been drinking all evening. Karen had seen Liz happy at office parties, but never to this extent. She felt a tug of pity. Happy drunks always seemed lonely to her.

"How about some coffee?" Karen offered. "I was about to put on a fresh pot."

"Coffee! Hell, no. I came to ask if you've got any tango music."

Karen's jaw dropped. "You've got to be kidding."

"No, I'm shee...serious. Tangos happen to be very provocative, let me tell you."

"Maybe so, but I still don't have any."

The woman scowled. "Oh, well, I guess it doesn't matter. I can do it without music. Come out here, you two. I've promised the others a demonstration, and I don't want you to miss it."

Touching the small of her back, Donis led Karen into the living room. "This should be fascinating," he whispered.

"Bill's agreed to be my partner," Liz said and pulled a somewhat sheepish William Miller onto the floor.

"My dad?" Karen said, unbelieving.

Mick had turned off the stereo, and the guests assembled to witness what promised to be entertaining, if nothing else. First, Liz rearranged her partner's flaccid stance into a semi-recognizable tango pose—faces nearly touching, arms out, right feet pointing outward. "All right, remember what I taught you?" she said to William.

He sighed. "I wouldn't count on it."

After whispering final instructions, Liz began the makeshift music. "Pa-rump, pum, pum, pum. Pa-rum, pa, pum, pum. Rum, pum, pum, pum. Pa-rum, pa, pum, pum."

Within seconds, everyone was howling. It was quite simply one of the most hilarious displays Karen had ever witnessed. Liz resembled a slightly bedraggled Carmen Miranda, while William looked exactly like what he was— an Ontario farmer being dragged through a tango.

Donis, laughing, let his head drop to Karen's shoulder. Unconsciously she reached up and laced her fingers through his hair. Her consciousness reared however when Donis captured Karen's hand and ran his tongue along the inside of her palm.

Fortunately her gasp was drowned out amid the gales of laughter. But if she'd had any doubts before as to Donis's intentions, they were more than clear now. Her own reaction was no less candid. She wanted him every bit as much.

When Liz and Bill's demonstration was over, it became obvious that the party was, too. It had been a perfect evening, Karen thought, and still was, with Donis beside her.

Father Peter, wiping tears of laughter from his eyes, was the first to get up and say his goodbyes to the others. "I have early mass in the morning, so I must leave. Thank you so much, Karen, for inviting me. This has been unforgettable."

Karen walked the priest to the door. "I'm so glad you came. I know how much it meant to Donis."

"Giving him this party was the nicest thing anyone could have done. He was fortunate to have gotten you as his counselor, not to mention his friend."

"Oh, speaking of friends," Karen said, "aren't you driving Liz home?"

"I made the offer, but apparently your dad insists on taking her home."

Her eyes widened. "Really? How about that?" She hugged the priest. "Good night, Father. Talk to you soon."

Karen returned to the living room and found her dad and Liz on the love seat, heads close together, giggling. Her dad never giggled, and he hadn't drunk more than a couple of beers all evening. It must have been the news of an impending grandchild that brought out the youngster in him.

Karen was pleased that her father had made the offer to take her supervisor home. Despite Father Peter's generosity, Karen knew that Liz lived in the opposite direction of the seminary. But for William, it was right on his way.

The others soon followed the priest's lead. Donis and Karen saw the guests to the door. Hugging Sue, congratulating Tim, Donis seemed so relaxed, as though he were the host, bidding his visitors good-night. Karen even had to acknowledge that Mick wasn't such a bad fellow, studded ears and all. But she was glad when everyone had finally gone, and she and Donis were alone.

In the silent aftermath, they looked at each other, as if neither one was sure what should happen next. Donis put an arm around her shoulder. "I'll help you clean up," he said.

The cleaning Karen would have gladly relegated to the morning, but decided not to voice her opinion. She was traditional enough to believe that the most a woman could do was set the stage for seduction. Ultimately it was the man who decided when to act.

Not that she minded Donis being in no hurry. Her physical desire, though acknowledged, was not something she felt at ease with quite yet. There would be complications. But when it came to giving oneself to a man, Karen reasoned, there always were.

Accompanying him to the kitchen, she began loading the dishwasher while Donis rinsed plates. Their conversation hovered around neutral topics—the party, the gifts, the food. Donis was generous and gentlemanly in expressing his appreciation. But all Karen could do was contemplate how it would feel to lie naked in his arms.

Donis, she concluded, was an overwhelming man. And Karen, despite her years and relative experience, had never been overwhelmed.

One day she would look back on this evening and tell herself they should have spent more time tidying the apartment. They should have kept their hands busier, their eyes safely diverted. But suddenly they found themselves in the living room, the last of the glasses emptied, the last of the crumbs swept away.

Donis held out his arm. "Come here, sit with me."

Once again Karen sensed the plea in his voice and responded. She took his hand, and they crossed the room to the sofa. A single lamp burned, one that cast far more shadow than light.

Donis gently took Karen's face in his hands. "I never dreamed someone as special as you would come into my life."

Though they were only words, they made her soar. But how could they do anything else?

"There's nothing special about me." Karen's response wasn't meant to be coy. Despite Donis denying he'd ever fallen in love, Karen was mature enough to realize there would have been many women attracted to him. And their roster, though totally imagined, was intimidating. Sultry Mediterraneans, stylish Europeans, elegant women, seductresses. How could a farm girl from Ontario even rank on the list?

"You make me laugh," he said, playing with a tendril of her hair. "You make me feel worthwhile, whole." He brushed his lips against her, but the touch was much too light for Karen. It wasn't a kiss, only a teaser. Karen had to struggle not to pull his face to hers again.

"I'm glad I can do that for you," she whispered. Even conversation, as long as it retained a certain intimacy, was better than nothing.

"I would like us to make a pact."

"Pact?" His choice of words puzzled her, but then Karen dismissed it as a loss in translation. A pact wasn't usually romantic, but it meant the same as a promise or a vow—and those were things that lovers made. "What kind of pact?" she asked, scarcely breathing.

"I want us to think well of each other, always. No matter what happens."

She fought the ridiculous wave of disappointment. "I already do. Why would you think things would change?"

Donis ran his hand along her sleeve. "Because things always do change between a man and a woman. Even now, I wonder if it's too late for us."

"Too late? Why?"

His gaze filled with wisdom and sadness. "Because you are falling in love with me."

A bucket of cold water would have accomplished the same thing. Karen, wide-eyed, began to splutter. "How can you...how could you come right out and say such a thing?"

"It is true, isn't it?"

"Whether it's true or not is irrelevant. I mean, of all the arrogant..." Words finally escaped her. Karen pushed herself from the sofa and stomped across the room. But when she reached the opposite wall, she had no choice but to whirl around and face him. Her face burned with rage, all the more humiliating because Donis sat there looking utterly guileless.

"I have upset you," he said. "I did not intend to do that."

"Yes, you've definitely upset me."

"Why?"

Dammit all, but Donis didn't look the least bit arrogant. He looked like a little boy who had no idea he'd done something wrong. She answered him, "Because... because a man just shouldn't say something like that to a woman, not...before she's even admitted it to herself."

"I wasn't trying to anticipate your feelings. I assumed you knew, and I was trying to keep things honest."

Karen sank into the nearest chair. "Honest? Good grief. Listen, maybe in Sanvito, that's considered honesty, but here, it's just—well, not the thing to say when a woman is feeling...intimate. There's too much pride at stake."

"Pride? What does pride have to do with love?"

Karen stared at Donis. He was obviously trying hard to understand. She wondered if this was a result of two years in solitary. Maybe social dictates were the first things to blur in one's memory. If that were true, then she wasn't being fair by reacting with anger.

"All right, I'll try to explain," she said. "As soon as you said that I'm falling in love with you, you put me on the defensive. And when that happens, a person automatically feels the need to...defend herself, if not retaliate."

Donis came over, sat cross-legged on the floor beside her and put his hands on her lap. "Do you think I would ridicule you or hurt you simply because I understand how you feel?"

"Those things crossed my mind," she admitted. The plaintive tone in Donis's voice was nearly enough to draw tears. Karen longed to clasp him to her breast; she longed to stroke his hair and tell him it didn't matter. But it did matter. And so she bit her lower lip and did nothing.

His hands fell from her lap. "Then I am truly sorry. I did not mean to imply that I don't want you, that I no longer want us to be close—because I do. But at times, I forget the—how shall I say it—the disguises a man and woman must wear in each other's presence."

Karen sighed. "It's unfortunate, but I guess the disguises are there for a reason."

"You are still angry with me."

Good Lord, Donis, don't expect consolation five minutes after you rip my heart out. Even if I want to console you.

Call it foolish pride, call it what you will, but there was still one overriding reason why Karen couldn't forgive him. He hadn't said a word about falling in love with her.

"I think it's best that you leave," she said at last.

"Could we not talk for a while, let me hold you?"

Karen turned her head away, so he wouldn't see the pain and, God forbid, mention it. "I think we've done enough talking and holding for one night."

Donis got up from the floor. She knew from the slope of his shoulders that he hurt, that he deeply regretted hurting her. But they each had their own anguish to deal with.

"Thank you for the party—" he began.

"No thanks are necessary." She didn't trust herself to see Donis out. She stayed where she was, listening to his footsteps, hearing the door open. There was a prolonged silence, as though Donis was thinking of coming back. But then she heard the door close, and the silence stretched on.

She half expected the rage to rise up again, the humiliation to resurface. But strangely enough, all Karen could think of was something Donis had said. "I want us to think well of each other, always. No matter what happens."

It was to have been a pact between them, and Karen had already broken it.

SHE MUST HAVE SLEPT, although she had no recollection of resting. One minute Karen was tossing and turning, the next she was peering through scratchy eyelids at the clock on the nightstand.

It was Saturday morning, barely eight o'clock. Anyone with sense would sleep till noon after a night like last night. But not Karen, oh no. Why sleep when she could wake up bright and early and agonize that much longer?

She sat up, then fell back again. What did a person do at eight o'clock in the morning when she wanted to forget? It was too early to drink, too early to go visiting. She didn't even have a garden to putter in. Her plants needed watering, but that would take five minutes if she dragged it out.

An idea finally came to her, one that a psychologist might have diagnosed as some kind of regression. She would visit her father, something she did most weekends anyway. There was no reason to attach special significance to this visit.

Karen felt better after a long hot shower and decided this was definitely a morning made for self-indulgence. One of her favorite indulgences was to go out for breakfast, so she drove to a truck stop on the outskirts of town. They were known for their he-man servings—two eggs, three strips of bacon, hash browns, toast, juice and all the coffee you could drink—for a ridiculously low price.

An hour later, Karen stared down at her greasy plate, wishing she were dead. Or at least, wishing she hadn't forced down those last three hash browns. Food was no antidote; it was just another form of misery.

She paid the bill and staggered to her car. Outside, the sun blazed, a disgustingly beautiful day. It was a day made for new lovers waking up and discovering each other, for picnics, for lying on the beach. Karen recalled similar fantasies of her own not so long ago. Now, here she was, all alone and running home to Daddy.

The newspaper on the front step was Karen's first indication that something wasn't right. The *Saturday Star* was delivered early, and her father always took it inside to read with his first coffee of the day.

Karen tried the door and found it locked. She rang the bell, but no one answered. She took out her own house key and let herself in.

"Dad?" The silence alarmed her. "It's me, Karen. Are you still sleeping?"

Oh, please, let him still be sleeping. Karen crept down the hallway to her parents' bedroom, trying not to imagine the worst. Accepting her parents' mortality was one thing, but to be the one who found her father dead was unthinkable. She was only a middle child, for heaven's sake.

The bed was vacant, the covers pulled up half-heartedly. Mother would have had a fit to see it like this. She was such a stickler about tucking the bedspread under the pillows.

Karen allowed the first wave of relief to wash through her as she combed the house and called out her father's name. Next, she went out to the sunny backyard. A hundred feet behind the lawn was the hay field, all that remained of his former acreage.

He might be in the fields somewhere, although Karen couldn't imagine why he'd be out before reading the paper. He was utterly predictable that way.

Finally Karen couldn't stand it any longer. She turned and rushed back into the house to phone her brother. "Tim, it's me. I'm at the farm and I can't find Dad anywhere."

"Wh-what time is it?"

Karen glanced at the clock on the kitchen wall. "Almost ten-thirty."

"Ten-thirty? Don't you realize this is the weekend?"

"I know, but I'm worried. The *Star* was outside, the door was locked. He's nowhere to be found."

"Maybe he's gone to the store. Is the car in the garage?"

Karen could have kicked herself. "I forgot to check. Hold on." Ignoring her brother's shout of protest, she dashed out the front door.

The garage door was closed. If Dad were at the store, he would have left the door open. She peered through a cobwebbed window; the car wasn't there.

Karen told her brother what she found. "What do you suppose could have happened to him?"

While she was gone, Tim must have heard something funny. There was no other reason for him to chuckle. "Sue and I have a pretty good idea. Don't you?"

"What are you talking about?"

"Dad gave your boss a ride home last night, right?"

"Liz? Yes, but I don't see what that has to...nooo, Tim, you don't really think..."

"Why not? They're consenting adults."

"I know, but..." Now that Tim had put it into words, it seemed so obvious. But Dad? Liz? He was sixty-nine, and she was Karen's supervisor, for heaven's sake!

"Are you still there, big sister?"

Karen sighed, suddenly feeling more rejected than ever. "I'm still here. How would you like some company for the day?"

DONIS HADN'T INTENDED to let so much time pass without calling Karen. Nearly a week had elapsed since the party. She deserved better from him.

But then he ought to be accustomed by now to letting people down. It seemed to be his unfortunate lot in life. He shouldn't even be in this country, cowering, hiding from a responsibility he neither sought nor wanted.

A nameless priest had given his life so that the great "Deliverer" could continue with his mission. And what had happened? Donis had led people to their deaths like lambs to the slaughter. Some hero he'd turned out to be.

Now, to feel guilty because he hadn't called a woman was almost laughably anticlimactic. But what could he say to Karen? He knew her feelings. He also knew that a relationship between a man and a woman could only grow or die on the vine. Wouldn't it be better for both of them to let this one die on the vine?

The knock on the door made Donis jump. It was late, almost eleven. His roommate was at work. Donis was expecting no one. At least, no one with good intentions.

He wondered if the visitor could see the light beneath the door. It might be wiser not to answer.

"Donis, are you in there? It's Father Peter."

Donis struggled with a sense of relief and disappointment. Had it been Karen, like it or not, his mood would have lifted.

He swung the door open. "Hello, Father."

"So you are still on the face of the earth. Some of us were beginning to wonder."

Donis chose not to press for details as to who the some were. "I've been working."

The priest stepped inside. "Twenty-four hours a day?"

"Practically. Can I offer you something? Coffee, tea?"

"Nothing, thank you. I apologize for the late hour, but you are a difficult man to get a hold of."

"Yes." Donis led him into the living room.

"If you don't mind my saying so, you look terrible."

"I don't mind hearing the truth." That was another reason he'd been reluctant to phone Karen. Donis had seen the marks of fatigue etch deeper on his face with each passing hour. Idiotic male pride, perhaps, but he had this need to always appear invincible with Karen. What would she think if she knew how desperately vulnerable he really was?

"How many jobs are you holding down?" Father Peter asked.

"Three." Donis fell heavily onto a recliner. "Do you think I'm abusing my privileges?"

"Not at all. Canadians could learn much from the work ethic of immigrants."

Donis longed to ask the priest if he'd spoken to Karen, but refrained. The fewer people involved, the better. "What can I do for you, Father?"

"You told me to get in touch with you after the party."

"Ah yes, the money, I'd almost forgotten. I won't be paid until the end of next week, but I can give you the details of who to contact. Can you remember a name and address without writing them down?"

Father Peter nodded. "Of course. I too have fled my past."

Donis gave him the information. The priest repeated it aloud, then closed his eyes, apparently committing it to memory. "That's it, then. I'm sorry I can't give you more to go on, but the effort is highly secretive, as I am sure you understand."

"I do. Please, try not to worry. You are doing all that you can, probably too much. Let me handle this area myself," Father Peter said.

"I appreciate your interest. There will be many in Europe who appreciate it as well."

"Why haven't you contacted Karen?"

The abrupt change of topic caught Donis off guard. He felt his color deepen, an alarming reaction for someone who'd once coolly engaged in subversive activity.

"You have spoken to her?"

"Several times. Don't you think you owe her at least a phone call?"

"Owe her?" Donis tried to keep his expression noncommittal. "I thanked her for the party, if that's what you mean."

The priest gave him an admonishing look. "She's a friend, Donis. She cares for you deeply."

"Did she tell you that she cares for me?"

"Not in so many words, but I've known her a long time."

Donis didn't want to sound callous, but there were some things a third party could do nothing about. "You haven't known me for long, Father. If you did, you would realize that I am not one who seeks gratification or commitment lightly."

Father Peter raised an eyebrow. "Those seem to be somewhat conflicting goals, Donis. What exactly do you seek?"

He couldn't come up with an answer as quickly as he would have liked. "Solitude. That's what I seek. The God-given right to be alone...if I so choose."

"Why, when you have so much to offer?"

Donis nearly laughed. "Me? What do I have to offer, other than the curse of my bloodline and a reputation that I do not deserve?"

"Don't you see? Those things don't matter here, Donis. Karen doesn't look upon you as a hero or a failure, any more than I do. By the grace of God, you've been given a chance to start a new life. But part of that grace demands that you learn how to live again."

"That's why I need time alone, to think about living again."

"You're not alone, Donis. You're lonely. There's a big difference between the two. I will not sit by and watch you drown in your own self-pity."

Donis slammed his fists against the armrests. "Then, by all means, turn away and don't watch!" He immediately regretted his words. "I'm sorry, I did not mean to..."

"It's all right. You're tired. I shouldn't have bothered you this late." The priest got up from the sofa. "You can call me when you have the money ready. If I'm not in, leave a message with the secretary. She can be trusted."

Donis nodded, too weary to walk his friend to the door. "Thank you for coming."

Alone again, Donis dragged himself to the bedroom. On his nightstand was an envelope; inside were two tickets to *Carousel*, a birthday gift from Father Peter. He took them out and read the date. They were for Saturday night's performance.

Donis smiled when he turned out the lights. His friend was right. It was time to learn how to live again.

CHAPTER NINE

LIZ CORNERED KAREN in the photocopy room. "Hi, there," she said over the roaring and clunking of the Xerox machine. "You've been awfully busy lately."

"Have I?" Karen picked up a pile of fresh copies and lined up the edges.

"We haven't had a chat in ages. What'd you do—give up coffee breaks altogether?"

"No, it's like you said. I've been busy."

"Then it's time you took a breather. Let's go for lunch. My treat."

Now Karen was retrieving each new copy as soon as it landed on the tray. "Gosh, I don't know, Liz. I was planning on grabbing a quick sandwich and getting some paperwork done."

"Hang the paperwork. You and I have to talk."

She hadn't been avoiding her supervisor. Not deliberately. It just seemed there'd been fewer reasons to speak to Liz lately. Come to think of it, there'd been fewer reasons to speak to anyone this past week and a half.

"Is it about work?" Karen asked. "Have I done something wrong?"

"It's about your father."

Karen reset the copier and picked up her documents. Sooner or later, she knew the topic was bound to come up. Dad and Liz had been seeing each other almost every night since the party. Whenever Karen called home to chat, Dad would invariably cut her off with a chipper, "Gotta pick up Liz. We're going dancing." Or out for dinner . . . or out to a movie.

There was no sense putting things off. She could appreciate Liz wanting to talk; so did Karen. "Let's have lunch." They went to a Chinese restaurant near the office that served food buffet-style, ideal for civil servants short on time. Not that Karen felt much like eating.

Liz took greater care selecting her food and arrived at the table a few minutes after Karen. "Okay, kiddo, let's be totally honest with each other. Does it bother you that I'm seeing your father?"

Karen studiously unfolded her napkin. "Don't be silly. Of course not." She could feel Liz staring relentlessly across the table and knew she wouldn't get away with her reply. "Well, maybe it bothered me a little, at first."

"I thought so. Why?"

"Gosh, I don't know. It's almost embarrassing to talk about. I realize Mom's been gone for two years, and she would approve of Dad getting on with his life . . ."

"I sense a 'but' coming."

"But is too strong a word." Karen snapped a corner off her egg roll and chewed it slowly. "It's more like . . . however."

Liz laughed. "All right. However, what?"

"If I tell you, please don't take this the wrong way. I don't want my supervisor coming down on me."

"Forget the supervisor bit. This has nothing to do with work."

"Okay. What worries me is that you're so much more . . . well, experienced than Dad."

Liz bit her lower lip. "Experienced?"

"You know what I mean. You're accustomed to an active social life, but Dad hasn't dated in almost half a century. Even when he married, the only time he and Mom went out was on their anniversary, and they were still home by ten."

"That's understandable. They were raising six kids and trying to keep a farm afloat."

"Yes, but—"

"What you're really afraid of is that I'll hurt him, right?"

Karen gave a sigh of relief. "Right."

"You think that I might bowl him over with my vast sexual experience, then dump him."

"Um, well...I guess you could, maybe, put it that way." Karen felt herself redden, no doubt a Freudian reaction to the thought of her father and Liz...together.

"What if I told you we haven't done anything yet?"

Good grief, this was awkward, Karen thought, squirming in her seat. "There's no reason to pretend with me, Liz. I may be handling this conversation badly, but I'm not a kid anymore."

"It's true, though. Despite my best efforts, your father and I are not sleeping together."

Feeling suddenly like a relieved parent, Karen stared at Liz. "You're not? How come?"

The woman laughed. "I thought it might come as a shock to you. Your father's an old-fashioned guy. He still believes in courtship, holding hands and all that."

"But the night of Donis's party. Dad never came home."

"We sat up until dawn, talking. Then he slept on the couch. He always sleeps on the couch whenever he stays at my place."

"My goodness."

"Now that you know, do you feel better?"

Facing up to one's hypocrisy was not an easy thing to do. Karen wished that Liz hadn't posed the question at all. "I guess maybe I do."

Liz reached over and patted her hand. "I understand, and I'm glad we had this talk."

"Could I ask you just one question?"

"Shoot."

"Are you falling in love with him?"

Liz let out a long, slow breath. It was obviously her turn to be put on the spot. "Let me put it into words that a farm girl can understand. I don't want to count my chickens prematurely, but this time, honey, I think I've found what I've been looking for."

KAREN, FEELING strangely muddled after her heart-to-heart lunch, was heading for her desk when Molly chased after her. "Hey, Karen, guess who called while you were out?"

Her mood rose, then just as quickly plummeted. She knew from Molly's expression who it was, and Karen wasn't in the mood to hurt. She had almost reached the stage where it didn't bother her not hearing from Donis. Now she would have to start over.

"Gee, don't look so thrilled," Molly said, handing her the memo. "I thought you liked the guy."

Karen forced a smile. "I do. That's the trouble." She glanced at the slip. Donis didn't leave a number. The message simply said he'd call back later.

Like hell, Karen thought at closing time when she locked up her desk and left the office. She'd taken precisely thirteen phone calls since lunch, and not one of them had been Donis. What did he mean by calling back later? Later in the week? Later in the year?

Even while riding in the elevator of the Federal Building, Karen imagined her office phone ringing, which was not only impossible, it was depraved. She stormed out of the building and did the only rational thing she could think of. She marched straight to the London Market and bought half a dozen cream puffs.

Being a disciplinarian, Karen promised herself she would put them in the freezer and only eat one pastry per day. By the end of the week, she'd be fully recovered from her trauma.

She brought the box home and dropped it on the kitchen table. Maintaining a routine at times like this was important. First she would get out of her work clothes and have a shower. Then she would take the pastry out of the box, walk calmly to the window seat and pig out.

The telephone rang while Karen was kneeling beside the tub, adjusting the water temperature. Giving the faucets a quick yank, she dashed naked into the kitchen.

"Hello?"

"Karen? This is Donis."

Smiling rapturously, she sank cross-legged onto the floor. As she sank, Karen grabbed the box of cream puffs and tossed it in the trash.

DONIS HAD TO WORK until seven on Saturday evening, so they weren't going to have time for a drink or dinner before the curtain rose. But Karen didn't care. She was going to be with Donis. The circumstances of their togetherness was the least of her worries.

He arrived at her apartment at half past seven. Her first sight of Donis after two weeks was alarming. He was freshly shaved, neatly dressed in a white shirt and tan slacks, but he looked exhausted. There were deep lines around his mouth, and shadows beneath his eyes that even an olive complexion couldn't hide.

"Are you sure you feel like going out tonight?" Karen asked, tossing an ivory linen jacket over one arm.

"Do I look that bad?"

He touched her back lightly as they stepped into the elevator. To be touched again was exquisite.

"You do look tired," she said. "You must be working horrendous hours."

"Today at the warehouse was longer than usual. An extra shipment arrived, so we had to stay and unload. The other jobs, the hours aren't so bad."

"Other jobs? How many do you have?"

They walked through a lush and hazy twilight to the Grand Theater. Rain had fallen steadily for most of the day, but had stopped, and now the air tingled with moisture. Even the leaves hung heavier than before, sated by their summer shower.

"I have three," Donis replied.

"Three? A few weeks ago, you didn't have any. How did you manage to find them so quickly?"

"It was not difficult. The restaurant where I used to wash dishes promoted me to sommelier, and I work there six evenings a week."

"Where did you learn to be a wine steward?"

"In Spain while I worked my way through school."

"Amazing. So you work at the restaurant and the warehouse."

"Yes, the warehouse job is full-time—they have trouble finding people willing to work. And I also deliver pizza from eleven to two on the weekends." He grinned, looking as proud as a boy with his first paper route.

"You got your driver's license too?"

"They accepted my international license. Meanwhile I am learning my way around London in a yellow Volkswagen with a pizza soldered on the roof."

Karen laughed. "I've seen those cars around town. They're so cute." Donis glanced away, as though her remark had made him uncomfortable. Regretting her thoughtlessness, she linked her fingers with his. "I'm happy you've found work, Donis, if that's what you want."

He looked at her and smiled. "There is not much demand for experts on Sanvitan economy. But someday I will once again be doing what I love best."

"I know you will, Donis."

He slipped an arm around Karen's waist and kept it there all the way to the theater.

Carousel was schmaltzy and gloriously old-fashioned with colorful sets and an exuberant cast. It was a shame that Donis fell asleep during the second act.

Not that Karen was surprised. He'd been rubbing his eyes and yawning through the first half of the show. The plush seats and the music had finally knocked him out like a lullaby.

She didn't wake him. She knew how badly he needed the rest. During the finale, when the cast sang, "You'll Never Walk Alone," Karen sobbed happily into her hankie. By the time she woke Donis during curtain calls, she'd mopped up her face and repaired the damage.

Donis woke totally disoriented. He blinked at Karen as though she were a stranger, then looked around at the applauding crowd. The first words he uttered were in some other language—Sanvitan probably. Then with a sheepish smile, he came to his senses. "When did I fall asleep?"

"Right after Billy Bigelow went to heaven."

Donis sat up, rubbing his hair, a gesture that could only be described as endearing. "Did he get the chance to atone for his past?"

"Oh yes, he returned to earth, saw his wife and daughter once more and gave them hope."

"That's good. I like happy stories."

For someone of Karen's achievement-oriented generation, hope seemed such an old-fashioned sentiment. It suggested passivity, submission to whatever came along. Yet when it came to Donis, she found herself returning to that feeling over and over. Hoping he was all right, hoping he would call, hoping things could somehow work out between them.

Karen knew there were ways of making things happen, of forcing an issue, even in romance. But she couldn't bring herself to behave that way with Donis. He didn't need more pressure in his life. He didn't need walls closing in on him again.

There might come a time when Karen would assert her feelings, but right now their relationship was too fragile. All she could do—all she dared do—was hope.

"Do you have to deliver pizzas tonight?" she asked as they left the theater.

Donis smiled. "No, I don't have to work anywhere until tomorrow evening."

There was no hesitation in Karen's voice, no second thoughts when she said, "I have a bottle of wine at home. Would you like to share it with me?"

She saw the flicker in his eyes, then the uncertainty. "Are you sure you wouldn't like to go dancing or something first? We haven't been out much, you and I."

"What I really want," Karen said, linking her arm around his, "is to kick my shoes off and relax."

"So would I," said Donis. For once, Karen knew, they were perfectly attuned.

At home in her kitchen, Karen brought out glasses while Donis uncorked a bottle of pale dry cabernet. He poured, then carried the goblets into the living room, the crystal glistening and sparkling in the lamplight. He handed Karen a glass, and it was as though he was handing her a star, a wishing star. She drew in a deep breath and savored the magic.

"I have been wanting to tell you how much I regret what happened the last time," he said.

Karen took his hand, urging him to sit beside her. "That's not necessary."

"But I didn't mean to upset you."

"I know that, but please let me say something first." She watched the pale amber spotlights shimmer from the wine. The words were coming slowly; she was grateful for Donis's patience. "The only reason I reacted so strongly to the things you said was because they were true. I was . . . I am falling in love with you."

"Karen, you don't have to . . ." He moved a hand along her thigh, a gesture as affectionate as it was seductive.

She set down her wineglass. "Yes, I do." Then more softly, she added, "I do have to say this while I still have the nerve. My feelings for you are mine alone, Donis, and I'm the one who has to deal with them. I'm not asking anything from you, and you don't even have to see me anymore. But I just wanted you to know that . . . you were right."

Donis drew in a deep breath and pulled Karen to himself. "Wherever did you get the idea that I was expecting a confession?"

She closed her eyes, drawing strength from his embrace, from the slow, steady beat of his heart. "I don't know what you were expecting. I just wanted to make sense of what went wrong last time."

"But don't you see? Nothing went wrong. Except perhaps that I should have been more sensitive to you, and you should have given me time to explain."

Karen slid her fingers along his jawline. She loved the rasp of his whiskers, the smoothness of his skin. "You've got all the time in the world now."

He laughed softly and kissed her. "So we have. Or at least until tomorrow evening. I will try to explain. The night of the party, I could see how quickly things were progressing between us. Not only in the physical sense, but as two spirits, two souls. It astounded me, almost frightened me that there we were—two people from totally different worlds, talking like old friends, like family . . . like lovers."

"Why did it frighten you?"

"Because I didn't think we could give each other what we needed."

"I don't understand."

He took a sip of wine, then held his glass to Karen's lips for her to drink. "You see, I've always believed there are three types of love—that of friends, family, and lovers." He drew her even closer. She felt the last of her resistance softly float away, and along with it much of her fear. No matter what Donis said, she no longer feared to listen.

"Of the three," he went on, "friends have the finest love. They choose one another, and when they offer of themselves, they ask nothing in return."

So far, she followed his reasoning. In the back of her mind, Karen was trying to envision a platonic relationship with Donis, but she couldn't do it.

"What about family?" she asked.

His arms tightened their grip, as though he was resisting something inside. "With familial love, we have no freedom of choice. We are bound by our blood ties, and if our family is less than ideal, we suffer the consequences all our lives."

Karen thought of her own scattered family. Did they actually love one another? Probably, but the love was seldom, if ever, acted upon. Certainly never expressed. "And lovers?" she whispered, stroking his chest.

Donis kissed her hair. "Ah, lovers. How often they blend the worst and the best of the other two. Sometimes we try to choose who we love. But likely as not, love appears without our even asking for it. Unfortunately a lover's affection is never unconditional."

Karen had never thought of love as being conditional, but Donis was right. How else to explain the mental agony, the insecurity, the divorce statistics of people who were meant to stay together?

"So when you told me I was falling in love," she said, "you were warning me."

"Yes. I didn't want to see us take that path and ruin what promised to be a fine friendship."

"But why should admitting one's love ruin a friendship?"

"Perhaps it's my own male prejudice, but whenever a woman says, 'I love you,' I have the feeling she is silently adding, 'So what are you going to do about it?'"

Karen couldn't object. She knew exactly what Donis was talking about. She'd been guilty of it so often. She would find herself mentally projecting a new relationship into situations prematurely. What if he didn't get along with her parents? What if he wasn't handy around the house and garden? What if...what if... Finally, the good things they had enjoyed together were no longer enough. The scary thing was, if Donis hadn't spoken up the night of the party, she might have made the same mistake again.

Karen looked up into his soft, misty eyes. "Now I understand."

She could see how badly he wanted to believe her. "Listen to me, Karen. Whatever expectations you have, I'll probably fall short of them."

"What if I told you I had no expectations?"

"Then I would tell you freely that I want you more than anything in the world."

"As a friend or as a lover?"

"In whatever way you choose to give."

Karen drew up her legs, bringing her body closer. Donis moaned, a delicious, wanting sound. His reaction made her feel so strong, so sure of herself that the words, for once, came easily. "I want to offer myself tonight, Donis, as a lover. No conditions, no expectations."

He looked at her for a long time. Then he kissed her deeply, and she sensed the ebb of hesitation. When they drew apart, he murmured, "You would do that for me?"

"I would do it for both of us."

Donis lifted Karen from the sofa to straddle his lap. He hugged her and he held her; he nuzzled her with warm, moist kisses. "I must warn you, dear lady. As a lover, I am sorely out of practice."

"So am I," she said, his honesty delighting her. "But I'm told it's a lot like riding a bike."

He raised an eyebrow. "A matter of balance?"

"No, silly." Karen gasped as he slowly unbuttoned the front of her dress and kissed each spot his fingers revealed. "You . . . um, you never forget how . . ."

"Ah, I see. That is a relief."

Donis slid the dress from her shoulders, so that it fell in a silken, floral drape around her waist. Karen only wore panties underneath and reveled in Donis's reaction as he gazed at her near nudity.

When it came time to undo his shirt, Karen wasn't nearly as adept or controlled. But how was a woman to maintain decorum while a man did the things he was doing to her?

Her legs spread across his thighs was hardly a ladylike position, but Karen knew the lady wasn't in control now. The woman was.

And this particular woman adored running her hands across her man's lean chest. Her eyes feasted on the straining hardness between his legs. When she ran a finger along the taut cloth of his zipper, Donis moaned. Lord, how she loved that sound.

"This will never work," he muttered, grappling with the lacy triangle of her panties. "They're too pretty to rip. Couldn't we go someplace where we could enjoy each other with less struggle?"

"My bed, perhaps?"

"An excellent suggestion."

When Karen stood up, her dress fell to the floor, but she made no attempt to retrieve it. Wearing only her bikini panties, she took Donis's hand and led him to the bedroom.

There was nothing so wondrous, Karen learned, as the touch of a new lover. To shed clothes shamelessly, to lie naked together even though, in so many ways, they were still strangers—what an astounding, illogical experience it was.

To stroke a finger along a thigh, to respond to each other's deepest needs were expressions so intimate they seemed almost dangerous. Yet Karen knew instinctively that was as it should be. And so she embraced the danger.

Donis arched back on the bed, lost, helpless, while she gave him what she knew of pleasure. "Ah, Karen..." he murmured, his fingers clenched in her hair.

But when the moment called for the mastery of a man, Donis drew Karen's sweat-slicked body upward, locked his arms around her and gently rolled her onto her back.

She didn't resist; she couldn't have. Every fiber of her body was eager to mold itself to him.

Yet, though she was in every way ready, she was staggered by the first thrust. Such heat, such power, she had never come close to knowing before.

At first she almost feared it might be too much. How could she appease the depths of his hunger? But it was only her mind in a momentary state of panic. Her body adjusted, as a woman's does, and soon they were riding the course together.

The soaring, the crashing, the giddying heights, Karen rode them all and gathered them into the soul of her being. Ravenous, she drew from Donis, and freely she gave back again.

At the last she cried out, and so did he.

"My woman..." he murmured and collapsed to her breast.

CHAPTER TEN

SUNSHINE SPREAD like watered silk over Karen's bed, nudging her awake softly. She opened her eyes to the pale dawn and wondered why everything felt different.

Then she rolled over, saw the indentation on the other pillow and remembered. Donis had spent the night, holding her, loving her. But he wasn't here now.

Slowly she climbed out of bed and put on her robe. She told herself not to panic. Just because they hadn't wakened in idyllic unison didn't mean he'd left, or that anything was wrong. He was probably in the bathroom.

The bathroom door was open. Okay, so he must be in the kitchen. Karen tiptoed down the hall. She couldn't hear any sounds, no water running, no kettle boiling. The apartment was so quiet she could have been alone.

Then she saw him. Donis was sitting on the window seat, arms draped over his knees. Rays of diffused sunlight shone about his shirtless body like an arc. If there was such a thing as a male vision, it was Donis at this moment. The sight of him quite simply took Karen's breath away.

He didn't seem to see or hear her. He was staring out the window, but Karen surmised that whatever he saw was thousands of miles away.

She would have loved to leap into his arms, to celebrate their night of ecstasy with a delirious greeting, but Karen felt reluctant to disturb him. "Good morning," she said hesitantly.

He turned. Recognition seemed a long time coming, but then maybe she was overreacting. The sun, after all, was behind his face; Karen couldn't quite see his expression.

"Did I wake you when I got up this morning?" he asked.

"Not at all."

"That's good." Donis opened his arms in invitation.

Karen sighed happily. It was all she needed.

Her shyness this morning was as delightful to Donis as her abandon the night before. He wrapped his arms around her silk-clad body and breathed deeply of her essence. How long it had been since he'd known such contentment, such pure and utter serenity. *Ah, Karen, to think you'd be the one to make me feel this way.*

"You looked so far away," she said. "I hated to disturb you."

He rested his bristly cheek against her hair. "I am not far away, angel. I am here . . . with you."

"Did you have trouble sleeping?"

Donis shook his head. "I rested well, but I am not a heavy sleeper. I thought it best to get up rather than risk disturbing you."

She sounded different this morning, but perhaps that was the way it was with lovers. He honestly could not remember the nuances of "mornings after" with other women. Karen seemed so caring, so concerned for his well-being this morning.

He smiled to himself. She needn't have worried. He hadn't felt this well in years. If only he could learn to trust the feeling, instead of fearing that something or someone would snatch it away.

"Last night," he said, "was exquisite."

Karen lifted wide green eyes to his. "It was for me, too, Donis."

"Then why do I see doubt in your eyes?"

"It's not doubt. I just...I can't really believe you're here. I can't even believe last night happened."

"Regrets?" he asked, half dreading her reply.

"Good heavens, no. It was...perfect."

Donis felt the shudder of her body and realized that the same tremor had passed through his own. As though she mistrusted perfection as he did. He'd felt this way before, and this moment only confirmed it—that despite their vast differences, they were kindred spirits.

"It's all right," he said in reply to her tacit message. "We'll take whatever comes, together."

She wrapped her arms more tightly around him. For a long time, they simply clung until the trepidation passed.

Donis shook himself from the disquieting mood. Karen deserved better from a lover than this. If he was not yet a whole man, the least he could do was make an effort. "Have you made any plans for today?" he asked.

Her hopeful smile tugged at him. "Not really."

"Would you like to spend the day together?"

"That would be nice." Donis knew she was trying to keep her exuberance in check. He wished she wouldn't. He needed Karen's exuberance in his life.

Maybe it was his fault for being so dour. "Have I ever mentioned my first impression of you?" he said teasingly.

Karen sat up, eyes twinkling. "As a matter of fact, you haven't."

"I thought you were a cold fish."

She feigned offense. "Well, thanks a lot."

"But only for the first few minutes. I soon amended my opinion, deciding that you were probably quite passionate beneath that severe exterior."

"And now that you know me better?"

Donis kissed her soundly. "My suspicions were confirmed, if understated. You are, most definitely, a woman of passion."

She buried her face into his shoulder, as though she were embarrassed. But he could tell his admission pleased her. Donis's heart swelled. To please such a woman was a privilege he wouldn't have dared hope for a year ago. God willing he could continue during what time they had left.

"And now that I've flattered you," he said, "it's time you learned what is expected of dutiful Sanvitan women."

"I'm not Sanvitan."

His mouth curved upwards. "You are now. It's part of a long-standing Sanvitan tradition. Make love with one, and you're as good as a citizen."

"Oh, great. You could have warned me beforehand."

"I didn't dare. You might have balked."

Karen laughed as Donis scooped her into his arms and led her into the kitchen. "Don't tell me, I have to start cooking and scrubbing, right?"

"Nothing so drastic. Not yet anyway. All you need to do is turn on the coffee maker while I adjust the shower. Then you can join me."

"Is that what Sanvitan women do? Shower with their men?"

"Among other things." He dropped her gently near the sink, then disappeared.

They made love beneath the gentle spray of water while their bodies were slick and soapy. They dried off, wrapped up completely in towels and in each other. Then they went to bed and made love again.

Though it would seem impossible, Karen thought, to improve on perfection, each time they came together was more exquisite than before. Like a rosebud as it opens to a fully blossomed rose, every stage of their lovemaking was flawless and beautiful unto itself.

Later, they sat in bed, drinking coffee and savoring the stillness of the morning. "Can you ride a bicycle?" Karen asked.

Donis, stretched out languidly beside her, threw Karen a look of desperation. "Please, woman, I am a lover, not an acrobat."

Karen laughed. "That's not what I mean, silly. I was thinking it might be fun to go to Springbank Park and have a picnic. I have a neighbor who might loan you his bike."

"A picnic sounds wonderful. Too bad we hadn't planned ahead of time. I could have prepared a few San-vitan delicacies."

Karen rolled onto her side to gaze at him. "You cook, too? I would never have expected that of a Mediterranean male."

"Now you're stereotyping. Don't you realize that most of the great chefs in Europe are men?"

"And I suppose you're one of the great chefs?"

"One of the great, unsung geniuses." Donis urged her body onto his. Karen closed her eyes, committing every nuance of this embrace to her memory. No matter what happened, no matter how great their happiness or their sorrow, she knew nothing could compete with the total bliss of this moment.

"Then I am one lucky lady," she murmured, only half in jest.

ALTHOUGH IT WAS NEARLY NOON by the time they reached Springbank Park, the day was still shrouded in a gauzy yellow haze. The mist floated in evanescent shreds over the Thames River.

An elusive, disturbing day, Karen thought, reminding herself that this was only an atmospheric phenomenon, not a reflection of her new relationship with Donis. Still, when she looked over her shoulder, Karen was relieved to see that Donis was behind her on his bike.

So what did you expect, she asked herself in exasperation. *That he's just going to disappear into thin air? Just* because he'd come into her life with no prior warning, didn't mean he'd depart the same way.

They found a grassy spot near the river to spread out their blanket. Nearby was a stand of spruce trees with boughs overhanging like an awning. To complete the sense of fantasy, Storybook Gardens, a children's theme park, rose up through the haze with the turrets of Cinderella's castle.

Donis pointed to the gates. "Could we go there after lunch?"

"Sure, if you like. Shall we borrow someone's children?"

"Why not pretend we're children ourselves?"

His remark tugged at Karen's heart in a way that was almost maternal. She couldn't recall other lovers making her feel that way. Maybe that was why other lovers left her feeling incomplete. "Why not?" she said, leaning over to kiss his cheek.

They ate salmon salad sandwiches and drank lemonade. This was the closest to happiness Karen had felt in ages, yet the feeling was unnerving. She knew happiness shouldn't come about because of another person. What happened when the person was no longer there? *You go back to the way things were before. That's all.*

"Donis," she said, "would you ever go back to Sanvito. I mean, if things were different there?"

Donis was lying on the blanket, staring up at the clouds. "Never," he said without hesitation.

"Don't you miss it?"

He seemed to consider this a while. "I miss what Sanvito used to be. I miss what it might have become. But the country is a nightmare now. People scavenging on the streets, brother turning against brother." Donis pulled up a long stalk of grass. "I would never return of my own accord."

"Isn't your grandmother still there?"

"As far as I know, yes." His expression eased. "I used to be terrified of her as a child."

"Your own grandmother?"

"You'd have to meet her to understand. The woman is tiny, but has such a commanding presence. Not until I was older did I understand why she had that effect."

"Why did she?"

"She had what I believe you call in English second sight."

"You mean she was psychic?"

"Yes."

"Could she actually predict the future?"

"Not with a crystal ball or anything so obvious. But Grandmother could enter a roomful of people and know at once who could be trusted and who could not. She used to have death dreams the night before a friend or neighbor died."

"Good grief. I can see why you might have been scared."

"Most people dismissed her as prematurely senile, but that was because she tried to keep her gift a secret. Sanvitans are a superstitious lot. They read omens into everything—the shapes of clouds, the color of mud, even potato peelings."

Karen chuckled. "You sound like a skeptic."

"I don't hold credence with potato peelings, that much is true. But I am forced to acknowledge that most of us are given the power to look beyond. Whether or not we choose to heed that power is up to us."

She stretched out beside him, smiling when he reached for her hand. "Do you really think so? I used to read books about creative energy and all that, but I've got to be the least intuitive person in the world. If I think it's going to rain, you could safely leave your umbrella at home."

Donis laughed softly. "I used to feel that way myself, but Grandmother and I spent hours on end talking about it. She used to say we all have instincts, which are not to be confused with...how would you say it in English... wishful thinking. Wishful thinking, she said, was tampering with the Divine Plan and a complete waste of time.''

"What do you mean by instincts?''

He turned onto his side to look at her. There was a solemnity in his eyes, a profoundness that stirred Karen deeply. "Instinct is an inner wisdom that's always there, whether or not we are aware of it. On rare occasions, however, you might experience a sudden flash of certainty, a rock-hard knowledge of something you didn't know before. It most often happens in a time of crisis, and try as one might, such instincts are impossible to ignore.''

Karen found the theory fascinating, if somewhat beyond her scope of experience. "What happens if you do ignore them?''

A shadow crossed his face, one that could not be attributed to the clouds overhead. "You could spend the rest of your life regretting it.''

IT HAD BEEN YEARS since Karen visited Storybook Gardens. Typical of a Sunday, the place was swarming with people, but Karen scarcely noticed. Arm in arm with Donis she felt herself to be at the center of her universe. What went on around them didn't matter.

They came to a fenced compound with three houses made of straw, twigs and bricks. "I know that story,'' Donis exclaimed. "'The Three Pigs.' And look, they're real.''

The creatures were pink and fat, but too muddy to be called cute. Still, Karen stopped to watch them with amusement. "Did you grow up with the same fairy tales as I did?''

"That's hard to say unless I knew what stories you grew up with. Most of these are familiar—Pinocchio, Snow White—but we Sanvitans have legends of our own.''

"Really? What kind of legends?"

"My favorite is the one of how Sanvito came to be."

"I'd love to hear it."

They continued walking, Donis happily munching on the cotton candy he'd bought earlier. "It's a long story, but in essence, they say that Sanvito is a slumbering giant and the sea a temptress who has loved him forever."

"Sounds romantic."

He glanced at her and grinned. "Then one day, when you are craving romance, I shall tell you the whole tale."

"Okay, I'll hold you to that."

"Who is this egg person?"

"Humpty Dumpty."

"What an unusual name."

Donis paused to read the nursery rhyme on the wall. That was when Karen saw a pair of familiar faces coming her way in the crowd. It was Miguel and Estelle Garcia, and they were holding hands, a couple again!

"I don't believe it," Karen said.

"Believe what?"

"Clients of mine. I thought for sure they had..." Leaving the remark unfinished, Karen waited to see whether the Garcias would acknowledge her.

They were giggling about something, heads lowered together, apparently oblivious to anyone except each other. Karen was amazed. This was no staged display of affection. Maybe she'd been wrong about them from the start.

Then Estelle caught Karen's eye, and it was as though a shutter had been yanked down. By now the Garcias were only a few feet away, so Karen could hardly pretend she hadn't seen them.

"Hello, Estelle, Miguel," she said, adding what she hoped was a noncommittal smile. "Nice to see you again."

Estelle's wan complexion grew even paler, in contrast to the gaudy flowered muumuu she was wearing. "Hi," she replied and dropped her gaze.

Miguel's dark eyes, as if in challenge, slithered along Karen's figure. "Hey, Miss Miller, lookin' good."

He wore what was probably the Garcia interpretation of macho chic—stone-washed jeans tight enough to cripple, a black shirt open to the navel and an arsenal of fake gold chains around his neck.

"How've you been?" Karen asked, directing her question to Estelle who was still staring intently at the ground.

Her husband answered for her. "We're doin' okay. What's it to you?"

"Why, I...I didn't mean anything." Miguel's hostility and Estelle's discomfort confused her. Karen would have thought they'd be delighted to flaunt their reconciliation in front of their biggest skeptic.

"You haven't come around to see us since Estelle came back," Miguel muttered.

"No, I..." Karen glanced over her shoulder and felt relieved to see Donis standing nearby. "Were you...away, Estelle?"

Estelle looked up, but her eyes would not meet Karen's. "Yeah, I was visiting friends in Ingersoll for a few days. Miguel told me you came over."

"Yes, I just wanted to see how you were doing."

"Oh, sure, tell us another one," Miguel jeered.

Karen chose to ignore the remark. "Last time I spoke to you, you'd been laid off, Estelle."

"They called me back."

Karen turned to Miguel. "How about you? Has that allergy cleared up?"

The man scratched himself rudely. "I'm okay as long as I stay away from tomatoes." He yanked his wife closer. "Except for this juicy tomato. Can't stay away from her."

Karen smiled with effort. "I'm still waiting for your medicals."

Estelle glared at her husband. "Haven't you gotten those done yet? I thought you told the lawy—I thought you said everything was taken care of."

"I got an appointment for next week, all right?"

Folding her arms across her ample chest, Estelle fell silent.

"Next week?" Karen said, determined to inject brightness into her voice. "That's great. So I can expect to hear from you shortly?"

Estelle brought a hand to her mouth, while Miguel gave a gruff laugh. "Oh, yeah, Miss Miller, don't you worry. You'll be hearing from us. Real soon."

THE TRANSITION from being alone to being in love was incredibly smooth, and for that, Karen gave much of the credit to Donis. The circumstances of his past had shaped him into a man who took nothing for granted, who made the most of every precious minute he and Karen spent together.

The only drawback was that all too often, minutes were all they had. Donis's working hours were endless, and although he required little sleep, his job at the warehouse was physically demanding. By the time his sommelier duties at the Trattoria Palermo were over, he was exhausted. Still, not an evening went by that he didn't stop in to see Karen on his way home.

Occasionally he spent the night, but Karen worried about Donis getting his rest. Heaven knew, she had reason to worry. There had been nights when their passion took the place of sleep—a euphoric state in its way, but a body could only keep up with those demands for so long.

Karen learned to adjust, not only to the constraints of her lover's workload, but to their nebulous future. It was now mid-August, a month since the hearing, and still no word from the Refugee Status Advisory Committee.

She wasn't concerned about the delay; it was still too early to expect an answer. And with each passing day, she grew more confident that his claim would be allowed. It was impossible for the committee to decide otherwise. Donis could never return to Sanvito without endangering his life, and technically, no other country was required to admit him if he was deported from Canada.

Yet once in a while, Karen worried about what would happen if Donis stayed. Would the two of them continue to be as happy, or would their relationship crack under the strain of a different reality? At times she feared that what they had was good simply because there were no guarantees.

On this sunny August weekend, however, Karen's blue mood was as distant as the clouds soaring overhead. She and Donis were in the car heading to her father's farm.

The occasion was a family barbecue, entirely Liz's doing. No one else could have orchestrated a minireunion with so little apparent effort, which certainly said a lot for the power of love, Karen thought as she drove.

Donis, who'd never really understood the dynamics of the Miller clan, seemed content to watch the tobacco farms passing by on the highway. Karen knew that for someone who'd never seen such large land holdings, they were impressive. The broad-leaved tobacco plants were five feet high and fully grown, green at the top and tapering to a yellowish shade at the bottom.

Donis pointed to the tractors moving through the rows. "Look, they're harvesting."

"They've been picking for about a week," Karen explained. "You can see they've already picked the bottom three leaves. Those are called sands. Now they're working on the seconds, the next set of three."

"Do they actually have names for the leaves?"

"Yes. There's a big difference in quality, depending on the leaf's location on the plant. The lower the leaf, the smoother the tobacco. The green ones on top look nice but produce a harsher product."

"You seem to know a lot about the industry."

"I picked tobacco for more summers than I care to remember. Dad used to have fifty acres of tobacco rights, and you'd be amazed at how much work that involves. I'm just as glad he's out of it now."

"What are those little cabins?" Donis gestured toward a group of wood-frame buildings painted brick red.

"Kilns. That's where the leaves are cured after they're picked. Dad still helps out with the curing on our neighbor's farm—or I should say, our landlord's, the Martins."

"Your father took it hard, no, losing his farm?"

"Hard does not begin to describe his reaction. He went into a terrible depression. He started drinking and drove Mom crazy. You'd think he had been forced to sell his children. Thank heavens, he wasn't given the choice."

Donis stroked her arm tenderly. "It's not like you to sound so cynical, Karen."

"I know. If I were honest with myself, I guess what really bothered me was that Dad grew tobacco."

"Instead of a food crop, you mean?"

She nodded. "I grew up in a generation that knew the health risks of smoking, and even though a lot of my classmates were tobacco farmer's kids, I was still ashamed that Dad's job contributed to sickness and death. That's an awfully ungrateful attitude, isn't it?"

"How did your father feel about his work?"

"He was proud. He used to come home from the tobacco factory loaded down with free cartons of cigarettes. You'd think they'd given him gold, instead of something that was slowly killing him."

"Did he know how you felt?"

Karen had never openly admitted her feelings of guilt to anyone. She wasn't surprised that Donis was the first to listen. He was, among other things, a wonderful listener. "I'm sure he knew. Kids don't hide resentment well. And it's not that I don't feel for him. Losing the farm was a dreadful humiliation, and then to lose Mom a few years later..."

"You still miss her, don't you?"

"More than ever, it seems. I never realized it at the time, but she was the one who held our family together. We used to gripe about coming home for the holidays, but we always came home. Now I'd give anything to bring those days back."

Donis's smile was filled with understanding. "We can never bring back the past, but at least we are compensated with a future. And now it seems your father has a future."

"Why do you say that?"

"He has someone to love. He has Liz."

Karen glanced at Donis, appreciating the unspoken parallel. "You're right," she said softly. "He does have Liz."

THE MILLER'S YARD was nearly an acre of rolling land adjacent to the hay fields. Along the edges of the lawn, a few scraggly perennials clung to sandy topsoil.

Karen could recall when the Miller garden was the pride of the neighborhood. Her mother and father used to spend days on their hands and knees, putting in tulips and daffodils, sweet Williams and canna lilies. Wisteria and impatiens of every color imaginable spilled from the hanging baskets that adorned the front of the house, welcoming all who turned into the drive. But now the baskets lay idle and empty in the toolshed.

These days, Karen braced herself for the inevitable lurch of disappointment when she saw the neglect of her family home. Except for today. She could hardly believe her eyes when she turned the car into the driveway. Dad was on a stepladder, reattaching the baskets to the eaves.

Liz was sitting on the front steps surrounded by crates of ivy. To Karen, she looked like an upscale charwoman—hair tied in a scarf, turquoise pedal pushers and of all things, an apron. Her expression suggested someone who'd suddenly been saddled with a dozen wailing infants.

"What is going on around here?" Karen said when she got out of the car.

Her father came down the ladder, grinning. "It's a little late in the season, but we thought it might be nice to have some greenery around the place again."

"Notice how he says 'we'?" Liz remarked drolly.

Donis took a seat beside her on the steps. "You look troubled. What's wrong?"

"Troubled is an understatement," Liz said. "William and I just got this stuff from the nursery, and now I wish I'd stayed home."

"The plants were your idea," William reminded her. "I only went in for a rake."

"Yes, but the ivy looked so gorgeous hanging around the cash register."

"So what is the problem?" Donis asked.

"Well, I thought they'd let us buy the plants they had on display, but no. We get these crates of teeny newborns. Do you realize I'll actually have to put my hands in dirt?"

Karen laughed. "That's usually what's required."

"You've never seen the plants in my apartment, have you? I buy only the silk and dried variety. They last forever, and they look great."

William groaned. "I've seen your plants, Liz. They look like what they are—dead."

"Would you like some help with the potting?" Karen asked.

"Potting?" Liz gasped. "Lord, it sounds like toilet training." Grimacing, she poked an impeccably manicured finger into one of the plants. "I'm sure I can manage. Bill's a good teacher."

Karen glanced at her father. He actually appeared to be blushing. It was strange seeing her dad in love. Almost embarrassing. "Let's get the food out of the car, Donis."

Donis had stayed up half the night preparing a Sanvitan speciality for the barbecue. Karen had been dying to try it, but he would allow no taste tests beforehand.

Soon after Tim and Sue arrived, Karen's dad had coals heating on the grill. Tim and William were in charge of the steaks, while the women kept a wide berth. Sue and Karen had warned Liz that barbecuing was the only form of food preparation Miller males ever engaged in. It was wise to stay away in case the men were tempted to relinquish that responsibility as well.

Donis moved between the kitchen and the barbecue, helping out where he could. But Karen sensed that he felt out of place with the men. Tim and Dad, being unusually amiable with each other, were discussing local sports—the Loblaw's softball league, Ray's Shell slow pitch. A person would have to dig deep to unearth more tedious topics of conversation.

Karen cornered Donis in the hallway and slipped her arms around him. "Are you sure you don't mind being here?" she asked, looking up into a face that grew dearer every day.

"Not as long as you're here," he replied.

"But it must be so boring for you."

He stopped her protests with a kiss, his tongue sampling hers with unabashed desire. Then he drew back and smiled. "If I appear bored, just take me aside and let me do this to you again."

She laughed delightedly. "You can count on it."

The announcement that the steaks were ready came as a relief to nearly everyone. For a while, they were pleasantly occupied passing food and filling their plates at the large picnic table.

"Take another potato, Sue," William urged his daughter-in-law. "Remember, you're eating for two now."

"That potato is bigger than the baby," Sue retorted. "I'm sure he won't mind sharing mine for now."

Karen noticed Donis probing his steak discreetly with a fork. Knowing he'd asked for rare, she leaned over and whispered. "I should have warned you. Dad only knows how to do medium and well done."

He squeezed her hand under the table. "I'm sure it will be fine. Stop worrying about me."

"Great potato salad, Karen," Tim said.

"Thanks. Here, Dad, try one of these." She held out a platter. "Donis made them. They're a Sanvitan speciality."

Her father looked at the food, then at Donis with equal reticence. "What are they?"

"They're similar to Greek dolmas," Donis explained. "Seasoned lamb and pine nuts rolled in grape leaves."

Karen heard Tim snort into his napkin. She figured that he would find it funny. Only her well-aimed glower prevented her father from saying, "I'll pass."

Instead, he held out his plate. One would think from his expression that Karen was about to lop off his arm. She realized that her dad knew virtually nothing outside the world of tobacco and southwestern Ontario. And like many of his peers, he was quite happy to remain that way. But Karen hoped that maybe this once, for her sake, he would be willing to stretch his horizons.

She watched with bated breath as her father sawed off a tiny corner of grape roll and slowly lifted it to his mouth. At least she'd warned Donis not to expect raving approval. William chewed impassively, then set down his fork. "Different, aren't they?"

Karen's shoulders slumped. She might have known. Her father had single-handedly set back Canadian-Sanvitan relations a decade.

"Well, I think they're delicious," Liz chirped.

"So do I," Sue added, poking Tim in the ribs.

"Hey, yeah," Tim said. "Could you pass the ketchup?"

Donis gave Karen a look that told her it didn't matter, which stood to reason, she supposed. Donis was a man who'd endured worse things than the narrow-mindedness of an Ontario farmer.

As the rest of the meal progressed, Karen was willing to admit she'd set her father up for a test he was doomed to fail, and that wasn't fair. She knew without being told that Donis made her father uncomfortable. It made no difference that Donis was charming and an excellent conversationalist. The cultural chasm between him and William Miller was simply too vast. The only way her father could handle it was not to handle it at all.

"Apple pie for dessert, folks," Liz announced as she began clearing dishes.

"Did you pick it up at a bakery when no one was looking?" Karen asked in the kitchen.

Liz grinned proudly. "Nope, I baked it myself from scratch."

"No kidding? But listen, aren't you overdoing this domesticity routine just a little?"

"You're a fine one to talk, a girl who used to come home every weekend and fetch her father's slippers."

"That's different. I grew up with a mother who waited on him. But you're a . . . you're my supervisor, for heaven's sake. You work in an office and wear fake nails."

Liz tossed her head imperiously. "We're never too old to change. I happen to enjoy doing things for your dad, and if it means I have to adjust my feminism to fit his chauvinism, I'm willing to make the effort."

Karen sighed. "Okay, have it your way, but don't say I didn't warn you. You'd be surprised how quickly Dad starts taking these domestic gestures for granted."

Liz's apple pie was carried to the table with great pomp and ceremony; all that was missing were bagpipes. Liz served William first.

Everyone dug eagerly into the dessert except Liz. She was too busy watching William's reaction, just as Karen had done at the beginning of the meal. What was it about patriarchal families, Karen wondered. One would think the sun rose and set on a single, intractable palate.

William sunk his fork into the filling, then pressed hard. He pressed again, harder. Finally the pastry snapped in two, and he brought a piece to his mouth. Karen shut her eyes, knowing exactly what was coming.

"This crust is kinda tough, wouldn't you say?"

She was right. Why did her father have to be so damned predictable?

She had not, however, predicted Liz's reaction. The Liz Karen knew would have upended the pie onto his lap and told William to stuff it. No, actually, the supervisor Karen knew would have bought an apple pie at the market and fibbed.

This new and different Liz looked at William with a hurt expression. "I followed the recipe on the shortening can."

"Yeah, well," said William, the epitome of male largesse, "They say there's a knack."

"Which I'm obviously lacking."

"I think the pie is delicious," Donis offered.

Liz shot him a dark look. "Thanks, sweetie, but what does a Sanvitan know about apple pie? Bill doesn't like it, and that's all that matters." She got up and began clearing the last of the dinner condiments. "So I guess I'll just keep right on mixing flour and rolling dough until I get the knack. I'll just keep baking pies until Bill thinks I'm ready, then we can have another *pleasant family get-together*."

Liz launched these last three words like heat-seeking missiles. Karen lowered her head to mask a smile. *This* was the Liz O'Connell she knew and loved. *This* was the kind of woman Dad needed in his life, not some faded imitation of his late wife.

"No need to overreact," was William's attempt at apology.

Liz glared at him. "You're right. I shouldn't have overreacted. I should have been grateful that you were willing to point out my failure in front of everyone. Heaven knows, women appreciate hearing these things. It reminds them of who's in charge, wouldn't you say?"

Sue began to pick up cutlery. Tim got up to douse the coals. Karen coughed while Donis studiously picked up the pitcher of iced tea. "Drinks, anyone?"

"I WISH I DIDN'T have to work tonight."

Donis and Karen were in the car outside of his apartment. Karen was resting her head on Donis's shoulder. "I wish we hadn't wasted the day at the farm. I'm so sorry I put you through that."

"Don't apologize. It was...enlightening for me to see where you come from."

"Good grief, all the more reason to have kept you away."

"Don't worry. You are not going to turn into a female version of your father, but you shouldn't be so hard on him. He's a product of his upbringing, as we all are."

Karen took Donis's face in her hands and kissed him. "You have got to be the most diplomatic soul I have ever met." *And I love you, do you know that?* But she wouldn't say it aloud. Oddly enough, she'd come around to understanding his way of thinking. It was wonderful to hear the words, but in a way, they were the easy way out. Karen would much rather prove how much she loved him, as Donis so often did with her. Enduring a day at the Millers for her sake was a prime example.

"When do you have to be at the restaurant?" she asked.

"Six."

Karen glanced at her watch. "Gosh, that doesn't give you much time. Why don't you shower and change, then I'll give you a ride to work."

"If it's not inconvenient."

"For you, gorgeous, anything. Besides, I've always wanted to watch you get into that sexy tux, one piece at a time."

He returned her lusty gaze. "Isn't it more exciting to watch me take it off?"

"Yes, but I've seen you do that so often," she teased, walking her fingers along his chest.

"Enough of that, woman, or my reasons for being late will be less than honorable. You may come inside to wait, but only if you behave."

"Okay, spoilsport."

Karen had only been in Donis's apartment a few times. His roommate worked shifts and slept odd hours, so it made more sense for Karen and Donis to spend time together at her place.

She followed him through the kitchen entrance to the living room. The place was neat, the furniture adequate, but typical of furnished flats, nondescript.

Karen stretched out on the sofa while Donis went into his bedroom to undress. A short while later, he emerged and headed for the bathroom wearing a terry robe.

"What's this sudden display of modesty?" she teased.

"Precautionary measure," he retorted with a wink.

There was nothing to do in the living room, not even a TV. The only magazine in sight—Sean's presumably—featured a motorcycle and a half-naked girl on the cover.

Restless, Karen got up and strolled the room. She battled a sense of irritation at the way they'd spent their day. What she wouldn't give to have this evening alone with Donis.

From the open door of the bedroom, she could see his clothes lying on the bed. The least she could do was fold them or throw them into a hamper, if there was one.

The room was small and like the rest of the apartment, strictly functional. Karen shook out his jeans and folded them on the crease, hugging them briefly before laying them over a chair.

She smiled when she picked up the Blue Jays shirt he'd worn that day. Tim and Sue had been pleased to see him wearing the gift they'd given. Donis was thoughtful that way, an openly appreciative man. To think, not so long ago, he used to make her nervous.

Karen placed the folded T-shirt on the chair. Just then her eye caught a small framed photograph on the dresser. The quality of the black-and-white picture wasn't very good; the people's faces were too distant to make out features. But the photo was the only visible memento in the room, so it obviously meant a lot to Donis.

She was studying it when he walked in, smelling fresh and soapy. Karen looked up at him and smiled. "You'll have to take that robe off eventually, you know."

He didn't return her smile. His gaze was flicking warily from Karen to the photo in her hands. "My family," he said, as though she'd requested an explanation.

"I didn't mean to pry," she said, thinking she'd upset him.

He came closer. "It's all right. I should have shown you before now."

That he was willing to show her filled Karen with a sense of warmth. Strange how something as insignificant as an old snapshot could bring a man and woman one step closer. "Who are they?" she asked.

He pointed to the elderly woman in the middle. "That's my grandmother."

She was tiny and dressed in black, just the way Karen had imagined she would look.

"These are my parents, and this is my aunt who's been dead for years. She was a widow when this picture was taken."

"And the three children?"

"The one with the knobby knees is me. I was ten at the time. That's my cousin Talia. She's two years younger and living in Spain."

Karen looked up. "She's the one you helped to escape, right?"

"Yes," he said, his face strained.

"Who is this other boy?"

"He is . . . my other cousin. Talia's brother."

Karen was standing close enough to Donis that she could feel him shudder. "Where is he now? Is he dead?"

Donis's jaw clenched briefly. "No, my cousin is not dead. His name is Salvo Gibrian. He is the president of Sanvito."

CHAPTER ELEVEN

DONIS CAREFULLY UNCURLED Karen's fingers from the photograph and led her to the bed. "Here, sit down."

Karen stared at her hands as though they were still holding the small brass frame. She'd never experienced the sensation of drowning, but this was how it must feel. Cold, smothering, helpless.

"I should have told you sooner."

She looked up. "Why didn't you?"

"Would it have made any difference?"

A drowning person will grasp at anything—a twig, a rag—whatever comes by that might postpone what seems inevitable. That must have been why Karen grabbed onto the passing thought—at least Donis hadn't just confessed that he was married.

A lingering vestige of professionalism was what surfaced first. "The refugee hearing," she mumbled. "That's when you should have told me who your cousin was."

"That would have been the worst time."

"Why?" She heard and hated the note of cynicism in her voice, yet she was unable to suppress it. "Because I wouldn't have gone out with you afterward?"

A rare look of impatience crossed his features. "Let us disregard you and me for the time being, Karen."

She dropped her gaze.

"I did consider telling the refugee committee and decided against it. The purpose of the hearing, as I understand, was to establish whether or not I could return to

Sanvito. I believe there was more than enough evidence to establish that without entering into details of my family ties."

"On that, we agree. But to deliberately withhold such a crucial fact—"

"Was it crucial, Karen? Or would I have ended up trying to establish the nature of my relationship with Salvo?"

"I'm not sure I understand."

"I gave you evidence to show that he wanted to see me psychologically destroyed, if not dead. I provided details of my escape from prison. But how could I have proven that my cousin did not have a change of heart? How could I prove that I wasn't sent here as a spy or a terrorist for the Sanvitan government?"

God knew, she hated herself for asking, but Karen was barely coping on an Immigration level. She hadn't even begun to deal with the situation as a lover. "Are you either of those things?"

Donis slammed a fist against the wall. "My God, woman, you've seen the marks on my body! Not to mention the deeper scars . . ."

Karen covered her face with her hands. "I'm sorry, I wasn't implying that you *wanted* to work for your cousin. I just mean that maybe, because of the torture you'd endured . . ."

"Listen to yourself. Do you see now what I mean? You and I are lovers, and I cannot even convince you that I am not the president's henchman. How much better would I fare with a committee of bureaucrats?"

Karen did see, and what she saw of her own reaction both shamed and frightened her. The shame arose from her lack of confidence in Donis. This was the man she loved. How could she not believe him now, after all they'd been to each other?

What frightened her, even in hindsight, was the realization that if she'd learned of Donis's blood ties during the hearing, she might never have agreed to go out with him. It didn't change who or what Donis was. But dear God, what did it say about her?

Donis was well within his rights to toss Karen out of his life forever. He didn't have to come over to the bed and sit down. There was no need for him to put his arms around Karen and hold her.

"From what I have observed of your culture," he said, "families do not maintain close ties beyond the immediate parents and children. In Sanvito, we maintain loyalties for many generations. Salvo and I are, I believe, what you would call second cousins."

Karen shook her head. "I'm a little fuzzy on how that works."

"Salvo's grandfather and my grandmother were brother and sister."

"Then you're not really that closely related."

"Genetically, no, but you might as well know that Salvo and I grew up together. As children we were best friends, inseparable."

It was like getting a second dose of the same bitter medicine, yet strangely enough, this time the effect was palliative. Donis must have gambled that this added measure would either kill her or render her immune. It seemed to be doing the latter.

"You didn't have to tell me that part," she said, her voice somewhat calmer.

"I know."

He trusted her. Somewhere, through her pitiful display of cowardice, he must have sensed some glimmer of support. He must have sensed the unconditional love of a friend.

"It must have been terrible for you," she said, "to be friends as children . . . and then to realize how far the two of you were drifting apart."

Donis stared at Karen for a long time. Then he drew her head to his chest and sighed. "It was more terrible than you can imagine."

MONDAY MORNING, Karen came into work looking pale and nervous, but with her mind made up. She had dropped Donis off at work the night before and gone to bed early. She didn't sleep, but spent the night agonizing.

The night, however, wasn't a total loss. During the long dark hours, Karen came to two separate conclusions. As a woman, she decided that Donis's revelation did not change her feelings, except in her determination to love and support him all the more. He had no control over who his family was, any more than she did.

But there was another element to consider, one that Karen was too professional to ignore. She could appreciate Donis's misgivings about bringing up his relationship to Salvo during the hearing. She was even willing to agree that the nature of the transcript might have changed considerably. But all that aside, the committee still had a right to know.

She didn't even bother going to her desk. Karen proceeded immediately to the office at the end of the corridor and knocked on the door. "Mr. Rathbone, I'd like to speak to you, please."

DONIS HAD MONDAY evenings off. When Karen finished work, she went to Donis's apartment hoping to find him at home. But when she rang the bell, there was no answer. Karen rested her head against the door, fighting tears of frustration. She needed to see him. She needed desperately to tell Donis what she'd done.

The possibility that he would hate her was very real, that he would look on her as the lowest kind of reptile. But she'd already considered that risk when she decided to talk to her manager—considered it, and still acted on the instructions of her conscience.

As Karen walked along Dundas Street, she became aware of a void inside, an aching emptiness she'd never felt this acutely before. When she dropped Donis off at work last night, they hadn't said a word about seeing each other today.

Not that it was necessary. They were in touch every day anyway. And there was no reason to believe today would be any different.

Yes, there was, Karen argued with herself. There was reason because things were different.

She didn't head deliberately for Victoria Park, but she couldn't bear the thought of going home to an empty apartment, and shopping certainly held no appeal. The park had come to be a favorite place for her and Donis to be together. So partly for consolation and partly as a form of self-punishment, Karen went there.

An artist had set up a display in the same area as the chamber quartet had performed some weeks ago. She'd never seen this artist's work before, and his oils were definitely a cut above the usual living room landscapes.

She wandered among the easels, and a seascape caught her eye. The harsh coastline was unlike any she'd ever seen before. The water was choppy, the sky a bone-chilling zinc white. Rocks jutted from the shore like stumps of old teeth; the beach was more gravel than sand.

But the focus of the painting was something unexpected—a brilliant patch of crimson slapped against a rock. Moving closer, Karen saw that it was a shred of clothing, so skillfully depicted she knew at once it must be silk. Whose was it? How did the cloth get there?

Karen didn't care. She only knew she wanted to buy the painting. From the price tag, she saw that it cost more than she could comfortably afford, but that did not dissuade her. She would go to the bank at once and withdraw the cash.

The YMCA building was on her way. It was one place she hadn't thought of looking for Donis. Karen went into the lobby and checked through the register lying on the desk. His name was there. He'd gone in over an hour ago.

"Are you looking for me?"

Karen's head shot up. "Donis!"

He was carrying his gym bag, and he looked tired, though whether from exertion or emotion, Karen couldn't tell.

"I went to your apartment first," she said.

"Did you?"

"You weren't there."

He smiled. "No, I was here."

Karen had meant to tell him what she'd done, and now the words stuck in her throat. It wasn't as though he *had* to know. He would never see a copy of the transcript or the addendum.

Donis swung the bag over his shoulder. "You told them, didn't you?"

She reddened. "How did you know?"

"Apart from the guilt that's written all over your face, I knew you had no choice but to advise the committee."

They walked outside together. "I did so have a choice." Innate guilt refused to let Karen off this easily. "I could have kept quiet."

"If you had, it would have eaten away inside you and eventually destroyed what we have with each other."

Karen, abandoning public decorum, threw her arms around his neck. "Oh, Donis. I was so frightened of how you would react. I didn't want to do it, but I had to."

"I know, and there's no need to worry. My feelings for you haven't changed."

"And even if you had been angry, I would have done everything I could to..." Karen trailed off, vaguely aware that she was arguing with herself. "You really aren't upset?"

"Not at all," he said, stroking her hair gently. "But now that we are being honest with each other, there is something I think you should know."

Still braced for the worst, Karen dropped her head back. "What?"

"I love you."

The birds didn't stop singing in the trees; fitness buffs on their way to the "Y" weren't suddenly suspended, mid-step. To Karen, they only seemed to do those things. "I don't believe I heard you correctly. Would you mind repeating what you just said?"

Donis laughed and drew her face to his for a kiss. "I said, 'I love you.' There, I have now said the unspeakable twice in my life, within a space of thirty seconds."

Karen grinned happily. "It wasn't so bad, was it?"

"Not at all. And now, aren't you supposed to return the favor?"

So he *did* need to hear the words after all. She'd always suspected as much. "I love you, Donis, but then you knew that even before I did."

Slipping an arm around her waist, Donis led her down the street. "I suppose I did. Let's go and have a drink. I need something to temper the shock."

In the flurry of events, Karen had forgotten all about the painting. Now that she remembered, she decided to show it to Donis first. "Come to the park with me. There's something I want you to see."

"All right."

But they were too late. The painting was gone. So was the artist and the entire display. Karen, near tears, looked down at the trodden grass. "It was right here. A seascape, the most beautiful painting I've ever seen."

Donis came up from behind and nestled his body with hers. "Don't be upset. There will be other paintings."

Karen leaned back into his embrace, trying to ignore her silly desperation. It had only been a picture after all, and a moody one, at that. Considering the cataclysmic event that had happened between then and now, she probably wouldn't even like it anymore.

Donis Sotera had finally told her that he loved her. That was all that mattered.

DONIS WOULD NEVER KNOW the number of times Karen consoled herself with that thought during the weeks that followed. She relived their encounter in front of the YMCA whenever her mood threatened to plummet, whenever the future seemed bleak.

The full moon of September brought on an early frost. Karen no longer lived on a farm where people dreaded the destruction of crops, but she was still susceptible to changes in the atmosphere. It was too soon for summer to end, too soon for cold nights and the itch of woollen clothing.

She tried to think about Donis as she marched to work the morning of the frost. She wore open-toed pumps and a light-weight trench coat, refusing to acknowledge she was damp and frozen. This time, however, thinking about him only stirred up her worrisome mood.

Precisely two months had gone by since Donis's refugee hearing. Karen knew the decision could arrive any day, and it no longer helped to tell herself that Donis had a solid claim.

She'd had upsets before—cases apparently airtight were turned down by the committee, throwing the poor claimant into an emotional maelstrom. Sure, there were channels for appeal, but once those were exhausted, the person had no choice but to leave Canada.

What if that happened to Donis? What if the committee for some unfathomable reason didn't believe his story or actually suspected him of subversive activity? Donis was under order of deportation. Once he left Canada, he would never be allowed to return.

And then what?

Somehow she could never get past that question in her mind. That was why she tried so hard not to think about it. And that was why she resented September's full moon for bringing on a frost and making her worry.

When she arrived at the office, there was a letter on her desk addressed to K. L. Miller. She glanced at the return address. It was from some government agency in Toronto. Karen was too preoccupied to pay much attention. But once she began to read the letter, other nebulous problems vanished from her thoughts.

Dear Ms Miller:

This is to advise that a complaint has been filed against you by Mr. and Mrs. Miguel Garcia of London, Ontario. They are of the opinion that their human rights have been violated by continued harassment and discrimination on the basis of national origin.

A Human Rights officer has been assigned to investigate this case and will be contacting you in the near future. As the respondent, you will be required to answer questions regarding the nature of your contact with the claimants. Please be advised that friends and colleagues may also be called upon to answer inquiries by the investigator.

Yours very truly,

The signature was illegible and irrelevant. Karen didn't know anyone at Human Rights, and if she did, this never would have happened. Harassment? Discrimination? Of all the ridiculous...

The Garcias had no right to do this to her! She had done nothing but pander and cosset to their whims from the very beginning. She should have written Miguel up for marrying to stay in Canada. She should have told Estelle up front that she'd found herself a loser and was better off without him. That's what a person got for giving people the benefit of the doubt—a kick in the teeth.

It dawned on Karen slowly and with frightening clarity that this was how it felt to be on the other side of the desk. No longer in control, but at the mercy of some anonymous bureaucrat who couldn't care less about her or her future. Was that how her clients felt when they sat down in her office? Did she ever manage to alleviate their worries, or had she become blasé with time?

Barney Coxwell chose that unfortunate moment to poke his head into her office. "Hiya, Miller."

"Go away," she muttered. Barney was the last creature on earth she cared to see. As the resident office bigot, this ought to be happening to him. He hated everybody.

"My, aren't we touchy," Barney cooed.

Karen tucked the letter under a file. "I'm having a bad day, okay?"

"I was just trying to brighten it for you, but if you don't want to hear my good news, that's fine with me."

"I'll hear your good news later, Barney. Right now, I've got to see Liz."

"I was afraid something like this might happen," Liz said when she saw the letter.

"Why?"

"I got a call from the Garcias' lawyer. He claims they ran into you at Springbank Park, and you were…" Liz was apparently having trouble getting the word out.

"I was what?"

"Rude. Not that I believed it for a minute, mind you. I told him I'd have a talk with you and get back to him, but frankly, it was so ludicrous, I never got around to it."

"I was not rude. If anything, I finally came to the conclusion I was wrong about them."

"I wouldn't worry if I were you. The Garcias don't have a leg to stand on."

"Maybe not, but there's still going to be an investigation. That's always the worst part, isn't it?"

Liz was kind enough not to offer false consolation. Working for the government, they had both heard horror stories about the effects of a discrimination charge on one's record. Despite constitutional guarantees, what remained in colleagues' memories was the laying of the charge. The dismissal of a case was often lost in the murk of innuendo, leaving the respondent with the equivalent of a scarlet letter on his forehead.

"You can tell me about the meeting at Springbank later. Meanwhile, let's pull the Garcia file and go see Mr. Rathbone," Liz suggested. "He ought to be forewarned, and he might even have some suggestions on how you should handle it."

Karen fought the rising panic in her stomach. "Good idea."

If Mr. Rathbone was surprised by the allegations in the letter, he gave no indication. He merely looked down his nose in that way of his and said to Liz, "Please advise Molly and the relief staff to cooperate with the investigator, but tell them he is not to disrupt counselors while they're with clients."

Liz nodded. "I'll tell them."

To Karen, he said, "Well, Miss Miller, what do you have to say about these charges?"

"What can I say? They're ridiculous." Karen crossed her legs, and noticing the glint of gold at her ankle, crossed them the other way. This was no time to appear brazen. "I've had my suspicions about the marriage from the beginning, but I've done nothing out of the ordinary in handling the case. I interviewed the Garcias separately and together—which is standard—and I had to remind them a dozen times about medicals. Hardly what you'd call harassment.''

''According to the file, you made an enforcement call with Coxwell.''

''Yes. I wanted to find out whether they were still together, and they weren't.''

''Karen could have written a report on Miguel then,'' Liz pointed out. ''The fact that she didn't, I would say, shows compassion, not discrimination.''

Mr. Rathbone continued perusing the file. ''I see the medicals were finally brought in.''

''Finally, yes,'' Karen said, ''but that was the day after we ran into them at Storybook Gardens. Otherwise, I'd probably still be waiting.''

''We?'' Mr. Rathbone repeated, his curiosity piqued.

''Well, yes. Donis . . . a friend was with me that day.''

''I don't see any notes to the file about your meeting at Storybook Gardens.''

''Of course not. It was a Sunday—''

''Is a client's status waived on Sundays, Miss Miller?''

''No, but . . .'' He was doing it to her again, making her feel totally inept. Karen exhaled, trying to lower the pitch of her voice. ''I didn't think it was necessary.''

''Aren't you aware that in the eyes of clients, you are, first and foremost, an Immigration counselor? That's how the Garcias would have interpreted seeing you.''

''I'd never thought of it that way.''

He turned to Liz as though Karen was the visual aid in a seminar. ''This is a prime example of what can happen when a counselor gets lazy.'' To Karen, he said, ''You must always keep detailed notes of every meeting, chance or otherwise. You must always cover yourself for any eventuality.''

What Mr. Rathbone said made perfect sense. She should have made the same meticulous entries she always made during working hours. Then an idea came to her. "I do have a witness to the interview."

"Yes, you mentioned a friend. Who was it again?" Mr. Rathbone turned one ear toward her. As far as Karen knew, he wasn't hard of hearing. It was just another thing he did.

She felt a growing pressure behind her rib cage. "His name is...Andonis Sotera."

Drawing his thick brows together, Mr. Rathbone turned to Liz. "Sotera. Haven't I heard that name before?"

Liz glanced at Karen, offering a tacit apology. "Er, yes, he's...one of our clients."

"Yours?" he said to Karen.

"Yes...that is, he used to be. He's filed a refugee claim, so I don't actually handle his case anymore..." Careful, Karen, you're talking too fast.

Mr. Rathbone stroked his long chin. "I remember now. Sotera's under deportation for unauthorized employment and passport fraud. Isn't he the one?"

"There were extenuating circumstances," Liz offered, for what it was worth.

"Do you really feel, Miss Miller, that a client under order of deportation would make a credible witness for a discrimination investigation?"

Her reply was feeble. "In this case, I think he would."

"Then I take it your being in the company of this Mr. Sotera was not coincidental?"

"No, sir."

Mr. Rathbone studied her a long while, then sighed. "Miss Miller, you've been working here for some time, so I'm not going to beat about the bush. Several days ago I observed you in the company of a dark-haired man at the market. On several occasions you displayed...shall I say, public affection. Was that man your beau?"

"Yes." She tried not to cringe at his archaic choice of words.

"Was he, by any chance, Mr. Sotera?"

"He was."

Mr. Rathbone drew in a shocked breath. "I have always believed you to be levelheaded and prudent, both in the office and in your personal life. Quite frankly I'm surprised that you've allowed yourself to get into this fix."

"Allowed myself? I had no idea the Garcias were going to do this."

"But as an experienced counselor, you surely could have anticipated the consequences of your behavior."

"I'm not sure I understand."

"How can an Immigration counselor accuse or suspect a client of marrying for convenience while said counselor is dallying with a refugee claimant herself—a deportee, no less? You are, I take it, familiar with the term, *conflict of interest*?"

"Mr. Rathbone, I don't see the connection at all. My personal life is my own, and it certainly hasn't affected—"

"We are talking credibility here," he cut in. "A counselor must not only be impartial. He or she must *appear* to be impartial. Being seen in public arm in arm with a deportee does not give that appearance."

"Are you telling me not to see Donis anymore?"

"You know as well as I do that as your manager, I have no authority to make such a demand."

"But you are suggesting it."

"All I am saying is that during a discrimination investigation, no stones are left unturned. For example, the conclusion could be drawn that you plan to marry Mr. Sotera if his claim is turned down, thereby enabling him to stay in Canada. Are you prepared to defend yourself against those kinds of conclusions?"

Karen swallowed hard. "I, uh...I hadn't thought of it, b-but, yes, I am prepared. And I will continue to see Donis before, during and after the investigation."

Mr. Rathbone folded his arms and leaned back. "Then there's little more that can be said. Your record speaks for itself, Miss Miller, and I'll certainly be forthright in my remarks to the investigator."

Liz picked up the Garcia file from the desk. "Thank you, Mr. Rathbone."

"Good luck," he said, as Karen left the office. In her imagination, she heard him add, "You're on your own now."

After lunch Karen was glancing through her phone messages when Barney Coxwell came in again. "Do you want to hear my news now or am I gonna have to write a memo?"

She forced herself to smile for the ignoble reason that Barney might be interviewed by the Human Rights investigator. "I'm listening. What's up, Barney?"

"Got a call from Windsor this morning."

"Don't tell me. They've arrested a truckload of illegal strippers and want you to help write them up."

"Wouldn't that be nice, but nah, it's nothing like that. Remember Scapiletti?"

The name sounded an immediate alarm. "Dominic Scapiletti? That's the man who charged Donis with assault and didn't show up in court."

"Right on."

"What about him?"

"The cops picked him up near Ambassador Bridge for driving without a license. The guy's an American—uses half a dozen aliases—and he's wanted in three states for armed robbery."

"Are you sure?"

"Positive. His prints check out. Looks like he planned to do a number on your buddy after all. No wonder he didn't show up in court."

"So he's not the Red Watch!"

"He's not what?"

"Never mind." There were times Karen could have throttled Barney. There were even times he struck her as funny in a strange sort of way. But until now Karen had never felt indebted to the man. "You're wonderful, Barney. I can't thank you enough for telling me your news."

Barney P. Coxwell grinned from ear to ear. "Hey, don't mention it. Maybe you and I could go bagging turkeys again some day."

CHAPTER TWELVE

DONIS SHOWED UP at Karen's apartment at ten-thirty that evening, carrying his wine steward's tux in a dry cleaner's bag. He looked tired, but his eyes held a familiar glint suggesting that sleep was the furthest thing from his mind.

Karen would have loved to indulge his fantasy, but there were more important things to deal with tonight. Things that wouldn't wait or go away.

Donis must have seen it in her eyes as soon as he stepped into the kitchen. "Something's troubling you, angel. What is it?"

She'd been struggling all evening to find a light way to broach the subject. She finally concluded there was no light approach. The impetuous, self-indulgent stage of their relationship was over. Maybe she'd been deceiving herself to think that stage had ever existed.

Karen poured two cups of herbal tea. "Sit down, please, Donis. I want to talk about us."

He sat down and stirred sugar into his tea. "You make the word *us* sound so ominous."

"I don't mean to. Well, maybe I do. Gosh, how am I going to say this? I need to know what's going to happen if... well, if you're not allowed to remain in Canada."

He didn't look overly surprised by the topic. But then Donis was a pragmatic man. Such thoughts could never be far from his mind. "I would think the answer was obvious. If I am not allowed to stay, I leave."

"Just like that? You would just accept their decision?"

"Why? Do I have other options?"

Karen kept on stirring her tea until Donis finally lifted her hand and the spoon from the cup. "There's the appeal board," she said, "and the Supreme Court. Why, your case could take years to be heard..."

"Since when did I retain Karen Miller as my legal counsel?"

"You didn't. I'm only trying to help."

"And I appreciate your help, you know I do. But I have no intention of living out my life in a state of bureaucratic purgatory. If the refugee committee decides that I am not a refugee, then there is something seriously wrong with my perception of things. I would have to go somewhere and reassess my life."

"But where would you go?"

"I don't know."

"You can't let them deport you back to Sanvito."

"Sanvito is the only country obligated to accept me."

"But your citizenship was stripped. Technically you're stateless."

"I was still born there."

Arguing with Donis, Karen felt as though she were sliding down a hillside of sand. "And when—if you go...what about me?"

She saw the slash of pain in his eyes and felt the respondent anguish in her own body. "You have your career," he said, "your family. Your life will continue as before."

Here goes nothing, Karen thought. If a man was ever going to feel threatened and bolt, this would be the moment. "I don't want my life to continue without you, Donis. As far as I'm concerned, it wouldn't be a life."

She had to give him credit. Donis stayed right where he was. He didn't even glance in the direction of the door. But he did look intensely sad. "We both knew from the start there were no guarantees. I thought we agreed to love each other for the time we had."

"We did agree, and I'm not arguing with that. But there's nothing wrong with being prepared either, with having contingency plans."

His shrug seemed a hesitant form of assent. "No, I suppose there isn't."

"If you were willing to make Canada your home and start a new life here, there is a way."

Donis took a long time to respond, and that bothered Karen. What could he possibly find elsewhere that he couldn't have here? He would have freedom, prosperity... love.

"You are going to suggest marriage, aren't you?" he said.

Karen squeezed her eyes shut. She should have anticipated he would do this to her again—pluck the thoughts right out of her head and hand them back. The man was a compulsive second-guesser.

But she wasn't going to let wounded pride or righteous anger get the best of her this time. She was going to see this discussion through to the end, bitter or otherwise.

"It's not as though we'd be marrying out of sheer convenience," she said. "I mean, we do... care for each other." Love was a word she preferred to leave out for the present.

"That's true."

"And even if we did get married, it wouldn't mean that you'd have to, you know..." The words were refusing to come out.

Donis frowned. "No, I don't know. Wouldn't have to what?"

Of all the times for him to be obtuse. "You wouldn't have to stay with me forever. Just until your status was rectified."

"For God's sake, Karen, what kind of insensitive beast do you take me for? First you offer yourself, body and soul, and in the next breath, you offer a way out. I have experienced enough martyrdom in my life. Don't you start now."

"Okay," she said, her voice small. She hadn't meant to come across that way, but there was no graceful method, she'd discovered, to offer one's hand in marriage. Even now she'd rather curl up on the floor and die than continue this conversation.

Sensing her distress, Donis took her hands across the table, not speaking until she was ready to look him in the eye. "I cannot tell you, Karen, how much your offer means to me. I understand the conflicts you must be facing—both professionally and personally—because you're seeing me. But don't you realize, if our situation had been different, I would have asked you to be my wife long before now."

Karen had been fighting tears of humiliation. Now they were becoming tears of another kind. "No kidding?"

He smiled tenderly. "No kidding. But I have not asked, nor can I accept your offer of marriage. I only hope you can understand my reasons."

"I guess that depends on what they are."

"The most important reason is your safety."

"What do you mean?"

"You know I am a marked man. For us to pretend the danger is past would be foolish. Today, tomorrow, one day my past will catch up with me, and when it does, I don't want a wife involved."

"You're talking about the Red Watch, aren't you?"

"Whatever name Salvo ascribes to his henchmen, yes."

"But they couldn't do anything to me. I'm Canadian."

"Under Sanvitan law, if I marry you, you automatically become a Sanvitan citizen with all the same rights and obligations."

"But surely that doesn't extend to... to the things that the secret police do." Karen couldn't bring herself to say the words murder and kidnapping aloud, but she knew Donis understood.

"To you the Red Watch may seem like rabid butchers, but remember, they are operating under a presidential mandate. As wife of The Deliverer, your danger would be no less than mine."

"Okay, I see your point, but I have reason to believe your fears might be exaggerated. Remember Dominic Scapiletti?"

Donis recognized the name as quickly as she had. "Yes? What about him?"

Karen told him what Barney had said and saw some of the tension drain from his face. "So he was after my wallet all along. That is good news, but it's an isolated incident. It is not proof that my fears are groundless."

"I know." After her initial elation had passed, Karen was forced to admit that herself. It had been nice for a while to think that one of their problems was behind them. "You said you had more than one reason for not wanting to marry me. I think I can handle hearing them now."

Donis kissed her fingers. "I didn't say anything about not wanting to marry you, my love, only that I could not. If it was meant to be, if we were to marry, I would want our lives to be totally different from what they are now."

"How do you mean?"

"I don't want us constantly looking over our shoulders or relying on government committees to decide our future. I would want us to be happy, free to live our lives the way we choose." His laugh was full of irony. "I don't ask for a lot, do I?"

Karen had intended to tell Donis about the Human Rights investigation. Now she decided that could wait. There had been more than enough government interference for one night.

"I don't think you're asking a lot." Karen took his hand and led him to the bedroom.

KAREN SPENT the next three days documenting foreign students at the university campus. Up to her ears in paperwork, she had little time to worry and wonder about her future.

Returning to the office brought it all back. She lugged her briefcase into Liz's office and dropped it near her desk. "I'm back," she said, searching Liz's face for signs of news. "I thought maybe you might have heard something while I was away."

"About Donis's claim?" Liz smiled. "You know I would have phoned you right away."

"Yeah, I knew that." She sat down heavily. "How have things been around here?"

"Crazy. Enforcement's been run off their feet. We've had clients three deep in the waiting room every day. The Human Rights investigator was here yesterday. So far, he's spoken to Mr. Rathbone and me."

"Really? What's he like?"

"Gee, I don't know...forgettable. I spent forty-five minutes with him, and I couldn't pick him out of a lineup. Don't worry, Karen. You can handle him."

"I hope so." She had more or less learned to live with the cloud of an investigation hanging over her head. Thanks to Donis's example, she had learned to live with a lot of things lately. Karen got up from the chair. "Guess I'd better see what my office looks like."

"Karen, wait. Are you doing anything after work?"

"No."

"Are you sure? You're not meeting Donis or anything?"

"Not until he's finished at the restaurant at ten."

"Could we go out somewhere for a drink? I need to talk to someone."

Karen had been too preoccupied to notice, but Liz wasn't her usual bubbly self. There were shadows under her eyes, and she looked strained. "Sure, a drink sounds fine."

They went to the Hungarian café across the street where Karen and Donis had first gone months ago. Funny, she'd been coming here for years and never waxed nostalgic about the place until now.

Liz ordered herself a double vodka martini. A heavy-duty drink for this time of the day, Karen thought, even for Liz.

"What's wrong?" Karen asked, stirring her spritzer.

"First, you have to promise not to tell another living soul what I'm going to say, especially not one particular living soul."

"I promise." Karen wrinkled her forehead. "But what particular soul are you talking about?"

"Your father."

"Oh. I should have guessed."

Liz wagged a finger. "Remember, you promised. This is just between you and me."

"I promise I won't breathe a word. But aren't you sort of putting me on the spot? I mean, I am his daughter."

"Believe me, Karen, if I could confide in anyone other than Bill Miller's offspring, I would. But you're one of the best listeners I know, and you probably understand him as well as anyone."

Karen appreciated Liz's confidence, though she didn't necessarily share it. "Okay, what's dear old Dad done now?"

"Dumped me."

"What?"

"Yeah. Last weekend. I'm surprised you didn't know."

"I had no idea. Donis and I dropped around briefly Sunday afternoon, and I asked about you. But Dad just said you were busy."

Liz guffawed. "I was busy all right, trying to put the pieces of my life back together."

"Did he give you any reasons?"

"One major reason. We made love."

Karen nearly choked on her drink. "Oh, gosh. Now I'm really not sure I want to hear this."

"Why not? Can't you accept your father's sexuality?"

"Of course I can, but if I know my father, I'd guess he's having trouble with it."

"You're right. The evening started off perfectly. We went out for dinner, came home and danced to Nat King Cole, his favorite. I knew he'd had a fair bit to drink, but he seemed willing enough when we went to bed."

Karen could feel herself turning red. This conversation was harder than she'd imagined it would be. "Don't tell me, he doesn't respect you anymore."

"Come on, he's not that bad. No, your father fell victim to a good old-fashioned case of guilt. He couldn't accept what he'd done to dear departed Alva Miller, to whom he'd been faithful for forty-some years. No offense to your mother..."

"None taken. I'm sorry to hear that, Liz. Really I am."

"I should have seen the signs. Making love was just the final straw. He'd started criticizing the stupidest little things—the grunge that had built up around my kitchen faucets, the way I sliced banana bread—never mind that I baked the damned stuff for him in the first place."

"I get the picture." Karen took a sip of her drink. "I can't say I'm surprised. He's never been an easy man to get along with."

"I shouldn't be surprised, either. At my age, I've known more than my share of widowers. They spend forty-five years with the same woman at their beck and call and come to expect it from anyone in a skirt. I was beginning to get the feeling that sex was to be a reward for good behavior in the kitchen. I think I was proven right."

"Good grief. A real joy, isn't he?"

Liz pushed her martini aside and leaned closer. "That's just it, Karen. He is—that is, he can be a real joy. Get him in the right frame of mind, and he's a darling. It's not that Bill is naturally miserable. He just got stuck in his ways out on that farm and forgot how to enjoy life." Liz stabbed her olive and popped it into her mouth. "For a while, I thought I could change all that for him."

"Are you sure he wants to change? Dad's been living with his misery for a long time."

"Give me a break, Karen. He's not happy. Don't you think he knows what's happened to his family since your mom died? You and Tim make it so obvious that your visits are obligatory. Don't you realize how that makes him feel?"

Karen was stunned by this sudden turn of the tables. "He's talked to you about that?"

"He doesn't have to. I can see it all over his face. He's a farmer, Karen, not a man of words. His sensitivity lies in his hands. He'll die of a broken heart before he'd ever admit how much he hurts."

Karen felt the sharp sting of truth. "It's not that we don't love him."

"I know. And I'm not being critical. I can see how you kids have ended up the way you did."

"Listen to us." Karen had no desire to pursue this change in conversation. "We were supposed to be talking about you and Dad."

Liz smiled sadly. "There is no me and Dad now, remember?"

"You really loved him, didn't you?"

"*Love* him," Liz corrected. "He dumped me, remember?"

"Oh, yeah. What an idiot."

"Karen, a little respect, if you please. He is your father."

"I know, but I was thinking of him in terms of a man. Are you sure you don't want me to put in a good word?"

"Good grief, that's the last thing I want. I only needed a sounding board. The best thing you can do is forget we ever had this conversation."

"Okay, if that's the way you want it."

Liz O'Connell shook her head. "When it comes to men, it seems things are never the way I want it. But this time, I came close...damned close."

THE YOUNG MAN sitting across from Karen's desk was blond and blue-eyed, but not the robust beach bum variety. One would more closely associate his coloring with chronic anemia.

Karen leaned across the desk. "What did you say your name was again?"

"Harcourt. Ardell Harcourt."

She repeated the name three times silently, but knew she would never remember it. Not that she wanted this man or his name lingering in her memory. He was the Human Rights investigator from Toronto, and the sooner he was out of Karen's life, the better.

He crossed his legs and poised a pencil above his notepad. It was all Karen could do not to lean back and dictate. Instead, with appropriate meekness, she said, "Where would you like me to begin?"

He spread his lips apart, no doubt an expression meant to put her at ease. "Why don't you start at the beginning?"

"You mean like where I was born and the name of my public school?" She didn't mean to act flippant, but something about this man made Karen want to scream.

"Not that far back," he answered, straight-faced. "The complainants, Miguel and Estelle Garcia, feel that they were harassed and discriminated against by reason of national origin. So why don't you tell me about the first time you met Miguel and Estelle Garcia."

Karen patted the file on her desk. "Am I allowed to refer to my notes?"

"Certainly. This is an interview, after all, not a quiz." Ardell laughed at what he must have considered his own joke.

Karen cracked a smile for his benefit. "Okay, the Garcias came into the office in early summer and wanted to apply for Miguel's permanent residence. Miguel had been in Canada for three weeks working as a farm laborer and had been married to Estelle for two days."

"How would you describe their behavior or their attitude that day?"

Karen thought a moment. "I'd say Estelle was reserved, shy. Miguel was a bit hostile, but we're accustomed to that in this office. Immigration isn't everyone's favorite place to visit."

"What was the first thing you told them?"

"I advised them that the proper method to obtain permanent residence was for Miguel to leave Canada and apply at the Canadian Embassy in Mexico City while Estelle made a sponsorship from here."

"The complainant suggests you instructed him to return to Mexico."

"No, that's not true. It's standard policy in our office to first advise clients of the proper procedure, but with husbands and wives, we almost always waive the requirements and proceed with the application. I only suggested that if Miguel had to return to Mexico to finalize other affairs, he might want to consider applying through the embassy."

"Which apparently he did not want to do."

"No. He said he didn't want to be away from Estelle that long."

"Did you begin processing the application that day?" he asked.

"Yes. I gave them a written list of instructions and medical forms and went over them step by step."

"Did they appear to understand your instructions?"

Karen tried to think of a way to cushion the truth. "Let me put it this way, Mr... er, Ardell. Estelle just nodded at everything I said. Miguel, on the other hand, kept interrupting the interview to ask me about welfare benefits and Unemployment Insurance. I did what I could to keep things simple. How much they comprehended is not something I can speculate on."

"So since the wheels were put into motion that day, there was no reason for you to conduct follow-up interviews."

"If this had been a normal case, no. There wouldn't have been any reason."

Ardell raised a colorless eyebrow. "Why did you not consider this case normal?"

"I strongly believed that this was a marriage of convenience; in other words, that Miguel Garcia married Estelle solely to remain in Canada."

"On what grounds did you base these suspicions?"

Karen phrased her response carefully. "There were several. First of all, the age difference. Estelle is thirty-eight, Miguel is twenty. There is also the vast... physical differences between them."

Whiffs of potential prejudice must have caught his nose, for Ardell Harcourt suddenly sat up and twitched. "What do you mean by physical differences?"

"You met them, didn't you?" Karen waited but received no confirmation, verbal or otherwise, that Ardell Harcourt had ever seen the Garcias. She was beginning to realize that Human Rights officials admitted to nothing. Ever.

Gamely, she pressed on. "All right, Estelle is nearly six feet tall and, well, large. Miguel is the size of the average Canadian twelve-year-old. But that's only a minor consideration. It barely colors the case at all. As I said earlier, Miguel had been in Canada only three weeks, and most of that time he'd been working. He and Estelle had spent virtually hours together before they decided to marry. Wouldn't you find that the slightest bit suspicious?"

Ardell, of course, didn't commit himself. He was too busy applying a period to the end of his sentence, raising an arm and stabbing the paper with the drama of a matador and his sword.

Karen nearly snorted, barely avoiding total humiliation by slapping a hand over her mouth in the nick of time. She could just imagine her case going to tribunal—the worst possible outcome—because she'd laughed at the investigator.

"Are you saying, Ms Miller, that the follow-up interviews—which the complainant regards as harassment—were conducted solely to determine whether this was a legitimate marriage?"

"That's right."

"Could you describe the nature of those interviews—what was said by the parties, their reactions, et cetera?"

"Yes, I spoke to Estelle first since she was the one sponsoring her husband. I asked if she'd ever been to Mexico, and she admitted she's never been outside of southern Ontario. Estelle has never been married, has never had a steady boyfriend, and she's worked at the cannery since she got out of high school."

"What do these facts have to do with their marriage?" Ardell asked.

"I'd say a great deal. I've seen many similar cases. The usual scenario, however, is a Canadian woman who meets a man while she's out of the country on holiday. These women are typically older—mid to late thirties—not attractive, but extremely lonely and vulnerable. The marriages never last. And except for the fact that Miguel and Estelle met here, the situation is virtually the same."

If she was making any headway in justifying her actions to Ardell Harcourt, Karen couldn't tell. She could only hope that somewhere behind those bland features lurked an astute and unbiased mind.

"The complainant, Mrs. Garcia, says that you said some unpleasant things about Mexico. She got the distinct impression you don't like the place very much."

"My job title is Immigration counselor. What I do is counsel, give advice, and with any luck, I occasionally enlighten. What I told Estelle was the bare minimum—and I mean the bottom line—of what she ought to know about her husband's homeland. Until I spoke to her, this woman actually thought Mexico was part of the United States."

"What specifically did you tell her?"

"I showed her a map of Mexico and the state of Chihuahua where her husband was from. I explained the economics of the region. Except for the Mennonite farms and the large ranches, most of the people in Chihuahua are unemployed and dirt poor. That was the reason Miguel came to Canada. He hadn't found work in Mexico for years."

"Please continue."

Karen took a deep breath, preparing herself for what she knew could be contentious ground. "I tried to explain to Estelle the notion of machismo, the attitude of men toward women that's still prevalent in much of Latin America."

"Why did you feel she should know that?"

"I had seen the way Miguel treated her in the office—he was bossy, belittling—and I sensed that Estelle was baffled by it. She is the kind of person who tries hard to please. I thought it might be helpful if I explained the kind of social upbringing Miguel probably had. She deserved to know at least that much, didn't she?'' Karen waited for a response and got none. "Obviously my counseling didn't have the desired effect," she added lamely.

"Are Immigration counselors trained in psychology and sociology?"

"We have training courses, though not exclusively in those fields. I read, and I watch television. Machismo is no myth. Its effects on Mexican society and marriage are well documented."

"Did you ever imply or suggest that Estelle had made a mistake in marrying a Mexican?"

"Of course not."

He startled at the sound of indignation in her voice. "Tell me about your interview with Miguel."

"Miguel was even more hostile than when I met him, although I suppose defensive is a better word. I asked him about dependents and previous marriages in Mexico. He was quick to point out that he had two children, but their mother was not his legal wife. She was married to a man serving time for manslaughter."

"Had you known about the children previously?"

"No, Miguel specifically denied having ties in Mexico during the first interview. But the truth was, he came here to earn money to support his illegitimate children. He did admit finally that Estelle knew nothing about his progeny."

"He claims you threatened to tell Estelle about the children."

"I don't threaten my clients. I merely suggested that it might be wise for him to tell Estelle because these things had a way of surfacing later on in a marriage. I was counseling him, Mr. Harcourt—not too effectively, perhaps—but counseling."

The interview droned on for another half hour. Karen rehashed the details of her enforcement visit with Barney, the missed interviews, the phone calls and finally, the encounter with the Garcias at Storybook Gardens. Donis had already been interviewed by Ardell the day before and assured Karen she had nothing to worry about. She wished she could share Donis's optimism. The investigator was certainly a Milquetoast, but Karen wasn't sure that was a good sign.

At last, Harcourt clapped his notebook shut and dropped it into his briefcase. "All done. Thank you for your time, Ms Miller."

"What happens next?"

"I have to conduct a few more interviews, then I'll be submitting a report with recommendations to the Human Rights Commission in Ottawa. When and if they concur with my findings, their decision will be handed down and you will be duly notified."

Karen hated that pompous phrase "handed down." It reminded her of Zeus and Mount Olympus, hardly an apt description for fallible senior bureaucrats. "How long will it take for them to reach a decision?" she asked.

Ardell Harcourt spread his lips once again. "Oh dear, that would be impossible for me to say. It might not take very long at all...then again, it might. Have a nice day, Ms Miller."

CHAPTER THIRTEEN

IT WAS EARLY OCTOBER, a few days before the Canadian Thanksgiving holiday, when Donis phoned Karen to say, "We've been invited to dinner."

She had just come out of the bathtub and was toweling her hair. "That's nice, but why are you calling me? I'm going to see you when you finish work tonight, aren't I?"

"Yes, but Father Peter needed to know if we were coming so he could know what to buy at the market."

"We've been invited to the seminary?"

"There's a diocesan conference in progress. One of the priests is from Sanvito and active in the relief efforts. Father Peter thought we might enjoy meeting him."

Karen was delighted that her friend had thought to include them. "Sounds lovely. When is it?"

"Tomorrow evening, seven-thirty. Father apologized for the short notice, but he's been so busy with the conference, he wasn't able to guarantee a free night any sooner."

"Tomorrow evening is fine. Do you have to work?"

"I have made arrangements to take the night off."

"It'll be nice for you to hear news of home," Karen said.

"Yes, it will. See you later, angel. I love you."

Her eyes brimmed, as they often did when Donis uttered those precious words.

DINNER WAS TO BE SERVED in an intimate, oak-paneled lounge off the seminary's main dining hall. A table for four had been charmingly arranged with a cornucopia

centerpiece and creamy linens. Karen, admiring the taste-
ful display, realized she must suffer from a reverse form of
chauvinism. Just because priests lacked women in their
lives didn't mean they were doomed to an inelegant existence.

"We'll have a small cocktail before dinner," Father Peter said, escorting his guests to a seating area in a corner of
the lounge. "Father Eustatius should be along any minute. Last I saw, he was debating with the monsignor—and
quite admirably—about universal health care. What can I
offer you to drink?"

Karen asked for white wine. Donis requested beer.

"A friend of mine brought some excellent Belgian beer.
You must try some, Donis." Father Peter disappeared to
get the drinks and returned a short time later with another
priest. "I found Eustatius. Monsignor had given up trying
to reason with him."

"One runs that risk arguing with a Sanvitan," Donis
pointed out.

The other priest laughed. "Only another Sanvitan would
dare make that remark."

Donis and Karen stood up while Father Peter made the
introductions. It was the only reasonable way for Karen to
greet the striking, silver-haired man who must have stood
at least six foot five.

"I have heard many fine things about you from Peter,"
he said to Karen.

"Thank you. It's a pleasure to meet you." Her hand was
lost in his grizzly-bear grip while her eyes swam in a vivid
blue gaze. Sanvitans must have a reputation for remarkable coloring, Karen decided, noting the olive contrast of
Father Eustatius's complexion.

Father Eustatius greeted Donis in a tone that was almost reverential. "At last I meet The Deliverer. This is indeed an honor."

"Here I am simply known as Donis, Father."

The priest smiled. "Humble as well as selfless. I have heard it said about you."

Father Peter, perhaps sensing Donis's discomfort, spoke up. "Why don't we all sit down and relax before dinner?"

Eustatius picked up a bottle of wine and examined the label. "A fine vintage. Ah, to be in Sanvito now, in the autumn..."

"The wine harvest would be going on," Donis reflected.

"That's right," said the priest. "My father owned a vineyard. I used to love harvest when people would come from all over the island to pick grapes and crush them in huge vats. There was singing and dancing and wonderful food. It was just like a carnival."

"Sanvito sounds like a beautiful place," Karen said.

"It is...or was," Father Eustatius agreed. "One day, God willing, Sanvito will be beautiful again."

"You're not living there now?" Donis asked.

"No, the political situation is as tense as ever. I run a small parish of Sanvitan exiles in Brussels."

"Father Peter tells me you're involved in relief work."

Eustatius glanced at the fellow priest. "Is it safe for us to speak openly in this room?"

"By all means. The staff has gone home. We have complete privacy."

"Excellent." He turned to Donis and said, "I'm glad you brought it up. I've wanted to talk to you about our relief work. Your efforts for the Sanvitan cause, Donis, have been greatly appreciated. One of our families in Germany has been provided with food, clothing and medicine for their ailing child. Our assistance network has become quite sophisticated."

"That is good to hear," Donis said, then turned to his friend. "I thought you said my contributions would remain anonymous."

"They have been—"

"You must not blame Peter," Father Eustatius interjected. "He has been most discreet about forwarding the donations, but rumors have been spreading among the relief workers that The Deliv—or rather, Andonis Sotera, must have made his way across the Atlantic. You've become quite a legend in your time. Even after your catastrophic disappearance several months ago, most people refused to believe you were dead."

"Wait a minute," Karen said. "I have a feeling I'm missing something in this conversation. What have you and Father Peter been up to?" she asked Donis.

The two men looked at each other with guilt all over their faces. "You've never told her?" Peter asked.

"I thought it would be best if I didn't."

"Didn't tell me what?" Karen wasn't offended, only curious. She loved and respected Donis too much to begrudge him his privacy.

"Haven't you ever wondered why Donis works twenty-four hours a day, seven days a week?" Father Peter said.

"I just assumed he was either compulsive or greedy," Karen said teasingly.

At this, Donis laughed. "In some respects, yes, but not with money."

"Donis has been giving me a substantial part of his earnings every week. I forward the money to an address in Europe, and the funds are used in the relief effort of exiles."

Karen folded her arms across her chest. "Really? And how long has this been going on?"

"Since my first job," Donis admitted.

"Not quite," the Hungarian priest cut in. "I refused to take any money from him when he was washing dishes illegally. I told him I had to maintain my credibility with Immigration."

"He's right," Donis said. "It was only after I received my permit that Father Peter agreed to assist me."

Father Eustatius raised his glass. "I propose a toast to these two fine gentlemen. There are so many indebted to their concern and generosity."

Karen clinked her glass with that of Father Eustatius. "To Father Peter and Donis," she said.

Donis leaned over and whispered in her ear. "Aren't you upset with me for not telling you?"

She shook her head, smiling. "I'm upset that you two have been keeping secrets from me, but no, I'm not upset. I'm proud of you both."

Conversation over dinner was lively, and Karen soon found herself caught up in the jocular mood of the three men. They were all excellent raconteurs, well traveled, well read. She'd never heard Donis speak so openly of his homeland and was pleased to see him relax.

The squab and wild rice was excellent. At the end of the meal, Father Eustatius leaned back in his chair. "If this is how you eat all the time, Peter, it's no wonder you've filled out since seminary days."

"Did the two of you know each other then?" Karen asked.

"No," said Father Peter, "but I think I mentioned once that I knew a Sanvitan priest and couldn't remember his name. As it turns out, Eustatius knew him."

"Yes, we were best friends for years. It's remarkable that Peter and I did not become acquainted sooner. Our paths have crossed many times."

"By the way," Peter said, "wasn't there a message you were to deliver to Donis?"

Eustatius slapped his forehead. "But of course, how could I have forgotten. Your cousin sends her love and best wishes."

Donis's eyes took on the burnish of pewter. "Talia? Have you actually spoken to her?"

"Many times. In fact, I saw her only last week in Brussels."

"How is she?"

Karen was moved by the warmth and love in Donis's face. She didn't even have to meet Talia to know that she must be a fine person.

"She is well. I didn't have the fortune of knowing her when she was younger of course, but she is a lovely woman."

"Last I heard, she was living in Spain. I haven't dared to contact her in case her mail and phone are being intercepted."

"She is still in Barcelona. Talia is one of the initial contacts for exiles and perfectly suited to the job. People love her."

Donis tipped his head. "People love her? Are we talking about the same Talia Gibrian? The girl I remember couldn't be bothered with people. Animals were the only creatures she had any interest in."

Father Eustatius laughed. "We are all God's creatures. It's a natural progression to go from animals to people."

Donis sat back, and his expression grew somber. "Has she encountered problems, Father, because of... who she is?"

"The president's sister, you mean. No, not at all. She is known in most places by her first name only. She seems to have overcome that hurdle quite effectively."

"Was she close to her brother when they were younger?" Karen asked Donis.

Donis smiled. "She used to follow us everywhere. Talia was only two years younger and such a...what is the word...tomboy. I would say, yes, they were close. We all were at one time."

"But you had to help her escape Sanvito, didn't you?"

"Yes. She and Salvo had been estranged for years because of his radical politics. When he won the election, and she refused even to acknowledge his victory, Talia rose quickly on his roster of state enemies. I don't know that he would have killed her, but he certainly wouldn't have been above throwing her in prison.''

Karen recalled the small, dark-haired girl in the photograph Donis kept in his bedroom. So that was Talia Gibrian, a girl who grew up to become the sister and enemy of a dictator. What an astonishing family they were.

Several hours later, Karen and Donis were on their way home. The evening had flown by, the laughter and conversation as relaxed as that of old friends.

"I can't remember when I've enjoyed a dinner party so much," Karen said, rearranging herself in the driver's seat. She'd have been wise to refuse the chocolate profiterole for dessert, but it was too late for regrets now.

"Nor can I," Donis said. "Peter is an excellent host."

"And Father Eustatius, what a sweetheart. I'll bet he broke a few hearts before he entered seminary."

Donis glanced at Karen with amusement. "What's this? I thought you had eyes only for me."

Karen batted her lashes at him. "My eyes, dear, I can't control. The rest of me, however, is for you."

"Ah, in that case, I have no objection."

They were approaching downtown London. Karen slowed the car for an amber light. "I feel guilty for even asking this, but were you planning to spend the night at my place?"

"Why do you feel guilty?"

"Oh, I don't know. I guess it's because we just came away from an evening with two priests."

Donis laughed. "You're not even Catholic."

"I know, but I still feel kind of funny."

"Father Peter does approve of our seeing each other."

"I know, but that doesn't mean he condones...you know."

Donis laughed even harder. "Now we refer to making love as 'you know.' Next I suppose, you'll be telling me we must wait until we're married."

The light turned green, and Karen pulled ahead. "I wouldn't go that far," she said. "By tomorrow I should be right back to normal."

"You're delightful. Have I told you that lately?"

She blushed softly at the praise. "Not in so many words."

"I have a suggestion. In order to appease your onslaught of conscience, I'll sleep at home tonight."

"Hold on," she protested. "My conscience isn't bothering me that much."

"That isn't the reason. I have to be at the warehouse by six-thirty in the morning, and it's already past midnight. If I come to your apartment, I have a feeling neither of us will get any rest."

"Okay." Karen turned reluctantly into the driveway of Donis's apartment. "Tonight, we'll be good. But tomorrow..."

"Tomorrow, we will be spectacular." He reached over and kissed her. "Sleep well, angel."

KAREN WOKE UP to Indian summer. Brilliant sunshine streamed through her window. Stretching and yawning, she rolled over and lazily peered at the bedside clock. Only seven forty-five...

Seven forty-five! This was no weekend. This was Friday, and she had to be at work in fifteen minutes!

Karen picked up the clock and stared at the face. Why hadn't it gone off? She checked the alarm switch. That was why. She hadn't turned the stupid thing on.

She was so tired after the dinner party last night. Lying there alone with Donis on her mind, she must have somehow forgotten about work.

Waking up late didn't bode well for the day. Karen hated rushing. She hated throwing on clothes haphazardly, applying makeup on the run.

She arrived at the office, gasping for breath, sixteen minutes late. And wouldn't you know it? Nobody noticed. She could have slowed down a little.

"Morning, Karen," Molly chirped.

"G'morning."

"Ooh, you sound as though you want to bite someone's head off."

"I overslept. I hate when I do that."

"Get yourself a coffee," Molly said. "There's nothing going on in here yet."

"That sounds like a terrific idea." Karen went to the cafeteria and returned a few minutes later with two styrofoam cups, already knowing this would be a multicup morning.

She had just sat down in her office when Liz O'Connell came skidding around the partition. "There you are! I've been looking all over for you."

"I was sixteen minutes late. I'm sorry."

"Pardon me?"

Bleary-eyed, Karen looked up. "You didn't notice? Then I was kidding."

"Never mind about that. I have two things to tell you. First, Mr. Rathbone received a call from the Human Rights Commission."

"And?"

"They're recommending the case be dismissed for lack of evidence. You don't have a thing to worry about."

Karen allowed herself a small sigh. "That's a relief."

Liz attempted to appear nonchalant. "And...we just got word from the RSAC this morning. They've reached a decision on Donis's claim."

Karen's heart tripped, then madly began to hammer. Her fingers pressed into the styrofoam. "Well? For Pete's sake, don't keep me in suspense forever."

Liz was doing what she could to keep her expression noncommittal. "They've allowed the claim. Donis can stay."

Molly, who'd been eavesdropping behind the cloth baffle, let out a raucous whoop. "Way to go! I knew it! Fantastic!"

Finally the news penetrated. Karen leaped up from her chair, and threw her arms around Liz. "He can stay! He can really stay!"

In no time, the three women were sharing a box of hankies and sobbing. Jim Evans, a veteran counselor whose office was next to Karen's, came to investigate the uproar. "What's going on out here?"

"Donis's refugee claim was allowed! Isn't that marvelous?"

"Who's he?"

"My client, my... my friend." *And my lover,* she was tempted to add.

Jim scratched his head and crawled back into his hole. "Just what this country needs. Another mouth to feed."

Karen was too elated to stick out her tongue at Jim's retreating figure. "So tell me, Liz, does Donis know? Has anyone called him? You haven't called, have you?"

"Calm down." Liz coaxed Karen back to her chair. "Drink your coffee and get hold of yourself. Why on earth would you think I'd call Donis? He's your man, and it's not every day a woman can give her man a future."

Karen wiped away a tear. "No, I guess it isn't."

"I'll leave you alone now," Liz said. "But the minute you've finished talking to Donis, I want you to tell me his reaction."

"Will do."

Karen's fingers were trembling as she looked up the number of the east-end warehouse where Donis worked.

When she spoke, her voice was breathless. "Hello, may I speak to Donis Sotera?"

"Hold on," a gruff voice replied. The voice returned a few minutes later. "He's not here."

"What do you mean, he's not there? Couldn't he be out in the yard or something?"

"Nope. Didn't come in today."

Karen couldn't believe it. She'd never known Donis to miss a day's work. "Did he phone in sick?"

"I'm not the supervisor, lady. All I know's Sotera's not here, and the rest of us are doing his job."

"Oh, okay, thank you."

Maybe Donis overslept, too. Karen dialed his apartment. A sleepy Irish brogue answered the phone.

"Sean, it's Karen. I've woken you up, haven't I?"

"No problem," he mumbled. "I was due to get up shortly anyway."

"Is Donis there?"

"I don't know. I'll go check." A short time later, Sean was back. "He's not here, Karen. May I take a message?"

"No, I...well, I guess so. When you see him, please ask him to call me right away."

"Sounds urgent. Nothing wrong, I hope?"

"No," she said too hastily. "N-nothing's wrong. It's...uh, good news, actually. Please, just ask him to call."

She hung up the phone with the unshakable feeling that something was wrong. It wasn't like Donis not to go to work without letting someone know. He was the ideal employee—punctual, reliable, dedicated. He wouldn't just not show up.

Maybe there'd been an accident. He took the bus to work. Something could have happened to the bus.

But it was almost 9:00 a.m. He said he had to be at the warehouse by six-thirty. A transit accident would have hit the grapevine by now.

Karen went to see Liz. "I can't find him."

"Find who?"

"Donis. He's not at work, he's not at home. I can't imagine where he could be."

"Maybe he's playing hooky. Everyone gets the urge to do that once in a while."

Karen doubted it, but she called the YMCA just to be sure. They paged the weight room, the gym and the locker room, but Donis wasn't there.

Liz had told her not to worry. He'd turn up eventually.

Karen tried to follow her supervisor's advice, but didn't have much luck. She got through the morning's interviews by sheer rote. Fortunately all of the cases were straightforward.

After lunch she phoned Father Peter, the only other person she could think of who might have some idea where Donis was.

"I haven't seen Donis since last night when the two of you left. You sound worried, Karen."

"I am, a little. We've just received word from the refugee committee, and I wanted to let Donis know."

"A favorable word, I trust?"

"Oh, yes, they've allowed his claim."

"Wonderful. Listen, I am sure Donis will show up soon. Perhaps he was overwhelmed by last night's reminiscence of Sanvito and has gone somewhere to be alone."

Karen was grateful for her friend's optimism. Father Peter's theory was the best one she'd heard yet. "You're probably right," she said. "It's been months since he's heard anything of his family."

"Precisely. I know how traumatic these things can be. Give him time, child, he'll be in touch. And if he shows up here, I'll be sure and tell him to call you."

"Thank you, Father."

Karen swore the day would never end. She leaped to the phone every time it rang, but the caller was never Donis.

Whenever Molly informed her about a client, Karen searched her face for signs of a practical joke.

Finally Molly couldn't take it anymore. "Karen, if he comes in, I'll tell you. So please stop looking at me like that. It's creepy."

Molly had grounds for her complaint. Karen felt creepy. And nothing anyone said, nothing they did could mitigate her growing sense of unease.

At four o'clock Karen practically fled the office. She didn't wait for the elevator, but ran nine flights of stairs to the ground floor.

She didn't exactly understand why she was running home. Home was only another place to wait, and she didn't even have an answering machine to take messages. But she ran anyway.

She stopped briefly to pick up her mail from the brass box in the lobby. A scrap of paper had been folded and inserted in the slot. Karen knew at once; it was from Donis.

The handwriting was barely recognizable—small and tight, nothing like his usual large flourish. The words, written with a dull pencil, were hard to read. Karen had to squint and hold the note up to the light.

By the time you read this, I will be en route to Sanvito. There is another woman—one whom I have loved for many years—and she needs me. I am going home to be with her. I'm sorry. I wish things could have worked out differently. Please, think well of me, as I always shall of you.

There was no one in the foyer, but she wouldn't have noticed if there had been. Falling to her knees, Karen crushed the note to her breast. A cry rose up from the depths of her soul—a cry of denial, a cry of pure anguish.

"No, Donis, please . . . !"

CHAPTER FOURTEEN

SOMEHOW SHE MADE her way upstairs. Somehow she managed to boil some water and make a cup of tea. Her movements were robotic, but at least she was moving. It was, for Karen, the only evidence that the world hadn't ground to a halt.

She brought her tea to the window seat, a place where she used to find solace. Now she could no longer look at it without thinking of Donis. She'd found him there lost in thought the first morning after they made love. The sun had been streaming, pale and white, like a halo all around him.

A halo. Karen winced. Maybe that was the problem all along. Because of his past, his strong sense of values, she'd idealized Donis, making him out to be something more than mortal.

She glanced over at the crumpled note on the table. How stupid of her to forget that he was only flesh and blood. Only a man.

And now he was gone. For three months Donis Sotera had been the mainstay of her life, and it was over. Without so much as an inkling that something might have been wrong. Karen thought back to the last words he'd said to her. *Sleep well, my love.*

The memory crashed through a floodgate that Karen could not control. The tears gushed and were far from soothing. They scalded her throat and tore at her gut. She doubled over, her body racked with spasms. For a time

Karen thought she might never stop crying. This was how they would find her at the end, hugging her knees and comatose like some poor creature left to die.

Finally like a dawn that rises timidly at storm's end, her crying stopped. Karen looked around, half-surprised to discover that everything in the room was the same. Her window still overlooked the park; her tea was still warm.

The only aberration was that Donis had somehow been replaced by a scrap of paper. Karen rose and crossed the room, picking up the note and smoothing it.

To look at the words still stung bitterly, but at least the shock was over. Perhaps if she read the note again, she might make some sense of it.

"By the time you read this, I will be en route to Sanvito." When could he have left? How did he leave? They had been together until after midnight last night. Surely he would have given some hint of his plans, even inadvertently.

Karen racked her brain and came up with nothing. As far as she could remember, last night had been like any other night. They were happy, they were in love and looking forward to being together the next day. That was no way to leave someone, she thought. Without any warning, without so much as a proper goodbye.

"There is another woman—one whom I have loved for many years... I am going home to be with her."

Another woman. Karen spoke the words aloud, as though to test how they would feel on her tongue. It was a strange sensation—both painful and numbing—like being impaled by an icicle.

She and Donis had talked on several occasions about their past loves. Karen told him of her ill-fated engagements, and he had told her about... she couldn't remember him telling her anything. He'd admitted to women, of course, but not "one woman." He'd been quite specific about it, that he'd never found anyone in Sanvito who interested him. And later, in Europe, he didn't have time to fall in love.

If there was someone in his past, why wouldn't he have told Karen? She stared at the note—"...one whom I have loved for many years..."

Part of her denied the notion outright, but her rational self was in control. The answer to her question was embarrassingly obvious. Donis wouldn't have told her about another love if that love was still ongoing.

"I'm sorry." Why did he say that? For what was he sorry? For hurting her, loving her?

Karen didn't know. But dammit, all hurting aside, she didn't want him to be sorry! Not for one single, solitary moment did she regret loving and being loved by Donis Sotera. Maybe she was naive and a hopeless romantic, but as far as Karen was concerned, there was nothing to forgive.

Just then, the phone rang. Karen gasped. It had to be Donis. She was going to pick up the phone and discover that this had all been some kind of joke.

Karen raced to the kitchen. "Hello?"

"Hello, Karen? This is Father Peter."

"You've found Donis! Where is he? With you?"

"No. No, he's not here. Get a hold of yourself, please."

Karen drew in a deep breath, trying to counter the horrible sinking feeling inside. "I'm sorry. I didn't mean to get hysterical."

"That's all right. The reason I called is...well, something very peculiar has happened."

Her knuckles turned white. "What is it?"

"Father Eustatius is gone. So is Sancho."

Karen felt a twinge of annoyance. "You called to tell me your car is gone?"

"And Father Eustatius too."

"He probably went somewhere for a drive." Karen was almost tempted to ask Father Peter to get off the phone. She needed to keep the line free in case Donis called.

"I don't think Eustatius would do that, certainly not without asking me first."

Karen caught the note of dismay in his voice and chided herself for being so insensitive. She knew how much Sancho meant to the priest. "It does seem kind of unethical for a guest to do that," she said. "Do you have any idea how long the car has been gone?"

"Not really. I didn't notice that he or Eustatius was missing until this afternoon, shortly after you phoned about Donis."

Suddenly something hit her. It came like a flash, a rock-hard knowledge of something that hadn't been there a moment ago.

Donis had once told her he would never return to Sanvito of his own accord. Now, two Sanvitans and a car were missing.

"Father," Karen said, feeling both calm and frantic. "I've got to see you right away. I think something terrible has happened."

"THE RED WATCH?" Father Peter sat across from Karen in his book-lined study. "I find that impossible to believe. The man is an ordained priest."

"I'm not questioning whether he's a real priest or posing as one," Karen said. "All I'm saying is that Eustatius has another mission in life with the Red Watch. Donis once explained to me that the Sanvitan secret police have infiltrated all levels of society. One of them could turn out to be your best friend, your doctor, a person you least expect."

The lines on Father Peter's brow deepened. "But he was such a gentleman, and so pleased to meet Donis."

"That's understandable, considering he probably had orders to bring Donis back to Sanvito."

"I don't know. It just doesn't sit right with me, Karen. I agree that both of them disappearing can be no coincidence, but perhaps Donis was acting on impulse. Having reminisced about Sanvito all evening, he grew homesick and decided to return to Sanvito with Eustatius."

"When was Father Eustatius scheduled to leave London?"

"Tomorrow, I believe."

"So why would he leave two days early, and in the middle of the night?"

"I can't imagine why, but—"

"And another thing, Father. Eustatius is a priest—or at least, we assume so. He couldn't return to Sanvito if he wanted to."

"No, that's true. I should have realized that myself." Father Peter thought awhile. "All right, you said that Donis would never return to Sanvito of his own accord. That doesn't necessarily mean he was abducted. From the way the note is written, Donis received alarming news that compelled him to change his mind and go back. These things do happen."

"It's got to be a trap. He's either going to end up in prison again or dead." Saying the words was terrifying for Karen, but she had to force herself to face the possibility for the sake of her own sanity.

"Circumstances change with time. The president is his cousin. Perhaps he has had a change of heart and sent Eustatius as an emissary to welcome Donis home."

"In which case, Donis would have told me. He would never just disappear like this."

"What if Donis only intended to go for a short time? It's possible he will stay in Sanvito only long enough to reconcile his business and then come back."

"Even if that were true, he can't come back. By leaving Canada, he's effected his deportation order and voided his refugee claim. He's inadmissible."

Father Peter sighed. "I don't mean to sound like a thick-headed oaf. Everything you have said is far more logical than any theory I have come up with. But the whole thing is so inconceivable. And to think I went to such pains to introduce the two men . . ."

Karen patted his hand. "Don't blame yourself, Father. I introduced you and Donis, so we're even."

The man suddenly looked older than his years. "My God, Karen, what have we done?"

She knew exactly how he felt. She'd been grappling with a horrible sense of guilt since the priest's phone call. "We've only been doing what we thought was right. Now the question is, what to do next?"

"We phone the police and report Sancho and the two men missing."

"Is there any chance that Sancho might have broken down on the highway?" she asked.

Father Peter smiled sadly. "I wish for once it would happen, but last week I took Sancho to the garage for a complete overhaul. The car runs like a real squire now."

"Then we're probably too late. It's only a two-hour drive to the Toronto airport, and we don't know how long they've been missing. They could have boarded any number of international flights by now."

"The police would check the passenger lists and perhaps alert Interpol."

Karen brightened. "You're right, they could do that."

"But without some proof of abduction, I don't know."

Her mood fell once again. "And Father Eustatius is hardly going to have Donis handcuffed. They're going to look like a pair of ordinary travelers."

"But if we could persuade the police to question them and interview Donis alone, he could tell them what was going on and have Eustatius arrested on the spot."

Karen shook her head. "I don't think Donis would risk exposing Eustatius. Whatever the priest used to coerce Donis into leaving, I'm certain the threat was greater than the loss of his own life."

"What greater threat is there?" the priest asked.

"The lives of others," she replied.

The priest nodded thoughtfully. "Yes, Donis would never jeopardize anyone for his own safety, and his abductor would know that. Also, if Eustatius is a member of the secret police, he would have safeguards built into his identity. For Donis to turn him over to Interpol could do more harm than good."

"So where does that leave us?" Karen asked.

Father Peter picked up the telephone. "We can still report Sancho missing and tell the officer the rest of the story when he gets here." He spoke to someone at the Royal Canadian Mounted Police whose jurisdiction extended beyond London's city limits. They promised to dispatch a constable to the seminary at once. "Could I see the note again, please?" he said to Karen after hanging up.

"I don't believe the part about the other woman," Karen said as she watched him read.

He looked up with a smile of compassion. "You don't believe it or you don't want to?"

"A little of both, I suppose. But tell me, Father, have you ever believed something to be true, and believed it so strongly that nothing could possibly convince you otherwise?"

"I'm a man of the cloth, remember? I live with those feelings every day."

Karen flushed slightly. "Of course you would, I forgot. Well, that's almost how I feel about Donis. He would never lie to me. He would never hurt me, either, unless he knew there was no other way. Donis once told me that feelings like this are impossible to ignore. He called them instincts."

"In my profession, we call it faith, but it's the same thing. Cling to them, Karen. Cling to those instincts with everything you've got."

AFTER FILING A REPORT with the police, Karen left the seminary and drove straight to Donis's apartment. His roommate fortunately was working the late shift and was there to let her in.

"Hi, Sean. You haven't heard from Donis, by any chance?"

"Not a word, and I've been here all day."

"It's all right. I didn't expect you would hear anything."

Karen hadn't discussed the details of Donis's disappearance, but Sean must have sensed her state of agitation. "Would you like a beer or a glass of wine?" he asked.

"No, thanks. But would you mind if I looked around in Donis's bedroom? He might have left some clue as to where he's gone."

"Go right ahead. Make yourself at home. I'll be in the living room if you need anything."

She thanked him and went down the hall. Donis's bed was made, which might have meant he didn't go to bed at all the night of the seminary dinner.

She opened the closet. His suit was there along with several shirts. The tuxedo he used for work was hanging in a dry cleaner's bag. Karen couldn't see that anything was missing.

Two dresser drawers were open with a few articles of clothing hanging out as though he had gone through them in a hurry. His shaving kit lay on top of the dresser, razor and toothbrush noticeably absent. But everything else— shaving cream, toothpaste, cologne—was still there.

Then she saw the small framed photograph of Donis's family and her heart wrenched. She knew how much this picture meant to him. After all he'd been through, he still retained this one memento from his childhood. He never would have left without it this time—not willingly.

Karen knew the police were likely to come and search the apartment sooner or later. She knew she ought to leave things as she found them. But Karen couldn't bear to leave the picture. All these years the photo had been Donis's only link to happier times. Now, the photo was her only link to him.

She slipped the snapshot into her purse and left the room. Thanking Sean, she informed him that Donis had been reported missing and not to be surprised if the police showed up.

THE NEXT MORNING part of her fears were confirmed. Sancho, Father Peter's station wagon, had been found in the parking lot of Toronto's international airport. The police had not yet been able to locate Donis and Eustatius on the passenger lists, but the investigation was continuing.

It was Thanksgiving weekend. Karen pondered the cruel irony as she drove to her brother's home. She was supposed to have made salad, but if Sue hadn't phoned that morning to borrow candles, Karen would have forgotten all about the holiday. Feeling anything but thankful, she stopped on the way to pick up candles and some ready-made salad.

Tim and Sue had never seemed happier. Impending fatherhood was working miracles on Tim, who announced over drinks that he wouldn't be selling the house in the foreseeable future. Sue was tired of moving, and she liked this place. It was a good neighborhood for raising children, and as Tim sagely pointed out, kids needed stability in their lives.

Sue took Karen and her dad on a tour of the nursery, cheerfully decorated in shades of peach and green. Her pregnancy gave her the classic maternal glow and made her bubblier than ever. Karen was delighted for both of them and did her best not to let her own loss overshadow the day.

It was a shame that Dad wasn't as considerate. Thanksgiving or not, he was the surliest he'd been in months. As soon as he arrived, he began to drone on about the Martins' disastrous tobacco crop, ruined by the frost.

When William was called to the dinner table, he barely acknowledged the majestic bird and the beautiful side dishes. Still, amazingly, Tim remained the ideal host.

The four of them sat down—the four that should have been six, Karen thought. She was feeling Liz's absence at the table almost as intensely as she did Donis's.

"Would you say the grace, Dad?" Sue asked her father-in-law.

William murmured a prayer of thanksgiving. The others said amen, then began passing food. Tim, at the head of the table, proudly carved the bird.

"Too bad Donis couldn't make it," he said, laying a slice of white meat on Karen's plate.

"It sure is," Sue echoed. "I know what it's like working on holidays. You feel so left out."

Karen choked back a sob. "I'm sure he's thinking about us." Maybe she was wrong not to tell her family what had happened, but Tim and Sue had worked so hard to make this day special. Karen couldn't bear to spoil it.

"He's really starting to feel like part of the family," Sue said. "I miss him when he's not here."

Please stop. Any other time, Karen would have loved to hear these sentiments. But dear Lord, not now...

"Has he heard anything about his refugee claim?" Tim asked.

Her fork clattered on the plate. "We, uh...we got word on Friday. He was...that is, he will be allowed to stay."

Sue clapped her hands together. "That is marvelous. You both must be so thrilled, and to think, it happened just before Thanksgiving."

Oh, what a tangled web we weave...

William Miller, who had thus far been silent at the table, finally spoke up. "This isn't your usual coleslaw recipe, is it, Karen?"

She turned to him, appalled. "What did you say?"

He looked up. "I just said, this doesn't taste like your usual coleslaw."

"Don't you like this recipe?"

"It's a little heavy on the vinegar—"

"Is it now? Well, that is too bad, but I can explain how it happened. I did something no Miller female has ever done for a family dinner. I bought the damned stuff at a deli on my way over here."

"Karen!" Tim and Sue said in unison.

"Sorry, guys," Karen said to the young couple, "but we had been discussing Donis's future, and not only does Dad have nothing decent to say about him, he has to interrupt because there's too much vinegar in his stupid salad!"

Nothing like this had ever happened at a family dinner before, and no one knew how to react. Even Karen felt vaguely disembodied, as though a part of her was standing aside watching the debacle.

"I certainly don't appreciate your behavior, young lady," William Miller admonished, "and I think you'd better apologize right now."

Karen lay her napkin on the table. "No, Dad, I'm not apologizing this time. You're the one whose behavior has been boorish up until I took over."

"What the hell do you think you're saying?" His eyes bulged in utter astonishment.

"It's true, Dad." Karen was on a roll. She couldn't have stemmed the flow of words if she tried. "You should have seen the look on Sue's face when you walked into the dining room and didn't say a damned word about the food. You know how hard she must have worked. You know how hard Mom used to work, but you never said anything to her, either."

"What's your mother got to do with this?" His face was apoplectic.

"You've been trampling over people's feelings for years, but you treated Mom worse than any of us. I don't know how or why she put up with it."

"Your mother knew how I felt about her," he said, some of the fight gone from his voice.

"Did she? How did she know? Did you tell her how you felt? Or did she interpret your silence as approval, the way the rest of us had to?"

"That's a low-handed remark," he growled.

"I know, but considering this is the first time that any Miller except you has spoken her mind, I think I'll just go on and finish what I've started."

"Karen," Sue said. "I don't mind about the food. I know he appreciates—"

"We're talking principles, Sue." Karen turned to her father. He was looking both murderous and cowed. "Did you hear her, Dad? She doesn't mind your lack of gratitude, but would it really hurt so much to say something?"

William didn't answer. He glanced at Sue, then quickly lowered his gaze.

Karen shook her head. "I guess it must hurt. And it must hurt when a father of six sits down for Thanksgiving dinner with only two of his children and not even a phone call from the others."

William slammed his fist on the table. "That's enough, Karen. What do you want from me?"

"It's not what I want, Dad. It's what all of us have wanted and needed and never gotten, dammit. Your love!"

The last word punctured his anger, and he moaned. "Is that what you think? That I never loved you?"

Karen, suddenly feeling like a child again, drew back. "There have been times..."

"Just because I didn't know how to say the words?"

"It wasn't only the words, Dad, but you couldn't even put your arms around us. When one of us did well at something, you grunted and walked away. But if we were feeling lousy, you told us to smarten up and stop sniveling."

Karen gestured toward her brother. "Why do you think Tim did so poorly in school? At least when you were giving him hell, he had your attention. Why do you think he busted his butt renovating houses these past few years? For the money? No! He wants your approval. He wants you to realize he's finally made something of himself. I mean, look at this place. He's only twenty-five."

She could see Tim's head was lowered; he was probably dying of embarrassment. Karen hated herself for upsetting him; she hated herself for upsetting Dad. But self-esteem was the least of her concerns right now. These were things that, like it or not, needed to be said.

"Is it true, son?" his father asked.

Tim looked up with red-rimmed eyes. "I suppose there's some basis to it."

"Why didn't you ever say anything?"

Tim's mouth opened, but nothing came out. Sue reached over and took his hand.

"How could he say anything?" Sue stepped in. "He's too much like his father."

"I do love you all," William said, pronouncing every word with deliberation, "I always have."

Karen fell silent. Heaven knew, she wanted to stay angry. Now that she'd finally broken through the walls of reserve, she didn't want to let her father off the hook so easily. A single "I love you" couldn't possibly make up for thirty-one years.

But, dammit all, it did.

Her heart bursting, Karen got up from the table and wrapped her arms around her father. "I love you too, Dad."

Tim got up and did the same. By the time Sue hugged him, there wasn't a dry eye in the room. A moment of awkwardness followed. Everyone returned to their seats and didn't seem to know what to say or do.

That was when William held up his wineglass. "I'm not very good at this, but I'd uh . . . I'd like to propose a toast to my wonderful daughter-in-law. Sue, this is the finest Thanksgiving I can remember. I'm just glad that Tim, in spite of being a chip off the old block, had the good sense to marry you."

Nothing could erase the anguish of Donis being gone, and Karen still wished that Liz could be with them. But in all other respects, her father was right. This was the finest Thanksgiving the Millers had known in a long time.

IT CAME TO KAREN the next morning—not with a flash, but with a slow, painful awakening. Despite the love she shared with her family over Thanksgiving dinner, she no longer felt a part of them. Tim and Sue's lives were filled with the anticipation of a child. Her father didn't seem to need her the way he used to, or perhaps she had simply come to terms with her own conscience.

Whatever the reasons, Karen knew she could never go back to her old existence. For years she'd been content as William's daughter, Tim's sister and Sue's sister-in-law. She'd been happy with her job, blithely assuming that uncomplaining diligence reaped its own rewards.

Those facets of her existence, once so fulfilling, were no longer enough. Donis had come into her life and boldly pushed back her horizons. He had shown Karen that the world did not cease to exist beyond a hundred-mile radius. By his very being, he had shown her the limitless capabilities of the human spirit. How did a woman go through loving and losing such a man, and then go back to what she used to be?

A woman didn't.

That's what Karen slowly came to realize as the autumn sun rose outside her window. The days of old movies and giggly shopping expeditions were over. Never again could she be content to live alone and loveless, as she had for years.

Karen knew what she had to do, and knew that nothing or no one would dissuade her. There was no naïveté to her decision, no overblown sense of the dramatic. For Karen this was an act of love, nothing more.

She waited until a decent hour of the morning to phone Father Peter. They chatted briefly about nothing in particular. Then he told her the police had come up with no new leads in the investigation. Somehow, Karen hadn't expected they would.

Finally she brought up the reason for her call. "I'm going to Europe to find out what's happened to Donis, and I'm going to need your help."

CHAPTER FIFTEEN

THIS WAS SHEER MADNESS—by far, the most reckless, irrational thing Karen had ever done in her life. Father Peter had said all he could to dissuade her, but Karen's mind was made up. She would never rest easy—could never get on with her life—until she knew the truth behind Donis's disappearance. The priest finally gave her the information she requested, only because Karen swore that, with or without his help, she was going.

As Karen stepped out of the Barcelona train station, the full impact of what she was doing assaulted her. Realization came in the cacophony of screeching traffic, in the austere grime of old buildings, in the mobs of pushy people shouting in languages she didn't understand.

As recently as the day before, Karen had felt almost smug, a latter day Mata Hari mingling with a Canadian tour group bound for Torremolinos. In the southern port city of Malaga, they parted company—Karen blithely heading east, the rest going west in search of bars and beaches.

Family and colleagues were led to believe that Karen was taking two weeks of R and R on the Costa del Sol. She'd dropped hints of Donis's disappearance, implying that theirs was a romantic falling out. What better cure for a broken heart than the sunny beaches of Spain?

Barcelona, however, wasn't sunny on this bleak October day, nor was Karen's mood. She was tired and dusty after the long train ride, far from the right frame of mind to begin her search.

But standing outside the station feeling sorry for herself wasn't doing any good, either. Karen hiked her travel bag high onto her shoulder and started to walk. Having pored over maps on the train, she knew that if she turned left out of the station, she would eventually come to the boulevard known as Las Ramblas. From there, the map would have to come out again.

The distances in Barcelona were greater than Karen had anticipated, but she was reluctant to hail a taxi. Maybe she was overestimating the impact of her mission, but Karen wanted as few witnesses as possible to her movements in Spain.

A cab driver might remember the nervous blond lady and the location to which he'd driven her. And Father Peter had been adamant. For the sake of the Sanvitans fleeing their homeland, Karen must be as discreet as possible with the scant information he'd been able to give her. And it was scant. A name, an address, nothing more. But at least it was a contact.

Her only personal precaution had been to contact the Canadian Embassy in Madrid upon her arrival in Spain. She didn't launch into detail, but told the official that she was traveling on her own through the country. If the embassy didn't hear from her after two weeks, she would appreciate their making inquiries with the Spanish authorities. She also left the address and phone numbers of her family, Father Peter and Liz.

By the time she reached Las Ramblas, Karen had relaxed somewhat. The exercise had done her good, and the pulse of the city no longer seemed so frantic.

The boulevard itself was charming. A wide median divided the thoroughfare, and on the median were kiosks and street vendors peddling everything from magazines to canaries. On both sides of the street was an endless array of shops and sidewalk cafés spilling over with people. The air was spiced with aromas of grilled meat, freshly baked bread and, of course, smog.

Karen finally came to the street that was supposed to lead to the Gothic Quarter, the area she was headed for. She had thought about finding a hotel for the first night, but decided not to. It wouldn't hurt to attempt an initial meeting with her contact; it might even make sleep remotely possible tonight.

But no sooner had she turned the corner than Karen's mood threatened to plummet again. Las Ramblas had been colorful and spacious, while the Gothic Quarter was drab and cramped. It was like stepping immediately into the Middle Ages. High stone walls encroached on either side of cobblestoned streets and blocked out what little remained of daylight.

Her map didn't show the street she was looking for, but Karen had hoped she'd be able to happen across it once she reached the Gothic Quarter. Now she knew that would be highly unlikely. The blind alleys and tiny lanes went on forever, crisscrossing or dead-ending at every turn. Karen soon found herself wandering in circles, more fatigued, more confused with every convolution.

At last she had no choice but to ask for directions. No fewer than five people she approached glanced at her notepad and shrugged. They'd apparently never heard of the street or the restaurant that was supposed to be on it.

Finally she approached an old man feeding pigeons in a tiny plaza. She showed him the address; he shook his head. At first she thought he didn't know the place, either, but with the use of gestures and a guttural language that didn't sound like Spanish, he explained that he was illiterate.

Clearly more embarrassed than he, Karen tried to say the street name aloud. Again the man shook his head. She told him the name of the restaurant, and this time his face cracked into a leathery grin.

He nodded eagerly and gestured for her to follow him, which Karen had little choice but to do. They seemed to plod on forever, and if the Gothic Quarter had struck Karen as gloomy before, it grew even gloomier. What little of the touristic charm she had subconsciously acknowledged earlier disappeared completely. Here, the stone walls were crumbling and streaked with the soot of centuries. The odor of what might have been rancid olive oil was so heavy, Karen felt nauseous. Just when she became convinced that the man was leading her to a den of thieves, he stopped and pointed at a doorway.

She would have missed the door altogether if it weren't for him. There was no restaurant sign to be seen from the street. All there was, was a small wooden plaque above the door, announcing that this was the Casa Suerte.

Karen thanked the man and rummaged through her purse for a coin. But when she brought out the tip, he waved his hand in good-hearted refusal. Then before Karen could ascertain whether the Casa Suerte was open for business, he ambled off and left her.

She pulled the door and pushed, but it wouldn't open. She peered inside through the barred window, but the interior was too dark and dusty to see anything.

Karen tried knocking and, listening against the door, thought she heard movement from inside. She knocked again, but another few minutes passed before someone finally came.

"*¿Sí? ¿Qué quiere?*" a man barked through the crack in the door.

"I, uh . . . I'm looking for a restaurant, and someone recommended this place—the, uh, Casa Suerte."

The door opened a tad wider. A round-faced, balding man took a good look at Karen. "Who are you?" he asked in English.

If this restaurant was supposed to be a front for subversive Sanvitan activities, they could do a lot, Karen thought, to make the atmosphere more convincing. "I'm from Canada," she said. "I'm a tourist."

"We are closed until dinner."

Karen glanced at her watch. It was after five. "When is dinner?"

"Ten o'clock."

"Ten!" That was bedtime where she came from. Karen considered coming back later, but that would mean walking these dismal streets after dark and perhaps finding out that the man was lying about the hours. For what it was worth, she was here, and Karen wasn't about to give up this easily.

"Couldn't I come in for a drink?" she asked. "I've been traveling all day, and I'm thirsty."

He gave her another cold assessment, and with obvious reluctance opened the door the rest of the way. Karen stepped inside but still couldn't see a thing. The man went on ahead of her and switched on a light behind the bar.

The place wasn't really so bad once you got a look at it. A bar, carved from some dark exotic wood, dominated the room. There were a few small tables, and the wainscoted walls were decorated with copper and tapestries.

Karen sat at the bar, something she'd never attempted in her life. But the gesture made her feel more assertive somehow, and she needed all the props she could get.

"What kind of drink do you want?"

Considering his line of work, the man would do well to take a course in public relations. "It doesn't matter," she said, "as long as it's cold and non-alcoholic."

He disappeared under the bar and came up with a bottle of what looked like condensed milk. That figured, thought Karen. She should have been more specific—anything except condensed milk.

He flipped the cap off against the side of the bar, found a straw and wiped it on his apron before sticking it into the bottle. Trying not to gag, Karen thanked him and gamely took a sip.

The beverage was thick, slightly sweet, and with a nutty flavor. Not bad at all. "What is this?"

"*Horchata.*"

"Oh," she replied, none the wiser, and continued to drink.

The man didn't budge from his spot, and Karen had the impression he wouldn't until she was ready to leave. Well, she wasn't leaving yet, not until she'd finished her drink and obtained at least some information.

"The person who recommended this place," she said, trying not to sound chipper, "said I might be able to meet a friend of his here."

The man's reply was a grunt with a question mark at the end.

Karen pressed on. "He thought this friend might be willing to...show me around Barcelona. You see, I don't know anyone here, and well, it would be kind of nice to meet a friendly face." *Which, so far in this restaurant, I haven't.*

"What's his name, the one you wanta meet?"

Karen pulled out her notepad, although she really didn't need to. It seemed prudent not only to appear harmless, but a trifle ditzy. The man didn't seem the type to appreciate intelligence in a woman. "Oh yes, here it is," she said. "His name's...Hannibal."

LYING ON A RICKETY four-poster bed, Donis glanced at the stark plaster walls around him. He'd obviously come up in the world. The food was good, the room was comfortable, and there were no bars on the window.

Yet the ache in his heart was far greater than he had ever known in his years of solitary confinement. He'd never tasted loneliness so bitter, so corrosive.

Karen, where are you? Are you thinking of me now?

Rolling onto his side, he clutched the pillow, fighting back tears of impotent rage. What kind of cruel god would entice him with such sweetness, such utter joy as he'd found with Karen, then snatch it away like a carrot on a stick?

Whoever said "'tis better to have loved and lost," could never have loved this deeply. There was no joy in clinging to Karen's memory, no relief in recalling the precious times they'd shared together. There was only anguish, only the bone-crushing despair of knowing he would never see her again.

Donis wiped his eyes and tried once more to take stock of his surroundings. It was crucial that he concentrate only on the present. The past was past. The future threatened to swallow him whole.

The door to his room was locked and bolted from the other side, but this, they had told him, was standard procedure for someone under "house arrest." Donis had found the term pathetically amusing. It stood to reason that Salvo, being the kind of host he was, would be forced to lock up his house guests.

Donis had been here nearly a week and had yet to see his cousin. The president was extremely busy, they said, attending to matters of state. Donis would just have to be patient.

Donis knew better. Matters of state had nothing to do with his cousin's reticence. Salvo delighted in mind games. As a boy he used to taunt Donis for his limitless patience. Now, it seemed, Salvo relished every opportunity to test it.

The first few days had been, by far, the worst, when the memory of deserting Karen was freshest. God, how he wished there could have been some other way.

But there had been so little time, so little warning. Even now, when Donis unwillingly recalled Eustatius stepping out of the shadows behind the apartment, it seemed like a misunderstanding or someone's version of a cruel joke.

But as soon as Donis saw the expression on Eustatius's face, he knew. No legitimate man of God could look so vainglorious, so evil. Even for one who considered himself impervious, Donis was shocked at the transformation. He had struggled not to show it.

"If it isn't the illustrious 'Father' Eustatius."

Donis saw the flicker of disappointment in the man's eyes. "Aren't you surprised, just a little?"

"Little surprises me anymore. How did you find out where I live?"

"Our dear friend, Father Peter, innocently pointed it out while giving me a tour of the city. He quite admires you, you know. But then so do I," the tall man had sneered. "It's such an honor to be the one who actually delivers The Deliverer."

"Get out of here, Eustatius, or whatever your name is. I am not going anywhere except to bed." Donis had stepped past him, employing all of his inner strength to appear nonchalant.

The man seized his arm. "Not so fast, Sotera. You are going back to Sanvito...with me. I have a car waiting around the corner."

"I don't care if you have a chariot." Donis yanked his arm away. "I should have known it would happen this way. Salvo always did suffer from a broad streak of sacrilege."

"He saw the gesture as poetic justice. To be set free by a priest, and then recaptured by one. Clever bit of artistry, no?"

Donis clenched his fists to control his rage. "What do you want from me? What does Salvo want?"

"You're an economist, one of the best. Our president wants you to come back and work for him."

His cousin's unmitigated gall made Donis laugh. "I would sooner die."

"Funny, that's exactly what he predicted you would say. He was quite specific in his instructions. 'Don't bother threatening Donis with torture or death,' he said, 'it won't do any good.'"

"Then what are you supposed to do? Appeal to my generous nature?" He'd been so glib with Eustatius, so sure of himself. But now...

"President Gibrian means you no harm," Eustatius had assured him. "In fact he intends to bestow you with the highest respect, befitting a man who is capable of restoring order to the chaos of our economy."

"And if I refuse?" The words were nearer a promise than a threat.

"Ah, that would be most unfortunate." Eustatius wrung his hands. "It's not that your grandmother hasn't led a full life, but to lose it because of her grandson's selfish disregard..."

Restrained fury rose up and boiled over. Donis lunged at the pseudo priest, pinning him against a brick wall. "He's taken Grandmother, an old woman? How could he?"

"With your record for obstinate behavior, the president had to resort to drastic measures."

"Where is she? What has he done to her?"

"She's in prison, the same cell block that you once occupied—isn't that a coincidence. The place is damp and cold—not very healthy for her old bones—but they are treating her well enough."

"That bast—" Donis stopped himself. "What is the price of her release—that I miraculously restore Sanvito to its former glory?"

Eustatius clucked his tongue. "Such sarcasm. Not at all becoming in a man of your station. President Gibrian only asks that you return to Sanvito and speak with him. He is certain that once you've had a chance to talk, everything will work out for the best."

"If I go to Sanvito, he will release my grandmother?"

"You have Salvo Gibrian's word on it."

Again Donis refrained from comment. No one knew better than he the value of Salvo's word. But he had no doubts that Grandmother was in prison. And he had no trouble believing that Salvo would murder the old woman to prove his omnipotence.

"Fine," Donis said at last. "I will make travel arrangements in the morning." He began to walk away.

Eustatius stepped forward, blocking the doorway. "That's not good enough, I'm afraid. There is a morning flight out of Toronto to Athens. It's as convenient a route as any, but we must leave now."

"I can't simply leave. There are matters that must be attended to first."

"Such as?"

Donis thought quickly. "My status in Canada, for one."

"Ah, don't give it another thought. Once you're back in your beautiful homeland, you'll forget all about this place. Now, let's go."

Eustatius, despite his age, was surprisingly strong and agile. He grabbed Donis, wrenched his body and pinioned both arms to his back. The pain was so excruciating, Donis could do little more than slow his assailant down.

"Th-there's . . . one other thing," Donis gasped, immediately wishing he'd kept his mouth shut.

"Don't tell me. Your lady friend."

It was too late. Donis knew he should have left Karen out of the discussion. But how could he leave Canada without letting her know? How could he leave at all?

They got to the curb, and Donis was horrified to discover Sancho. Poor Father Peter, what would he say when he found out?

Donis renewed his struggle to free himself, but when the barrel of a small gun appeared next to his heart, he ceased struggling. No matter which way Donis looked at it, there was nowhere to run tonight. And he didn't want to endanger his grandmother's life any more than necessary. Escape, he decided climbing into the car, would have to be attempted another time.

After Eustatius got behind the wheel, Donis risked the resumption of their conversation. "I can't disappear without letting someone know."

"Yes, you can."

"Let me leave a note, at least. You're welcome to censor what I write."

"A note to whom? Your precious Karen?"

The very sound of her name tore Donis to shreds. "Is it asking so much?"

"Hah! What would you tell her? That the dreaded Red Watch finally caught up and took you away? I am no fool. She works for the government. I cannot allow our departure to become an international incident. Discretion is one of our agency's greatest strengths."

Donis hadn't thought of it that way, but he supposed there could be some basis to Eustatius's concern. Karen knew more than the average Canadian about the Sanvitan secret police. She might conceivably report this to the proper authorities. For her sake, Donis desperately hoped she wouldn't.

"She's only a counselor," he said, hoping to deflect his assailant's suspicions. "She wouldn't have the authority to initiate diplomatic action."

"You are forgetting I met Karen. She's an ingenious woman, not to mention head over heels in love. I wouldn't put anything past her when it comes to you."

"Then my note will be vaguely worded. She doesn't have to suspect the worst."

Eustatius started the car, while skillfully keeping the gun aimed at Donis's neck. "I'm not sure I like it . . ."

"Listen to me. If Karen finds out the hard way that I've gone," Donis argued, "you can be sure she will contact the police right away."

The man considered this. "Perhaps you are right. The longer we can keep her from asking questions, the better. Go ahead then, write the note. But tell her something that will satisfy her curiosity. Where is her apartment? Does she have a mailbox?"

Donis gave directions, then rummaged through Sancho's glove compartment for a pencil and paper. He found it difficult to write with the car in motion and a gun at his jugular, but found it even harder to know what to say.

He considered mentioning his grandmother outright, but feared that Karen might catch on right away. God knew, he didn't want to deceive her. Yet he would far rather break Karen's heart, even force her to despise him, than to risk having her harmed by the Red Watch.

They were the hardest words Donis ever wrote. The muscles of his hand cramped around the pencil, as if to protest the writing of such untruths. But it was the only way he could think of.

And so Donis began. "By the time you read this..."

KAREN GOT NO REACTION from the proprietor except for the same relentless stare. She decided to wait out his response.

"Where did you say you came from?" he asked at last.

"From Malaga, this morning."

"I mean, before that."

"Oh, I see. I'm Canadian." She smiled innocently. "Have you ever been to Canada?"

"No."

"I've never been to Spain either. Are you Spanish?"

"Sanvitan."

"Oh, really?"

"What do you want with Hannibal?"

"Well, like I said, this friend of mine—"

"What friend?"

Karen drew in a sharp breath, not sure how much longer she could handle his interrogation. "Do you happen to know Hannibal?" she asked, hoping to deflect his question with one of her own.

"He comes in here once in a while."

"Is there any way I could get in touch with him, let him know I'm here?"

The man shook his head.

This wasn't going nearly as well as Karen had hoped. Obviously he suspected her of being an enemy or a spy. Not that she blamed him, Karen thought, glancing around. She, too, would be suspicious of a foreigner who showed up unannounced in this godforsaken spot.

There was no point in wasting any more time. She might as well be direct. She gazed briefly at the door, wishing there were more pedestrians or customers. The man had left the door ajar, but Karen wasn't sure she could escape in time if necessary.

"Have you ever heard of The Deliverer?" she asked evenly.

The man, like another Sanvitan she knew, was a master of the art of nonexpression, but that didn't matter. From the corner of her eye, Karen saw the movement of a curtain. So they weren't alone, after all. And whoever was in the back was listening to every word. She took that as a positive sign.

"Everyone's heard of The Deliverer. What do you know about him?"

It might have been wishful thinking, but Karen could have sworn the man's gruffness abated. "We were very close once."

"He's not the one who told you to ask for Hannibal."

"How do you know?" Karen asked.

"I know," he said, effortlessly calling her bluff.

"You're right. I'm looking for Donis, and that's why
need to see Hannibal. He might be able to help."

The man turned away and began to polish glasses. "Lik
I say, he comes in here sometimes."

"How often? Every day?"

"Maybe."

"When? In the evenings?" Karen was quickly becom
ing frustrated by the snail's pace of their conversation.

The man didn't answer. Karen would have to try a di
ferent tack. She pulled out a few bills. "How much is th
drink?"

He quoted a price and she paid him. "I'll have anoth
horchata," she said, "but I'll drink it over there." Sh
pointed to a table near the door.

"I told you we're closed."

"I know, but you let me in. And I thought I'd wait fo
the dinner hour in case Hannibal showed up. Don't fe
you have to cater to me or anything." She wondered if h
appreciated her sarcasm.

The curtain rustled again, and now she knew their cu
riosity was definitely aroused. Wherever and whoeve
Hannibal was, Karen had a hunch that news of a strang
Canadian lady would soon reach him. All she had to do i
the meantime was wait.

Karen waited three days, the most excruciating, infur
ating three days of her life. She found a small pension a
the edge of the Gothic Quarter, but used the place only t
sleep and shower. First thing in the mornings, she woul
return to the Casa Suerte with a sweet roll and juice, an
wait by the door, reading.

The restaurant opened at eleven for the long Spanis
lunch hour, which at least broke some of the monotony
Karen, of course, lunched there every day, repeating he
request to see Hannibal.

The customers appeared to be a mixture of Spaniard
Catalans—who spoke the guttural language she'd hear

from the pigeon feeder—and Sanvitans. At first, the patrons appeared openly curious about the blond lady who always ate lunch by herself, but by the third day, they'd dismissed her presence entirely.

The only reason Karen held out any hope was that the balding proprietor who first let her in never told her to leave outright. She had the unshakable feeling they were watching and testing to see how long she could endure.

During the hours between lunch and supper, she waited on a bench near the Casa Suerte with a book, discreetly watching every passerby for some sign of curiosity or recognition. This proved to be no easy task since virtually every Spanish male made eye contact and often misinterpreted her intentions by sitting on the bench and introducing himself. None of them was named Hannibal.

Finally, near midnight of the third day, Karen was nursing a glass of wine in the Casa Suerte, having just finished a passable *paella*. This was the worst time of day for Karen, knowing as it drew to a close that she was no nearer to finding Donis. That was the reason for the wine—not to celebrate, but to soothe tense muscles and frazzled nerves before walking back to the pension.

Most of the customers had left, on their way to nightclubs and livelier places. A shoe-shine boy came in and pestered some of the older gentlemen who brushed him away impatiently. Karen had seen the boy a few times before, but always during the day when business was brisk. She wondered why he was still out at this hour. Didn't his parents care or worry?

Having exhausted his other leads, the boy approached Karen. She shook her head and held out her foot. "See? They're sandals. They don't need to be shined."

He peered at her feet curiously. He was a cute kid in a scruffy sort of way, probably not much older than twelve. She was surprised when he spoke to her in English. "You're looking for Hannibal?"

Karen sat up, heart pounding. "Yes, I am. Do you know him?"

He wiped his nose across his sleeve, a gesture he somehow managed to make imperious. "I know him."

"Where is he? I've been waiting three days. Could you please let him know that I need to talk to him?"

The boy set his shoe-shining kit on the floor and boldly took a seat at her table. "Go ahead, talk. I'm Hannibal."

DONIS KNEW SOMEONE was behind the door even before he heard the creaking of the hinge. It was dark, but not so dark that he couldn't make out the silhouette of a uniform. Donis lay stock-still on the bed and waited to see what the soldier would do next.

"Are you awake?" the man whispered.

Donis didn't answer.

"Of course you are. There's no need to reply. Just listen." The floor squeaked as the man tiptoed closer. "Our forces have been mobilized. The president's days are numbered."

The bedsprings squawked when Donis sat up. "What did you say?"

"You heard me. I cannot tarry, but I am instructed to warn you. There will be an uprising. The best way for you to help is not to cooperate with the president's orders. Annoy him. Anger him, do whatever you can to distract him."

"When will this take place?"

"I cannot say for certain, but soon."

The soldier backed away toward the door. Donis realized too late that he'd never even gotten a glimpse of the man's face. "How do I know it isn't a trap?"

"You don't."

"Wait! Isn't there anything more you can tell me?"

The soldier paused. "Only that your cousin sends her love and promises she will see you soon."

Talia!

Perhaps it was true then. She'd always been active in the underground. But a successful uprising in this compound was virtually impossible. Salvo would sniff it out, and there would be more bloodshed.

The wave of optimism crashed over him and vanished as quickly as it had appeared. Once again, Donis was left alone with his thoughts. They were all he had. And God help him, they were all of Karen.

CHAPTER SIXTEEN

KAREN GAPED AT THE RAGAMUFFIN sitting across from her. "*You're* Hannibal—the person I've been waiting three days to see?"

"Why do you look so surprised?" He spoke in what Karen was beginning to recognize as a Sanvitan accent, but his English was excellent.

"You're a kid, for Pete's sake."

"That is why I do well at my job."

She glanced at the box on the floor. "Shining shoes, you mean?"

"Shining shoes is my cover. My real job is much more important. And anyway, I'm not that young. I'm fourteen . . . nearly."

Karen was fed up, tired, exasperated that so much time had been wasted. Tracing Donis might be impossible by now; he might even be dead. She quickly squelched that negative thought to concentrate on the present.

"All right, Hannibal, I'm here to find out what's happened to Andonis Sotera. I was given your name as a contact. Is there even the remotest possibility that you could help?"

"I haven't eaten all day," was his irrelevant reply. "Would you mind if I ordered some dinner?"

Sighing, Karen motioned toward the menu wedged between the oil and vinegar cruets. "Go ahead."

Hannibal didn't need the menu. He called out to the proprietor, ordering something in Sanvitan. Then he turned to Karen. "You are from Canada, no?"

"I see they've filled you in."

"Not really. I was listening behind the curtain the first time you came here."

"I thought someone was back there. Why didn't you come out?"

"We have to be careful of people who come here asking questions. I had to be certain that you were not the enemy."

"What makes you so certain that I'm not?"

"I've been watching you when I came in to shine shoes. There is so much sadness in your eyes. We've been hearing rumors about Donis being taken back, so when you showed up looking for him, we decided your story must be true."

"Who is this 'we' you keep referring to?" she asked.

"The people I work for."

"And the rumors about Donis? What have you heard?"

"That he is under house arrest at the palace."

"In Sanvito?"

"Where else?"

"What does house arrest mean in Sanvito?"

Hannibal shrugged. "Who can say? It means whatever the president wants it to, but at least we know Donis is alive."

That was something, Karen reasoned. It was basically what she'd wanted to know and would never have found out in Canada. So why didn't she feel better?

The proprietor brought a huge plate of fish and french fries to the table. He muttered a few words to Hannibal, who reacted with the indignation of a child being scolded. It stood to reason, Karen thought. Hannibal was a child.

The boy eagerly launched into his food with knife and fork. Between mouthfuls, he said, "The owner of this place, he thinks I'm talking too much."

"Why? You've hardly told me anything."

"I've told you more than I should," Hannibal said. "I am not the one in charge. I am only a—" he wrinkled his nose "—an emissary."

"What does an emissary do?"

"Many important things. I pick up the money people send for the exiles and see that it gets to the right places, I deliver messages—and I do what I am doing now."

"Eat at someone else's expense."

Hannibal gave her a lopsided grin. "That, too, but what I meant is, I meet people and report back to the others with my assessment. I am an excellent judge of people, you know."

"I see." Karen tried not to smile. It was impossible to dislike Hannibal. He was obviously a bright kid and might have gone far under other circumstances. Then again, he might still go far—either as an international statesman or a jewel thief. "Have I passed muster?" Karen asked.

"Mustard?" Hannibal looked at her, confused.

"Now that we've met, do you think you can trust me?"

"Oh, yes, no problem. Like I said, I've been watching you. Talia wants to see you right away."

The name struck an immediate chord with Karen. "Talia? Do you mean Donis's cousin?"

"The same."

"Where is she?"

"Nearby. I will take you to her as soon as—"

"I know. As soon as you've finished eating." Karen sat back and tried to stay patient. She'd come this far and waited this long. Another few french fries couldn't possibly make any difference.

Now that Karen prided herself on finding her way to the Casa Suerte, Hannibal led her through yet another tangled maze of laneways and alleys. After a few minutes they came to a wall with a door, indistinguishable from nearly every other wall with a door in this part of the city.

Hannibal rapped with an elaborate series of knocks, obviously a code. A short time passed, then finally at the top of the door, a wooden slot slid open. It was too dark to see the eyes on the other side, but Karen felt them as acutely as if they were touching her.

No words were spoken, and Karen wondered briefly how they could be certain that Hannibal was with her. He was too short to be seen through the slit. But before she could ponder this further, the door opened. Hannibal went inside, pulling Karen by the hand behind him.

They were in a small dark anteroom devoid of furniture. A hunched old man looked Karen over keenly, then beckoned for them to follow him into a central courtyard. Here, someone had taken greater pains to make the place pleasant.

Plants and lush tropical flowers were everywhere, spilling over the quarry-tiled patio. Lanterns had been strategically hung to give off fascinating patterns of shadow and light. And to complete the jungle ambience, there were exotic birds, perhaps a dozen of them, sleeping soundly in their wicker cages.

At first Karen thought no one was in the courtyard. She turned around and felt strangely reassured to see that Hannibal was with her. The old man was nowhere to be found.

Just then a woman stepped out from behind a broadleaved tree. A witch from the Dark Ages was Karen's first impression of the woman. But then she realized the surroundings probably had something to do with her opinion.

The woman was about the same height as Karen but voluptuously built, with masses of black hair that reached her waist. Barefoot, she wore a gathered blouse, gold hoops in her ears and a brightly patterned skirt.

Even more remarkable, however, was the brightly colored bird perched on her shoulder. The creature's feathers were long and exotic, curving delicately around its caretaker's torso. They seemed to belong together, woman and bird, as if each was wearing her natural plumage.

"You are Karen?" she said in a low voice that commanded one's attention.

Karen nodded.

"What do you want from us?"

"I want to find out what's happened to Donis."

"Why?"

"Because... because I love him."

"What makes you think anything has happened?"

Karen glanced at Hannibal whose eyes were wide with apprehension. Obviously he wasn't supposed to have told her about the house arrest. "It's just a feeling I have," she replied, feigning ignorance.

The woman, perhaps because she was a woman, didn't question the logic of Karen's response. "How long have you known him?"

"About four months." Sensing the woman's reticence, Karen reached into her purse, bringing out the items she'd been saving for a time like this. "I have a couple of things you might be interested in seeing." She held out the note from Donis first.

Talia—assuming this was Talia—approached slowly, not so much with caution, but with a bearing that seemed almost regal. She took the note and held it up to the light. Quickly she handed it back with a huff. "This handwriting is not his."

"I didn't recognize it, either, but I know it's from him. I have this as well." She handed Talia the small photograph from Donis's bureau.

This time the reaction was entirely different. Talia smiled, her face practically dazzling. She was an incredibly beautiful woman. "Look, look," she said to Hannibal. "It's the family. I haven't seen this picture for years. We were children then—Donis, Salvo and me. There's my mother, there's Donis's parents...and Nani. She looked just as old in those days as she does now."

Nani, Karen surmised, must be Talia's name for Donis's grandmother. But what struck her about Talia was her almost childlike spontaneity at seeing the picture. Love was evident not only in her glistening eyes, but in the way her fingers moved over the photograph, as though she were gently stroking the memory.

Karen no longer felt as intimidated in Talia's presence. She could even understand why the bird was willing to perch calmly on Talia's shoulder. Animals had a sixth sense about who could be trusted.

She handed the picture back to Karen. "Thank you for showing me. It's been a long time since I recalled those happy days. I know it's late, but will you stay and talk to me of Donis?"

Karen, feeling a lump in her throat, nodded. "I'd be happy to."

Talia raised her arms, and the bird hopped off her shoulder. "Here, Hannibal, you take Rasputin and put him in the cage. It's time for you to go to bed as well."

"Ah, do I have to?"

Karen had to laugh. For all his street smarts, Hannibal was still a typical boy.

"You don't hear Rasputin complain," Talia pointed out. "Now off with you."

Hannibal patted his shoulder, and the feathered creature promptly hopped on. Karen watched the two of them disappear through a door in the courtyard. "He's quite a boy," she remarked to Talia.

"Hannibal is...one of a kind."

"Does he have any family?"

Talia shook her head. "He lost his parents in the political upheaval of Sanvito. He still has an older sister and brother living on the island, but they felt Hannibal would have a better chance if he left. So I've been looking after him. We're a family, the birds, Hannibal and I." She gestured for Karen to follow her into the kitchen. "Do you drink tea?"

"Yes. I'd love some." She watched Talia move through the small kitchen getting cups and a tin of loose tea. Though she was tall, almost an imposing woman, her bearing was surprisingly delicate. One thing that could be said for Donis's relatives, they were far from forgettable.

"Where did the birds come from?" Karen asked.

"From everywhere. Rasputin is a bird of paradise. He was caught by a poacher in Papua, New Guinea, and brought to Spain. But the bird's wing was broken en route, making him worthless. He was left to die in a trash bin."

"You found him?"

"A friend did. I have something of a reputation for taking in abandoned creatures." There was a flicker of amusement in her eyes when she glanced at Karen, though she refrained from making the obvious comparison.

"Then I guess I've come to the right place," Karen joked, feeling much better than she had ten minutes earlier.

Talia put the kettle on a two-burner gas stove and sat across from Karen. "So tell me, was Donis happy in Canada?"

"I think he was the happiest he'd been in years."

Over tea she told Talia everything. How she and Donis met, how she got him out of jail and introduced him to Father Peter. Karen spared no details, up to and including the abduction by "Father" Eustatius. It felt wonderful to unburden herself with someone who cared for Donis as deeply as she.

"What did this Eustatius look like?" Talia asked.

Karen described his height, his silver hair, his intellectual bearing. "Does he sound familiar?"

"No, and I'm sure I would have remembered someone like him. Sanvito is not a large island. It is possible, though, that he's not Sanvitan. Lately, Salvo has been recruiting people who will kill for hard currency."

"You seem well informed about your brother's activities."

Talia looked away as if discussion of her brother made her uncomfortable. "There are security leaks everywhere, even in the presidential palace."

Briefly Karen wondered where Talia's loyalties really lay. Wasn't she as capable of treachery as anyone? "What does your brother want with Donis?" Karen asked, knowing she had no choice but to hope for the best. "Do you think he plans to...to kill him?"

"No, not right away at least. He needs Donis and his expertise. I only hope Donis isn't foolish enough to refuse."

Suddenly overwhelmed, Karen covered her face with her hands. "I don't know what I was thinking when I decided to come here. It seemed so reasonable. All I'd have to do was find out what really happened to Donis, and then I would somehow get on with my life."

Talia picked up the note that was sitting on the table. "Are you sure it wasn't the existence of this other woman you were obsessed with?"

Karen flushed. "Lord, I hope not. But maybe that was part of it."

Talia laughed, though the laughter did not light up her eyes. "If it will put your mind at ease, I've known Donis all my life, and he's never been seriously involved with anyone. Oh, he had the usual tempestuous affairs that went on for a year or so, but none that stand out as the kind of love he alludes to in this letter."

"Thank you, Talia. I guess I did need to hear that."

"And now that you've heard it, what will you do?"

Karen held out her hands. "What can I do? It's not as though I can go to Sanvito and visit Donis."

"I wouldn't be too quick to dismiss that possibility."

"What?"

Talia leaned across the small table. "One of the reasons our group made you wait three days was because we needed time to finalize the details. As it turns out, your presence here could be quite advantageous."

"Advantageous for what?"

She paused, as if to consider her words. "For our plans to rescue Donis...and to overthrow my brother's regime."

THE GREAT HALL of the presidential palace was an example of excess taken to absurdity with dozens of pink marble columns, enormous chandeliers, a grotesquely frescoed dome and at the end of the hall, a throne. There slouched the insouciant Salvo Gibrian, president for life. Didn't he realize that the immensity of the room made him look like an overweight dwarf?

Donis had been spared the indignity of shackles, but was still flanked by two armed guards as he was led up the aisle to his cousin. Ordered to halt ten feet from the throne, Donis waited for a command to kneel, which he would have refused. None came. Perhaps Salvo was aware of his own limitations after all.

"Well, well. At last, we meet again, dear cousin."

Donis said nothing, using the opportunity to observe his one-time friend. The transformation was shocking. Salvo Gibrian had quite simply gone to seed. There was no proud thrust to his jaw, only jowls. The barrel chest had melted to waist level, and even his hands looked flaccid.

"Come now, surely you have some word of greeting to offer me," Salvo urged. "We used to be so close."

"Have you released Grandmother?"

"All in good time—"

"You gave me your word!" Donis shouted, oblivious to the guards lunging at him from either side. When they received no orders from their superior, they backed down.

Salvo idly examined his fingernails. They were buffed daily by a personal manicurist. "Yes, well, I thought it might be premature to set your grandmother free until we had a chance to talk."

Donis steeled himself for an argument. "Go ahead and talk, Salvo. I'm listening."

The president motioned to his guards, dismissing them from the room. "Come up here, sit on the step," he said to Donis. "I want our conversation to be private."

Donis glanced around the cavernous hall. "You might have tried finding a more private spot."

"I thought the surroundings might impress you. It's all my own design, you know. But never mind that. Donis, I must be frank. This country needs you desperately. We are on the verge of financial collapse, and I cannot allow that to happen."

"Why? Would it disturb your sleep?"

Salvo frowned. "You would be wise to refrain from sarcasm. I will make it easy for you. I can provide you with all the information you need—statistics, financial reports, whatever. But our situation is critical. The inflation rate is over five hundred percent, foreign banks won't touch our currency, and they are constantly amending our terms of repayment, none of which are realistic."

Donis wasn't the least bit moved by Salvo spouting statistics and economic jargon. He was more concerned with what the situation meant to the average Sanvitan. A week's salary for a pound of meat—if meat was even available. It meant no new clothes for children, never mind luxuries like candy and toys. What had once been a comfortable existence was now reduced to a pitiful subsistence level.

"What you're asking, Salvo, is impossible for one man to correct."

"Then hire more experts. Whoever you need, I will ensure that he is at your disposal. My advisory board is nothing but a bunch of yes men. No one is willing to make a decision about anything."

"That's not so difficult to understand," Donis observed, "considering what might happen if they make the wrong decision."

Salvo was too egotistical to take offense. "Things have changed since you left, Donis. I'll have you know my campaign for political solidarity has been curtailed considerably."

"What is that supposed to mean—that you're not murdering as often as you used to?"

"Guard your words, Donis. I am still in the seat of authority."

"I have no intention of helping you, not in any way, shape or form. I only agreed to see you, and that was only so you would release Grandmother, your own great-aunt."

Salvo's face darkened. Glowering, he lifted himself out of the throne. "You *will* do as I ask, Donis. You owe me."

"Owe you for what?"

"For trying to kill me."

Donis felt the sweat suddenly break out on his forehead. "What are you talking about?"

"Don't pretend you've forgotten. You always were so damned sanctimonious. Remember that foggy morning on the cliff. Right outside the window of this palace, in fact. We were no more than twenty—full of plans, full of ideas."

How well he remembered, though he'd done everything he could over the years to blot out the event. And how typical of Salvo to erect his monstrous palace on the site of their childhood haunts. "I had no intention of letting you fall."

"Don't lie. I saw it in your eyes—the loathing, the ter-or, as though I were some kind of monster. You even oosened your grip on my arms."

"But I didn't let go."

"No, you didn't!" Salvo slammed a fist into his palm. 'But you've been regretting it ever since.''

For once Salvo displayed a glimmer of the second sight hat ran in Donis's grandmother's side of the family. Of all he times for him to be insightful, Donis thought ruefully. 'How could I not regret ignoring my instincts? Twenty ears ago, I was given a chance to prevent the ruin of San-ito, and like a fool, I let that chance go by.''

"Is that why you became The Deliverer—so saintly and noble—rescuing your countrymen from my evil clutches? Was it guilt that motivated you all these years?''

Salvo was nearer the truth than Donis had ever allowed imself to be. He was almost grateful to hear it put into vords. "I never set out to be a hero," he admitted. "I only did what I could."

"Then may I suggest you continue to help your long-uffering countrymen."

"I've already told you, I'm not going to repair your conomic disasters.'' Donis hoped his attitude of non-cooperation was convincing enough. He hadn't seen or eard from that soldier again. He couldn't even be certain t wasn't a dream.

The short, squat man landed heavily on his throne. 'Dear me, that is a shame. I was so confident you would isten to reason. You see, there are still a number of polit-cal prisoners languishing in our cells, and I would dearly ove to save the taxpayers further expense. It's a good first tep, don't you think?''

"By all means, release them."

"I would gladly. If you would agree to act as my eco-nomic advisor, the future of these eighty-six men and vomen would be assured."

Donis feared the tone in Salvo's voice. It bordered on madness. "What do you mean, their future would be assured?"

"As I said, they are much too expensive to maintain. But our firing squad still has plenty of ammunition, and lately my marksmen have been so bored...."

Donis raked anguished hands through his hair. "For the love of God, Salvo, are you utterly insane? When will all of this end?"

"It will end, dear cousin, as soon as you come up with a policy draft. You have until the end of the week—that's five days. If you have not come up with concrete suggestions at the end of five days, the prisoner in the first cell will die. After six days, the second will die, and so on. That gives you, what—ninety-one days in total. If you are still resisting at the end—which I doubt even you would be so foolish to do—then it will be your turn. Ultimately Salvo Gibrian will be free of all the political riffraff."

Donis had hoped, after falling in love with Karen, that he would never again experience a feeling of utter helplessness. She'd had a way about her that gave him strength, that made him feel worthy. How desperately he needed her now. And how futile was the very notion. Karen wasn't here. There was nothing she could do for him anymore.

Salvo, apparently interpreting Donis's silence as assent, summoned the guards. "Take this man to his room, and give him whatever he asks for. He has work to do."

"Release Grandmother," Donis called out as the men dragged him away.

Salvo laughed, and the sound echoed maniacally through the Great Hall. "Didn't I tell you? I released her a week ago."

THE SOLDIER APPEARED again, this time outside the window. Donis heard the rapping from his desk and got up to investigate. "The window is locked," he said through the frosted glass. "I can't open it."

"Go to the bathroom window," the voice replied. "It's been left unlatched."

Donis did as he was told, and now he was able to see the soldier face to face. He was a young man, barely out of his teens. Probably still reeked with idealism, as Donis once had long ago.

"I hope you have good news," he said to the young man. "I only have five days before people start dying."

"The wheels are already in motion. Go ahead and do what the president asks."

"But I feel so helpless, waiting around. Is there nothing more I can do to help?"

"Nothing. Your mere presence is of great assistance. People are clamoring for the release of their Deliverer."

Donis covered his face in his hands. Not that again. He'd had more than enough of martyrdom for one life.

"One more thing. Your Canadian friend is in Spain."

His head shot up. "What friend? Who are you talking about?"

"The woman. I don't know her name."

"Karen..." Her name was like honey on his tongue. "Are you sure? Why has she come?"

"She is looking for you. She's already met with Talia."

"Oh, God, no. I never thought, never dreamed she would..." Donis's first reaction was euphoria. Karen had come to find him! Did she really love him that much?

Joy was quickly tempered by distress. She was not supposed to have followed him. Donis had worded his note specifically to discourage it.

What kind of woman would go looking for her man after being led to believe there was another lover? *A woman who knew her man too well,* came the instinctive reply.

Knowing too well the dangers Karen might encounter, Donis covered his face with his hands. "Tell Talia to send her home right away."

"I can pass the message, but I don't think it will do any good."

"Why not?"

"Talia intends to solicit your friend's help. She could be very useful to us."

"No! It's out of the question!"

"Shh! Keep your voice down! Do you want to get us both killed?"

Donis lowered his voice, but not its intensity. "Karen must have nothing to do with the uprising. I insist that she go home at once."

The soldier hitched a machine gun higher on his shoulder. "Our plans are already laid. We cannot thwart the future of Sanvito for the sake of one woman."

Donis gripped the sill, knowing how easy it would be to jump out the window and escape. He could find Karen and force her to return to Canada. He could even take her someplace where the two of them could start a new life....

But Donis knew he would not do it. For now, his place was here. He was the decoy, the bait on which this uprising depended. It was perhaps his country's final chance to escape the tyranny of Salvo Gibrian.

"Then, please, promise me no undue risks will be taken."

"I will pass your message along. And now, I need your ring. The one with the cross. It's part of our plan."

CHAPTER SEVENTEEN

As THE SOLDIER had told Donis, the plans were already laid. Karen was too deeply involved, emotionally and physically, to consider going home.

Now, as the yacht approached the harbor of Muniz, Sanvito, she wondered how Donis would react when he learned she had not left. Would he be furious? Grateful? A light breeze fanned her hair as she stood on the upper deck. His reaction, Karen decided, didn't matter. What mattered was that Donis might soon be set free. With any luck, they would have the rest of their lives to deal with her obstinacy.

The island was like a sepia print superimposed on a turquoise sea. Muniz was made up of sand-colored buildings with flat roofs and arched windows, laid out in terraces along a rugged hillside. On either side of the city lay the ruins of fortress walls, their bastions and battlements still in evidence.

The skyline was dominated by two buildings. The cathedral, the older structure, looked as though it had been carved from the island itself. Solid, unpretentious, its cupola gleamed with a soft golden burnish. The second building on the stark northern coast was a Moorish monstrosity.

"That's the presidential palace," Talia pointed out.

"I guessed as much," Karen replied. "It must have cost a fortune to build."

"A fortune that Sanvito does not possess," Talia said sadly. "Salvo had the pink marble shipped block by block from Italy."

Karen glanced at her fellow passenger. Talia looked radiant with her luxurious hair tied back with a silk scarf. Outwardly, she appeared calm, but Karen sensed her tension as keenly as she felt her own.

On the deck behind them milled an equally anxious press corps—technicians, film crews, reporters. They had assembled that morning at the Barcelona docks, a motley crew from half a dozen countries clamoring for photos and interviews.

Karen gave Talia full credit for playing up their story so dramatically and with such success. Theirs was, after all, an unlikely collaboration—the sister of a ruthless dictator and the girlfriend of Donis Sotera, a Sanvitan hero and the dictator's nemesis.

From the questions they'd been asked at the press conference before sailing, it was obvious that the journalists would play up the drama—Talia's estrangement from her brother and subsequent exile, Donis's reputation for saving lives at the risk of his own. And Karen's poignant story, coming all the way from Canada to plead for her lover's release.

The publicity was crucial, Talia had explained to Karen. As long as the world was watching, as long as Salvo knew he was in the public eye, he wouldn't dare do anything rash. He had already promised, however grudgingly, to welcome the women and the reporters, assuring them he was more than anxious for frank discussion in the matter of Donis Sotera.

A wealthy Sanvitan exile, a friend of Talia's, had offered the use of his private yacht and crew for the journey. Karen only wished the circumstances could have been happier. She was in no frame of mind to enjoy the ship's luxurious amenities.

Hundreds of people were crowded on the wharf to greet them, cheering and waving Sanvitan flags. To Karen's surprise, there were even a few Canadian flags interspersed among them.

"Where do you suppose they found those?" she asked Talia.

The woman shook her head. "Who knows? But how sad that they consider our arrival a cause for celebration."

"Why do they?"

"It's because of you, the woman who captured their hero's heart. We Sanvitans could never resist a good love story."

A military escort led Karen and Talia to a convertible limousine, while the press piled into a bus behind them. The limo's top was down, so that the crowds along the street could get a good look at the two women.

"Good grief, you'd think we were visiting royalty."

"To them, you are," Talia answered with a fixed smile. "Wave, or you'll offend them."

Karen waved and smiled, but inwardly she struggled with an eerie sense of unreality. She'd never before been at the center of sensationalism and knew now she didn't like it one bit.

The road to the palace was twisting and tortuous, the limousine bumping and lurching the entire way. The greenery planted on both sides of the road looked out of place, as if opulence had been forced onto the unwilling landscape.

Inside the palace Karen and Talia were led up the aisle of the Great Hall, flanked by three guards on either side. Karen had never seen such ostentatiousness. The room looked like an effeminate railroad terminal.

Flashbulbs popped, shutters snapped, while Karen's nerves did the same. If their negotiations with Salvo were going to take place amid this hoopla, she'd be lucky if she could squeak out a single word.

At the end of the aisle was an unoccupied throne. If the president came out carrying a scepter, Karen told herself, she would probably throw up. They were ordered to halt a respectable distance from the seat of honor, and for the next few minutes, reporters and photographers jockied for the best positions. A few tape recorders were confiscated, but otherwise the guards treated the press reasonably well.

The president of Sanvito marched into the hall with a trumpet fanfare. Actually, he didn't march. It was closer to a waddle. Karen had pictured someone more imposing. Salvo Gibrian was short and stout with a receding hairline and soft jowls. He looked like Napoleon—no small irony, she supposed—complete with military uniform and a chestful of medals. He probably had the medals made to order.

The president gave a cursory glance at Karen, then turned his full attention to his sister, holding out his arms. "My dear Talia, how exquisite you look."

Talia slowly climbed the three steps to the throne and embraced her brother. Karen couldn't help but notice that Salvo's embrace seemed theatrical, while Talia's appeared poignantly genuine.

"Welcome to Sanvito, all of you." Salvo's sweeping gaze and unctuous smile took in the entourage. "I am honored that the world has chosen to share with us this touching family reunion."

His mention of the world reminded Karen that in Ontario, it would now be eight o'clock in the morning. She assumed that most of her family and friends would be watching the news, since the event had been announced worldwide for two days.

After careful thought Karen had decided not to call home. They would only beg her to leave before something terrible happened. She wondered how they were taking it. Probably not well.

Salvo snapped his fingers and called for a couple of chairs. When they were seated, Talia spoke up. "Tell me, dear brother, how is our cousin doing?"

"Splendidly, dear sister. I tried to tell you from the start. Donis is here because he wants to be. You needn't have gone to these elaborate lengths."

"So you would like us to believe," Talia countered. "I have difficulty accepting that Donis has changed his colors so completely."

Their conversation went on for over an hour by which time Karen was ready to scream. Salvo, she decided, was not merely unbalanced—he was stark raving mad. He rambled, repeatedly lost his train of thought and seemed to regard this whole episode as a huge joke.

Karen overheard one of the reporters mutter, "If Sotera is here voluntarily, we won't have much of a story."

"So we'll cover the love angle," his colleague replied. "It's better than nothing."

"If what you say is true, why don't you let Donis come out and speak for himself?" Talia said to her brother.

"I would have done so from the start, but Donis is extremely busy and specifically requested to be left alone. He promised to have a policy paper ready for me by tomorrow. He's been working night and day to finish it."

"I flew halfway around the world to see Donis," Karen argued, "and I don't intend to leave until I do. For all I know, sir, you could be lying...and Donis could be dead." Tedium and frustration had fueled her courage. Even the president's pout failed to stir up fear.

"You obviously know nothing about me, or you wouldn't have said such a thing. Has it not occurred to you, Miss Miller, that Donis's feelings toward you might have cooled since his return to Sanvito?"

Talia had warned Karen to be prepared for that eventuality. The messages from Donis had come by way of many mouths. They had no way of knowing how much was said for the benefit of the enemy.

"If his feelings have changed," Karen insisted, "I want to hear it from him."

Salvo swung his legs over the side of the throne. "All right, ladies, have it your way. I will ask Donis to come out. But I'm warning you he won't be pleased." Salvo issued an order to one of the guards who left the hall and returned a few minutes later with Donis beside him.

Karen's first sight of the man she loved made her knees go weak. They hadn't been apart for very long, yet it seemed like years. He looked gaunt, but healthy enough otherwise. He wore a white shirt with the sleeves rolled up, as though he'd been interrupted at work.

Donis turned to Talia and then slowly his gaze moved to Karen. She had almost forgotten the haunting color of his eyes—misty and pale gray—almost no color at all. "What are you doing here?" he asked.

Karen saw no gratitude in his eyes, heard no pleasure in his voice. Only the sharp edge of something—annoyance, perhaps, or fear. She swallowed hard, unable to reply.

"We came to see you." Talia spoke for both of them. "Surely you aren't so buried in your work that you failed to hear the crowds welcoming us on the street."

"I heard nothing. The palace is a long way from the common folk. You've wasted your time coming here. What Salvo told you is true. I am here of my own accord to review Sanvito's economic situation. I am not, as rumor has it, under house arrest, and am free to leave anytime I choose."

"I don't believe you," Talia countered.

"Your opinion is the least of my concerns."

As Karen listened, she felt the hairs of her nape stand on end. Donis's belligerence toward Talia was so convincing. Karen knew that was how it must appear. But that didn't make things easier to bear.

"I think you've been brainwashed by my brother," Talia said.

Donis laughed harshly. "I assure you, cousin, my brain is entirely under my control. Your brother and I have come to a cautious understanding. We were friends as children, and see no reason why we cannot be friends once again."

At this, Salvo grinned broadly, affecting a grandiose pose for the benefit of the press.

"Could you not at least say something decent to Karen?" Talia said. "She's come halfway round the world to see you."

Flashbulbs were popping in Karen's face like bulbous, prying eyes.

"I heard through the grapevine she had come," Donis replied, "and was most disturbed by the news. As far as I'm concerned, she is meddling in our internal affairs. This great romantic reunion you reporters have come to witness is a sham."

Salvo slapped his knee and laughed out loud. "I knew it!"

Talia touched Karen's arm. "I'm sorry. It looks as though we have misjudged the situation after all."

For Donis's sake, for everyone's, Karen struggled to keep her face expressionless. "At least, now I know."

Talia ran a hand dramatically across her face. "It was foolish of us to come. I must have been away too long. It seems I no longer know my family."

Salvo studied his sister's face. "No need to regret your visit," he said. "I've always wanted to show you how far I've come up in the world. Until now you considered yourself too good for my hospitality."

Talia lowered her gaze and made no reply.

"As it turns out, Donis and I have planned a little surprise," her brother went on.

"What surprise?"

"A private family reunion. We thought you might like to see Nani once before you leave, since I assume you have no desire to stay in your homeland."

Talia squared her shoulders. "I no longer consider this place to be my homeland . . . but I would like to see Nani. How is she?"

"Sharp-tongued and dotty as ever."

Karen allowed herself a small measure of relief. Donis had obviously regained Salvo's confidence, the most critical aspect of their scheme. She could only pray everyone else would be equally successful.

"Why would you do this for me?" Talia asked. "You've never made any secret of your feelings toward our great-aunt."

"Time mellows even the deepest of grudges. Nani is a harmless old woman. I have learned to disregard her unfounded prejudice against me."

"When can I see her?"

"This afternoon. The four of us will have lunch in my private courtyard. I think you'll find the place . . . appealing."

"The four of us?" Talia questioned.

The president smiled. "You, Donis, Nani and me. And my guards, of course. I haven't taken total leave of my senses."

Karen's stomach tightened. So she wasn't to be part of the reunion. Not that she was surprised. It was a contingency they had anticipated.

Talia tossed one end of her crimson scarf over her neck. "How do I know, dear brother, that you haven't made plans to assassinate us in your . . . private courtyard?"

Salvo looked around at the entourage of reporters. "Dear Talia, I am wounded. Even I would not attempt so flagrant and heartless an act with the world looking on."

"Then you will allow the press to join us."

"Out of the question. The courtyard is much too intimate."

Talia turned to Karen. "Would you mind spending a few hours on your own?"

"I don't mind, but are you sure you know what you're doing?"

The dark-haired woman shrugged. "There are times when we must trust our instincts. I would love to see Nani once more, and since Salvo has already made arrangements..."

"Then go ahead. I'll be fine."

In short order, Karen and the reporters were ushered to a lounge where they were served mint tea and sweets. Talia disappeared with two of the guards to another wing of the palace.

Karen did her best to mingle with the reporters, to behave like the innocent she was believed to be. But in truth, she'd never felt more terrified in her life. What did she know of treachery? Of danger? Talia was the sister of a demented dictator. What made Karen so certain she could be trusted?

As for Donis, he had publicly denounced their love. Was that also part of the performance? Or did he now see her as merely a link in an irreversible chain of events?

Karen dared not reach for the ring that she wore hidden beneath her collar. It was tempting to consider the gold band a symbol of Donis's affection, but in truth it had come to her by way of strangers for reasons that had little to do with love.

Angrily Karen pushed aside her thoughts. This was no time to feel sorry for herself. She had to concentrate on what Talia had told her. It was crucial that she remember everything.

Sources within the palace had provided them with details of the president's quarters. A sumptuous bedroom, several guest suites and a book-lined study overlooking a private courtyard by the sea.

The courtyard, she knew, was the critical element. If the right people weren't in their places when she staged her arrival, everything could come undone.

Time dragged. A few kind souls tried to persuade Karen to eat, but she couldn't. Her distress, at least, was understandable. To be humiliated in public by her lover was not an easy thing to endure.

As she paced the stuffy lounge, a guard entered and whispered a few words to one of his colleagues who was overseeing this pseudo reception. The two of them, machine guns over their shoulders, approached Karen.

"We have a message from Andonis Sotera."

She looked at the younger guard with feigned disgust. "Do you now?"

"He would like his ring."

"His what?"

"The gold ring he gave you. He requests that you return it to him."

She clutched her purse more tightly under her arm. "You can tell him from me that I have no intention of giving it back. Just because Donis finds it expedient to break his promises..."

The guards glanced at each other. "I am afraid we must insist."

"Or else what? Am I to be executed for refusing?"

"No, no of course not. You are under the protection of our president, Miss Miller. But we hoped that you would cooperate with Mr. Sotera's request."

Reporters were listening in, none too discreetly. Karen made sure she spoke clearly. "If Donis wants his ring back, let me give it to him myself."

The guard sighed. "So you do have the ring."

"Certainly. I never go anywhere without it." She brought out a gold chain from the neckline of her dress.

"Donis is having a private lunch with his family. He does not wish to be disturbed."

"I won't disturb him, and I promise not to create a scene. That's what he's afraid of, isn't it?"

The younger guard, apparently the only one who spoke English, conferred with his elder colleague. "Very well," he said at last. "We will escort you to the courtyard, but you will not be allowed to stay."

Karen tossed her head. "I haven't the slightest desire to stay where I'm not wanted. I only want this day to be over with."

The two guards led her from the lounge through endless corridors. Karen had taken the ring off the chain and was clutching it in a sweaty palm. Her heels clicked on the marble floors with a confidence she didn't feel.

Finally they came to a closed set of double doors. A soldier standing guard reluctantly allowed Karen and the others entry. Now there were three of them marching with her through the vast study to a set of glass doors on the far wall. She felt frighteningly outnumbered.

The private courtyard was built along a cliff edged with a small stand of cypress, just as Talia had described. "The giant's cowlick," they had called the place as children. It was walled off on three sides, the fourth side made naturally impregnable by a precipice. Karen could hear the surf roaring far below.

The scene that greeted Karen was surprisingly tranquil. A tiny woman dressed in black sat at a wrought-iron table, sipping from a teacup. Donis sat across from her, legs stretched out casually in front of him.

Talia and Salvo were squatting near the cypress, digging near the roots for something. A fourth guard stood watch nearby. Everyone turned to look when Karen entered the courtyard.

"Why is she here?" Donis demanded, straightening in his seat.

Karen held out her hand, amazed to see that she scarcely trembled. "I have your ring...sir."

"I thought I instructed the guards to bring it to me."

"You did. I ignored them. Here, catch the damned thing...."

While Karen diverted the group by tossing the gold band, two guards raised their guns and opened fire. Scrambling awkwardly to his feet, Salvo was riddled with bullets. Talia caught him in her arms. But Salvo proved too heavy, and she lost her balance. Before anyone could react, both brother and sister fell backward over the cliff's edge.

Karen ran to the precipice. She saw rocks like stumps of old teeth protruding from the sea. Salvo was impaled on one of them. But Talia's body was nowhere in sight. All that remained was her crimson scarf wrapped around a rock.

Donis's arms were around Karen in an instant. She could feel his anguish and his strength as he clung to her, weeping. "My dear love, it's over. Please forgive me...."

EPILOGUE

HE HOUSE WHERE DONIS grew up overlooked the south-
n shore of Sanvito, a gentler coast of fine sand and
vaying palms. It was a modest home with arched win-
ws and a flat, tiled roof. But it was home nonetheless for
aren and her husband of six months.

On the patio table, Karen's work was divided into two
les—one, a collection of Sanvitan grammar books, the
cond, an overflowing box of unanswered correspon-
nce. Karen meanwhile was stretched out on a chaise
ngue, trying to decide which pile she could ignore the
ngest.

"Lazing about again, are we?"

Karen looked up, shielding her eyes from the sun. "Hi,
rgeous. How's the inflation rate today?"

Donis leaned over to kiss her. "Holding its own, thank
u. Where's Grandmother?"

"Where you'll find her every day at this time."

"At the beach."

Karen smiled slowly. "Hannibal is with her. He's as
nvinced as Grandmother that Talia will come back some
y. Apparently there's some legend..."

Donis gazed across the unbroken stretch of sea.

"Yes, the legend. It's come to me so often these last few
onths. They say that if a woman falls from the cliff, the
a will spirit her to safety."

"Do you actually believe that?"

Donis looked at his wife. "I don't know. The impor
tant thing is Grandmother still believes that Talia is aliv
and will come back to us. I have every reason to tru
Grandmother's feelings."

Karen, who'd come to cherish the wise old woman, fe
the same way. She'd never fully come to terms with T
lia's disappearance. There was something unfinished abou
that day, some purpose yet to be fulfilled, and Talia G
brian was part of it. Only time would tell if their instinc
were correct.

"I almost forgot," Donis said, "I have a letter for you."

"Another one? Who'd believe we would still be gettin
mail six months after our story came out?"

"This one's from your father."

"Oh, in that case." Karen sat up and tore it open.
smile spread slowly across her face as she read. "Every
one's fine," she told Donis. "Our nephew, Benjamin,
three months old and has his first tooth...my gosh, I don'
believe it. Dad and Liz are looking at condos in the city
He's actually going to leave the farm."

The Sanvitan coup, it seemed, had far-flung repercus
sions. The entire Miller family had flown home to anx
iously watch the news coverage about Karen. Around th
same time, Liz and her father reconciled and were to marr
in the summer.

Karen held up a newspaper clipping from the *London
Free Press*. "Look what else Dad sent. Says he bought fift
issues of the paper, in case anyone wants a copy."

The headline read, "London woman to head up Sanv
tan Task Force." The article described ongoing negotia
tions to reopen the Canadian Consulate in Sanvito, heade
by Karen Miller Sotera, wife of Sanvito's chief economi
advisor.

"They even interviewed Mr. Rathbone," she said. "H
was quoted as saying, 'Miss Miller was an excellent coun
selor. I'm proud that my recommendation for her ap

pointment was accepted.' How about that, Donis? He likes me."

Donis sat down and slipped an arm around his wife's waist. "Of course, he likes you. You were the best counselor he ever had. How many others could have overthrown a dictatorship while vacationing in Europe?"

Karen winced. "Please, I'd just as soon forget that whole episode."

"It's not something we should forget. I was so proud of you that day. It was all I could do not to shout in the middle of the Great Hall—look, everyone, that is the woman I love!"

She studied her husband's face. Lines had etched deeper these past few months, but in her eyes, they made him all the more handsome. "We have come a long way together, haven't we?"

Donis gently touched her cheek. "We've only begun the journey, my love."

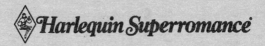
Harlequin Superromance

The elemental passions of *Spring Thunder*
come alive once again in the sequel....

SUMMER LIGHTNING

by

SANDRA JAMES

You enjoyed Maggie Howard's strong fiery nature
in *Spring Thunder*. Now she's back in *Summer
Lightning*, determined to fight against the resumption of logging in her small Oregon town. McBride
Lumber has caused nothing but grief for her in the
past. But when Jared McBride returns to head the
operation, Maggie finds that her greatest struggle is
with her heart.

Summer Lightning is Maggie Howard's story of
love. Coming in April.

SR335-1

Harlequin Superromance

CALLOWAY CORNERS

Created by four outstanding Superromance authors, bonded by lifelong friendship and a love of their home state: Sandra Canfield, Tracy Hughes, Katherine Burton and Penny Richards.

CALLOWAY CORNERS

Home of four sisters as different as the seasons, as elusive as the elements; an undiscovered part of Louisiana where time stands still and passion lasts forever.

CALLOWAY CORNERS

Birthplace of the unforgettable Calloway women: *Mariah*, free as the wind, and untamed until she meets the preacher who claims her, body and soul; *Jo*, the fiery, feisty defender of lost causes who loses her heart to a rock and roll man; *Tess*, gentle as a placid lake but tormented by her longing for the town's bad boy and *Eden*, the earth mother who's been so busy giving love she doesn't know how much she needs it until she's awakened by a drifter's kiss...

CALLOWAY CORNERS

Coming from Superromance, in 1989:
Mariah, by Sandra Canfield, a January release
Jo, by Tracy Hughes, a February release
Tess, by Katherine Burton, a March release
Eden, by Penny Richards, an April release

Harlequin
Superromance®

COMING NEXT MONTH

Harlequin Temptation dares to be different!

Once in a while, we Temptation editors spot a romance that's truly innovative. To make sure *you* don't miss any one of these outstanding selections, we'll mark them for you.

When the "Editors' Choice" fold-back appears on a Temptation cover, you'll know we've found that extra-special page-turner!

THE *Temptation*

EDITORS

Have You Ever Wondered If You Could Write A Harlequin Novel?

Here's great news—Harlequin is offering a series of cassette tapes to help you do just that. Written by Harlequin editors, these tapes give practical advice on how to make your characters—and your story— come alive. There's a tape for each contemporary romance series Harlequin publishes.

Mail order only

All sales final
